Shadows Lost

Book III of The Lost Trilogy

By Melyssa Williams

Red Team Ink
DBA of Zealot Solutions, Idaho LLC
5447 Kendall St.
Boise, ID 83706
Copyright© 2017 by Red Team Ink

This is a work of fiction. Names, characters, businesses, places, events and incidents are either the products of the author's imagination or used in a fictitious manner. Any resemblance to actual persons, living or dead, or actual events is purely coincidental.

For permission requests or information about discounts for special bulk purchases please contact: redteamink@gmail.com. Substantial discounts on bulk orders are available to corporations, professional associations, and small businesses.

Printed in The United States of America

Cover Design by Genesis Kohler

Library of Congress Control Number: 2017930466
ISBN: 978-0-9984881-1-0

Title: Shadows Lost
Description: First Edition

Chapter 1

I miss a lot about my old life, the life before my sister Rose, I mean. I miss Prue, my adopted grandmother, left behind in London. It seems everyone I love gets left behind eventually. I miss her cantankerous ways, her reminiscing, and the way she knew me better than anyone else. I even miss her dreadfully messy, and questionable cooking.

I miss my coffee shop drinks, the smell of sticky syrups used to flavor lattes and mochas, the roasted beans, and the sound of the espresso machine. I recently had an idea for a new concoction, a Baklava Latte, something with honey and cinnamon and maybe a pat of butter on the top.

I miss my guitar, and I also miss being able to play music on tiny devices that plug into my ears, allowing me to mute the outside noise. I wonder if I could still play the chords to my favorite songs, songs that Luke Dawes would say were depressing. The calluses on my fingertips from the strings are completely gone now, and I miss them too. I miss spray cheese and cars. I miss cars fiercely actually. I am beginning to really hate walking. It's completely overrated.

I miss bubble baths, fragranced with cucumber and melon or lemon and sage, and my old monogrammed washcloth. Yes, it was monogrammed with someone else's initials, but I didn't care. It was mine, and I mourn its loss like a tiny death. I miss my old clothes, despite them being unfashionable, I loved those overalls and my tie-dye shirt.

I miss Emme the most though. Sometimes I dream of her at night, and I wake angry because it isn't a nice dream. Emme deserved to be the star of a lovely dream, not a nightmare drenched in blood.

I dream that we are taking her cold, dead body out of the house, dressed in her pink dress. She sits up and beckons to me to follow her with a crook of her bone white finger. She is ghostly pale, and blood seeps through her bodice. When she summons me, I cannot withstand her. How can I? If her dying request is to see me dead with her, I will give in.

I can see straight through her to the other side of London, the side where she lived and worked, the side that ended up killing her. I see phantom young women in the street, swirling through the air and wailing horribly, desperate and murdered. Her red hair blows around her face though there is no wind in the house.

I wake whimpering, my heart hammering, and my hair sweaty around my face. I'm terrified that she'll speak to me in my dream because I know what she will say. I couldn't bear to hear her ask me why I let my little sister and Jack kill her like they did. I always struggle to wake myself before she can speak, but so far, I've succeeded. I take it one night at a time.

Africa is hot and dusty, though beautiful. It's a dismal time to be a lady in a desert, though I'd wager it is a dismal time to be a lady at all in 1888. I've abandoned all hope of a corset, those evil things, and have taken to wearing wide-legged, men's pants. The Africans find me bizarre anyway, so it hardly matters to them how I dress. I'd like to think if I slipped into something prettier, Israel might approve, but he's so busy with Dr. Smythe and the new clinic. He hardly notices me, and he's never been one to care what I look like anyway. At times like this, I suppose that's a bonus, since I look like a gangly teenage boy. A boy who hasn't quite grown into his legs and whose voice hasn't changed yet.

I almost miss Dad's drinking. It's a terrible thing to admit to, but his drying out period is nearly harder on us than it is on him. He's so melancholy that everyone hates to be around him. Even Bea has had it with his moping, and she's the gentlest one of our bunch.

Yes, your eldest daughter is a pant-wearing heathen, I want to say to my father. *Yes, your youngest daughter is pals with a serial killer, and your wife was murdered, I know, I know, but it's time to focus on the positive.*

If I could find one, a positive that is, I'd point it out to him. It isn't as though I want to hand him a scotch and soda or anything, but I wish they made a patch or something. Something to wean him off gradually, because the cold turkey approach is a slow, slow killer.

I miss some of the lightheartedness that used to be, in my old life, my pre-Rose life. Now she's gone, or to be more precise, we're gone. Her shadow remains lodged in my head, my dreams, and my heart. She blackened everything in our lives with her darkness, like a cold black wind that blew out a candle. Most light engulfs darkness, isn't that the way it's supposed to be? I don't believe that anymore. Some blackness can overpower the light, Rose is proof of that. She has a special kind of darkness in her. I can't be sure of whether we will ever see my sister or Luke Dawes again, and as a result, I am constantly watching my back. I wonder if I'll ever stop.

Israel has thrown himself into his work. I can see that this is his pattern, and I suppose it's not a bad one. I wish that there was more time for me, but even I can't be so selfish. How can he make it better anyway? There's nothing he could say or do that would remove the last year from my life. So, he works, he and Dr. Smythe, and I help. I practice my Chinese with Lu, the good doctor's wife, and I help with Joe, Emme's son. As far as Lu and her husband are concerned, I am Israel's wife, a lie that began in London.

This has made things a bit awkward.

"You can take the bed tonight. I'll take the floor," I offer to my not-husband. I help him with his boots as he yawns so big he looks like he could swallow me whole, and I'm hardly a dainty size. He is even more exhausted than usual because we've had a break in the weather. It's October now, but the season known as The Long Rains was extremely difficult and they've been working nearly around the clock.

"No, it's okay, Sonny. You take it." He rubs his eyes with his palms. In the dark of our bedroom, his black hands blot out the whiteness of his eyes, and he nearly disappears. In the last few months, he's taken to my nickname, which previously only my dad had ever used. I like it, except when he's romancing me, and then it's just odd. I told him that, and it made him laugh. *Fine*, he said, *when I'm whispering tender nothings in your ear I'll only call you Sonnet.*

"Rock, paper, scissors?" I pose with my hands ready. He's so tired that he'll be slow, and I can anticipate his moves. He's nearly always scissors anyway. I think it must be the surgeon in him.

Sure enough, I win or I let him win by choosing paper, and I tuck him into the bed. Some nights, with the new development between us, the tension in our room is palatable. A lighthearted kiss turns breathless and full of promises I'm not ready to cash in on. Things are still so new between us, but tonight I could be tucking in a teddy bear or a kitten for all the desire that unfolds. He is asleep before I even say goodnight.

A swift knock on our door makes me roll my eyes. My dad does this every night, just a reminder to his not-son-in-law that he'd better be behaving himself and a reminder to me that I'm still his little girl. You'd be surprised at how much an anticipated knock can be like a douse of cold water. I toss my pillow at the door in rebuttal.

I know I need to fall asleep as quickly as possible, of course. Being Lost, we don't mess around with insomnia, not if we're with someone we'd like to stay with. A constant worry in our lives is the fear of being left behind or going on ahead without our loved ones. As a result, the Lost can sleep pretty much anywhere, anytime. Ever see a homeless person, napping at a bus stop? He may just be trying to get out. When all else fails, and we have trouble sleeping, there's always the Nightfall pills. Invented by some Lost genius out there with a restlessness problem, they'll knock you out quickly enough. We're all so tired here in Africa that none of us are using them now, but we each keep a steady supply. Sleeping together becomes an art form, me, Iz, Dad, Bea, and Joe, all sleeping at once, never without the others, not even once. Once is all it takes, just ask my sister Rose. Leaving her behind one night when she was just a child was hardly intentional, but she won't forgive us.

Even so, tonight I find my mind wandering. I think about Rose and Luke and wonder where they are now. Have they stayed in London? Are they still in old man Tate's house, eating cake, sipping imaginary tea, and throwing dishes? Did they realize we'd slipped away after Emme's funeral? We had only traveled continents, not centuries, not yet (please, God, anytime), and I can almost feel them near me. It makes me shiver, and not just with fear, but with a sense of foreboding. Though I'd like to assume we are done with them for good, I can't be sure. If Rose is still determined to exact her revenge on us, she'll find us soon enough. She did before.

With that disturbing thought, I firmly shake my head, and find Israel's hand beneath the blanket. I pull it down so it dangles off the side of the bed, so I can hold it. With the practice of someone who has perfected it, I will myself to sleep.

* * *

When morning breaks, Israel is already gone, and though I've lain in bed sleepily, I don't fall back asleep. Travelings usually happen in the dead of night, which makes waking at different times acceptable for the most part, but still.

The mornings in Africa are best when it comes to the weather, the deluges and downpours will start in the afternoon. I'm used to having our room to myself to get ready for the day. I'd love a bath, but I make do with splashing some cold water on my face from the pitcher on our bedside. I also miss deodorant if I haven't listed that in my long list yet. I ponytail my hair low enough that it won't cause a problem with my wide brimmed hat and change out of my white nightgown and into a pair of trousers.

I can't stop yawning this morning, though I slept all night and mercifully didn't dream of Emme. Her loss is a physical thing to me, and I wince every time she comes to mind, which is at least a hundred times a day.

Breakfast is usually spent with Bea and Joe, and this morning is no different. They are already up when I come down to the eating area. Bea is sipping tea and Joe bouncing off the walls. Our home, if that's what it is (the name doesn't fit yet), is a boarding house for tourists. Israel says less than a decade from now this will be Nairobi, but for now it's just a village in Kenya. I try to close my eyes and picture it as a bustling, modern capital city with telephone poles, internet connections, hotels, and cars, but my imagination fails me. Already I've tumbled into the past and acclimatized to it.

Of all people, I should be perfectly able to picture it modernized, but I simply cannot. Right now, the people look at us with distrust, though we are only here to help them. Well, we are also here to escape from my sister. I hope we won't stay too long here. It's one place I won't mind waking up and being gone from.

Our boarding house mistress is a young woman named Asha. She's a startlingly beautiful widow, independent especially for this day and age, and she doesn't care for me a fig. I know this because she told me so. If I thought things were awkward in the bedroom, it's nothing compared to the awkwardness I feel around Asha.

She nods to me, the way she always does, and continues stirring something in a pot for her guests. We aren't really considered guests anymore, just boarders. The difference between the two, I am not entirely sure I grasp. About a month ago, she left us to our own devices when it came to meals. This has left us to scrounge around for our breakfasts and lunches. It has put me in the position of cooking supper for my pretend husband. He likes this arrangement even less than I do. I can't cook.

"Auntie Sonnet, I defended our whole house from lions last night!" Joe says with his mouth full of porridge. He tells me this nearly every morning.

I ruffle his messed up hair fondly. "Did you? Well, I certainly appreciate that. I wish you would have chased off the elephants too, though. I had three of them in my bed, and it was so crowded!"

Joe laughs and spits porridge everywhere. "That's incredulous, Auntie," he says. My father has been teaching him new vocabulary words, and he enjoys peppering his sentences with them whenever he can. Joe is only seven, but he can speak like an old professor when he puts his little mind to it.

Only seven. Suddenly, I remember his sixth birthday, over a hundred years from now. We were in America, and I was working at the coffee shop with my boss, Micki. Emme had come in and taken me shopping with her for his birthday gift. That was the day I realized she was Joe's mum, not his sister, like she pretended to be. That makes Bea his biological grandmother, not mother, but she always filled the latter role. Now, with Emme dead and gone, she always would. Just a year ago, but it feels like lifetimes ago. All our ages are a bit in question, especially since our travel to London when Rose pulled us there. Somehow, we missed a couple of months. Later, I realized we had missed my birthday. I'm nineteen, nearly twenty now, I think.

"You're incredulous," I reply mildly. "Now share your porridge, if you please."

"Make your own." Joe guards his bowl the way I knew he would, and bares his teeth growling.

"Oh, ho," I shake his own spoon at him playfully. "Who's the lion now?"

While Joe immerses himself in method acting by practicing his roars, I finish the last of his breakfast. Bea is staring into space, the way she does frequently these days. I hate to interrupt her thoughts, though if they're sad, perhaps it would be a kindness. I study her face for a moment. She has prematurely aged a bit in the last year, no small wonder. Her smooth face has slipped a bit, like butter left out on the counter. I long to lift the corners of her mouth like I would do if Joe were upset to make him laugh. I go ahead and speak though I'm not confident she's even listening to me.

"Israel asked me to get some things. Well, he asked me the other day, but I forgot until now. We could ride the train and make a day of it if you aren't too busy." I make a show of scraping my bowl clean though there's nothing left to scrape. I'm uncomfortable around Bea these days, though she's the closest thing to a mother I've ever had, beside Prue. Since her and my father are somewhat involved with one another, she could be my stepmother someday.

Even so, or because of those things, the guilt I feel for her only daughter's murder never leaves my mind. I can't help wondering if she blames me for Emme's death. Now she's left with her grandson to raise by herself, and I feel as though it's entirely my fault. If I hadn't become obsessed with finding Rose, if I hadn't pursued her, maybe she would have left us alone.

Bea looks up and focuses on me, just for a moment, long enough to reply. "They're doing the ribbon cutting ceremony today, remember?"

Oh, yes. I had forgotten about that. Though the clinic isn't really finished, it's finished enough to start seeing patients. They see a few at a time, while the rest of the building goes up around them. Israel and Dr. Smythe are excited to get back to practicing medicine, leaving the carpentry and such to their hired laborers.

Though Israel once confessed to me that he hated being a doctor, but the usefulness he feels when practicing makes him whole again. Traveling centuries through time and space has given him an edge in the medical world, and he plans to use his knowledge to save those who couldn't be saved before. He's much nobler than I am, and I'm proud of him. My only contribution to the world seems to be bad fashion and a lunatic family that I try to keep out of the general population. I typically fail at the latter.

"Oh, mercy, I forgot!" I smack my forehead making Joe chuckle. "I should probably wear a dress, and make myself look more professional like?"

Bea has already dismissed me in her mind and is no longer listening. Resting her chin in her hands, she is staring into space again. Asha bustles by, and I can nearly feel the iciness as she passes me. I don't know why she dislikes me, but I can guess. Israel is handsome, what more modern girls would call very fine, I'm a white nobody. I don't think she appreciates me taking him off any other eligible, more compatible, girl's hands. But then again, that's just a guess. Maybe I'm paranoid.

"Are you going to at least comb through this lion's mane of yours?" I make a show of giving Joe a Mohawk, sliding his carrot-colored hair through my palms. He is in desperate need of a haircut, but he won't sit still long enough, and truth be told, the only person who has ever cut his hair was Emme. I wonder if he'll ever cut it again, and if we'll have a male version of Rapunzel on our hands soon.

"Stop it!" He swats my hand away and smooths down his ruffled hair. "I like it the way it is. I gotta go! I'll see you there!" He speaks in exclamation points all the time at this age. Everything is exciting for Joe.

We've given him entirely too much freedom here, I think. He comes and goes without so much as a by-your-leave, and no one is making him do lessons or keeping him accountable for anything. Dad is teaching him big fancy words, but that's about the extent of his education and nurturing right now.

I make a mental note to start him on his letters and numbers soon, if I can broach the subject to Bea without insulting her parenting style. I remember being a little Lost child, and I was taught my letters by a silent monk in a Spanish monastery. I remember practicing my handwriting in the dim light of a candle while he inscribed sacred texts and illuminated manuscripts. I wish I could give that to Joe, but I'm sure he'll get his own unorthodox education all in good time. Who knows where we'll wake up next?

For the ribbon cutting ceremony, I wear my second best dress, the blue one that Lu found for me back in London. As usual, it's too short, but no one here will care or even notice. In order for it to button correctly and not look odd, I have to wear a corset, my absolute least favorite invention in the world. I complain the entire time Lu is pulling it tight. Hers is already laced up and ready, and she looks like a little China doll. Appearing older in appearance really than her years, but still attractive.

"I don't remember it being this tight on you last time," Lu admonishes in Chinese.

"Thanks a lot," I pant. "I think you just relocated my spleen."

"Are you sure you aren't with baby?" She steps around from the back of me and eyes me, up and down, hands on her hips.

I blush to the tips of my hair. "I'm sure," I reply firmly. "Are you really going to ask me that every day for the rest of my life? I promise if that ever happens, you'll be the first to know."

"Well, I don't know what's taking so long." Lu looks irritated by my lack of procreation. "I'm going to talk to Ethan about this."

"No, you will not talk to Dr. Smythe!" I am appalled. Really, my nonexistent fertility problems are the least of everyone's concerns. Why isn't everyone busying themselves with bigger problems? Why is the size of my waist the only thing on Lu's mind?

It probably would have been easier to just come clean with the doctor and Lu about our sham of a marriage, but we worried that they would be insulted that we started our friendship and work partnership on a lie. Plus, Africa or no, this is still a Victorian time we live in. It doesn't do well for one's reputation to be living in sin, even if there hasn't been much sinning.

"Finally," Lu grunts. "You're done. May I fix your hair?"

"So, I can shove it under a hat? No, thanks." I'm still miffed at her nosiness, and my tone is sharper than I had intended. "Sorry. The heat is oppressive already, and I miss my spleen, that's all."

Lu rolls her eyes and mumbles something that sounds like the Chinese word for baby. Whether she's mourning the lack of me producing one or is accusing me of being one, I don't know.

We head out into the sun.

Chapter 2

There's a newspaper man at the ribbon cutting ceremony that I take an instant dislike to. He totes around his mammoth camera and seems to be under everyone's feet at once. He reminds me of a little weasel. Maybe the reason I don't like him is the camera. The last relationship I had with a photographer did not go well, and my blood boils a little at the thought of Luke. Anyway, this weasel's name is Basil, and I'm worried about how far his audience spreads, and how he already knows all our real names. We should have traveled with aliases, but then we'd be back to the whole insulting of Dr. Smythe and Lu again. They know us by our real names, and there's no story ever penned that would give a plausible explanation for why we suddenly felt the need to change them. Well, there's the story of a mad sister chasing us through centuries as we travel through time, but I've not known that one to attract any friends.

"I don't want in the photo," I practically growl. I sound like Joe imitating a tiger. "That's final."

Basil, the oily thing, doesn't take no for an answer. "But your husband has been instrumental in the building and creation of this historical hospital! This is a monumental moment, a moment your children and grandchildren will want preserved for all time!" His voice has a nasal, whining edge to it that must have driven his own mother to drink when he was a child. I can just imagine him pleading for more dessert, and her giving in to keep him quiet.

"Why is everyone so dang obsessed with my imaginary children?" I nearly yell. "Israel, back me up on this." I turn to him, rather desperately. "No photos."

"No photos," Iz repeats, his voice hard. Basil immediately slinks off to pester someone else. I imagine him leaving behind a trail of slime, like a giant slug. I don't usually take such an immediate dislike to people, but lately I've been paying better attention to my instincts. Before Rose, I believed everyone had good intentions on their minds.

"Geez, Louise," I mutter, and fan myself with my hat. "I hate photographers. I really do, nearly as much as corsets, and definitely more than scorpions." I step on one savagely with my boot and hear a satisfying crunch. As I knew he would, Israel jumps backward a full foot and makes a sound like a nine-year-old Girl Scout. He hates creepy crawlies, probably even more than photographers. Though it's a tossup, his hatred of Luke Dawes runs pretty deep.

"Ugh." My handsome hero shivers. "That sounded like a big, squishy one."

"Don't worry, I'll protect you." I sidle up and throw my arms around him. "For a kiss, that is."

A moment of bliss is interrupted by the flash of an old fashioned camera. I'd like to beat that Basil with his own equipment. I really would.

*   *   *

The hospital here was started by an eager couple who were fresh out of some sort of religious school. They came with a zealous desire for missionary work and the funding to back them.

They lasted a few months and were happy to let Dr. Smythe and Dr. Rhode (as everyone calls my Israel) take over. We'll probably never know their story, but let's just say they had their suitcases packed when we arrived and barely showed us around before they took off back to the states.

The Lost are used to making do and surviving. We don't expect the red carpet treatment, so stepping into their spots was easy enough. I'm not saying I'd like to stay here. Of all the places I've called home, this doesn't make my personal Top Five List. Maybe it's Asha, maybe it's the feeling of looking over my shoulder for my sister. Perhaps I just don't belong here even more than I don't belong anywhere, which is really saying something.

At night, we pull out a handwritten letter, addressed to Ethan and Lu. Every single night we pull this letter out and leave it on our nightstand.

Every single morning, when we wake still here, we tuck it back inside the drawer for the next night. It's Israel's words, but it's my handwriting. How his beautiful hands can perform delicate surgeries, and softly stroke my wrist making me weak kneed, but can't legibly write his own name, is a mystery to me. The letter says this:

Dear Ethan and Lu,

The time has come to part ways. You know of some of our plight in London; indeed, it is worse than you believed. Our enemies are close, and we must put distance between ourselves and those we love, namely you. It is better this way so you will not be in danger, too. Thank you for your understanding, wisdom, and friendship. Forgive us for our abrupt departure.

Israel and Sonnet, Noah, Bea, and Joe.

It's unusual that we do this, but the thought of abandoning them without any kind of explanation is too cruel. They've allowed us to live with them, and we've gotten to know them through our travels and struggles. To disappear in the middle of the night, as we will inevitably do someday, would haunt us. Our explanation is shoddy, but the best we can do. Plus, it's a little bit true. They know of Rose and Luke, and without Lu, Israel and I might have met a bloody demise at the end of Luke's pistol.

Lu was our avenging angel, flying through the night and saving our lives. I still smile when I remember it. I doubt Luke smiles over it. He was so angry that I thought he might break right through the wardrobe door we locked him inside. I wonder how and if he got out. Did Rose return from wherever it was she had gone that day? Had she been cavorting with Jack the Ripper again? Had she traveled somewhere alone?

Rose is the only one of us who can control her travels. I'm jealous of that, I'll admit readily enough. To be able to navigate, and go where and when you choose is a luxury. Though it hasn't done her any favors, since she's as mad as a hatter. The weird thing is that I still love her desperately. We'll never be true sisters again, and I want nothing to do with her.

It's dark, and normally we'd all be asleep by now, but the ribbon cutting ceremony and all the excitement surrounding it has wired us all up. Joe is usually our bedtime reminder at night, but he is still up eating more dessert in Asha's kitchen. Bea and my father have gone for a stroll in the moonlight. I try not to imagine them stopping to kiss or some such thing. Lu is sewing by the light of an oil lamp, and Dr. Smythe and Israel are conversing out on the porch with a colleague. I tried to join in their conversation, but it was getting far too bloody and detailed for squeamish me.

I don't mind pretending I know what they're talking about when the conversation is tuned to turned ankles or fevers or coughs, but when they get into things like squirting blood vessels and violent bleeding, I feel a bit lightheaded. Actually, I think Iz does too, but he takes it like a man more than I do. When you're a good three or four inches over six feet tall and full of rippled muscles, people expect braver things of you (unless there's a scorpion nearby).

So, I wander up to our room, thinking I'll read until Iz comes to bed and we start our awkward dance of who sleeps where. Lu has given me a collection of Chinese fairytales. They're gruesome and eerie, and guaranteed to not to give me stellar dreams. I'll read a while and maybe comb through my mop of tangled hair.

I haven't had my dark hair trimmed in months and months, and I forget how long it is until I take the time to brush it. I decide if we travel to the 1920's flapper era, I'm going to cut it all off in a pageboy style. Of course, with my luck, we'd wake up the next day in Puritan Salem, and they'd burn me as a witch for such a wicked head of hair. I can't seem to win for losing.

I'm distracted by the sight of our letter to Dr Smythe and Lu perched on the nightstand. I frown perplexed. It's always the last thing we do before we fall asleep. Israel hasn't even been to our room since early this morning, and I distinctly remember putting it away when I got up, hours ago. Reaching for it, I realize it's not our letter. This one is a paler shade, not the same paper at all, and it's not folded like ours is. It's just a small rectangle of paper with one line written in familiar handwriting. I know it because I've seen his writing on the backs of his photos.

Gray,

I need to see you – life or death matter. It's about Rose.

My blood runs cold. The last person I ever wanted to see again had found me. My betrayer, my sister's lover, Luke Dawes.

* * *

"All in all, I think it was pretty successful." Israel yawns and stretches. "The natives are warming up to us, and even though I know Basil is a greasy skunk, the hospital needs the publicity. I made him promise me to give me the photo of us, though." He winks at me. "Want to reenact the moment?"

I'm too distracted for kissing. I haven't decided what to do about the note. Earlier, I had ripped it into tiny, unrecognizable pieces and threw them out the window. Then I bolted shut the window. The thought of Luke being in my room without my knowledge makes my skin crawl. I haven't told Israel.

Yet.

"I haven't brushed my teeth," I lie. "I have garlic breath."

"Yum!" Iz grins. "Come here."

"No, really!" I back up. "And I'm getting a cold."

"You should see a doctor." He wiggles his eyebrows suggestively. "I'd better examine you." What has gotten into him? The one night I'm far too distracted for flirting, and he goes all romantic on me. For crying out loud.

"For that cheesy line," I announce, "you totally get the floor. Down, boy."

"You're killing me, Sonny," Iz groans. "I'm not kidding."

"You just worked a twelve-hour shift. You're delirious."

"Delirious, but not dead," he mutters as I hear the familiar goodnight knock on our door. We freeze as though we had been doing something remotely questionable.

"Night, Dad," I say loudly.

"Night, Sonny!"

"See?" Crossly, I turn to Iz. "You call me that one minute, expecting goose bumps and passion, and then my dad comes along and calls me Sonny. Seriously."

"You're just looking for excuses." Israel's tone is teasing, but there's an underlying current to his words. It's probably true. I do look for excuses to not get too close. My emotional walls are as high as the moon sometimes. "Fine then, but if you're planning a booty call in the middle of night, missy, you'll be sorely disappointed."

I snort. "Thank you for the warning, Casanova, though I hardly know what that means." I take a deep breath and lick my lips. Then I chew on the bottom one. I can't get the words out, the words that will tell him our least favorite person in the world is lurking nearby.

"What?" Israel frowns. "What is wrong with you tonight?"

I already know what will happen if I talk. Israel will grab the rifle that Asha keeps for protection, and he will pace the house and the grounds until he finds Luke. Then, after he beats him to a pulp, he'll shoot him or maybe vice versa. I just know there won't be any conversation between them, and I may never know the meaning of the note.

It's about Rose? Is she dead? No, he wouldn't come find me for that news, there'd be no point. Is she locked up again? That's probably it, though what I could do about it is beyond me. Has she traveled without him? Again, what could I possibly do about that? Has she ... recovered? *Yes, Sonnet, she's all better now, full of sweetness and light,* my inner sarcastic voice ridicules me.

"I'm just tired and cranky," I answer with a shrug. "Are the doors all locked?"

Israel really stares at me now. "You know Asha. She's pretty into safety. Why, think Basil is going to sneak in and annoy you some more?"

"I've heard of paparazzi doing worse," I point out, glad my tone sounds normal. "He might climb the tree and come in through our window. I'll just double check the latch." I make a show of being silly and dramatic, but really I am jiggling the lock, testing it.

Did Luke just stroll casually through the boarding house to my room? How did he know where to go? Did he ask Asha for my room number, or did he really shimmy through the window? I don't remember now if it was locked or not. Like a dunce, I've locked and relocked it so many times in the past twenty seconds that I can't recall.

I look down, into the space below the window. It's too dark now to see the tiny pieces of paper I threw. Had I unlocked the window before tossing them out? I can't remember. I'm such a fool. I lean my forehead against the cool glass of the window. I feel Israel kiss the back of my neck, which would normally give me delicious goose-bumps, but tonight only serves to make me jump. I then hear him toss his pillow on the floor.

I crawl into bed and debate my options. I could wait until Iz falls asleep, then sneak down and get the rifle myself. I could then go find Luke, and demand to know what he wants from me, but I run the risk I always run if I'm not sleeping at the same time as the others. If tonight's the night for a travel, I'd be left behind. I would have chosen Luke, of all people, over my own family.

I close my eyes tight, and with obstinate resolve, I make myself fall asleep.

* * *

For once, I'm awake before Israel. I think I even wake up before the rooster out back, but that's not necessarily an achievement. Whoever says roosters only crow at dawn are mistaken. They crow all day and half the night or at least old Boris does. Asha told me his African name, but I couldn't decipher or remember it, so I call the mean old thing Boris. Boris and Asha have very similar personalities traits like snooty, snobby, and peckish.

I struggle to get my pants on underneath my nightgown, and then realize that's not half as difficult as putting on my chemise and shirt while still wearing my nightgown. I am practically stifled to death by a ruffle, and at one point I am concerned I'll have to wake Israel up just to get me out. That would defeat the purpose of me doing this in the first place, which was just to keep him from seeing me naked.

Flushed and feeling like I just ran a marathon, I finally closed the door softly behind me and set off downstairs. I'll have to wake him soon, but he had a long day yesterday and never gets to sleep much. Also, I'm pretty confident I heard a soft chuckle when I was tangled in my nightgown, so I don't think he's sleeping anyway. Overgrown brat.

I ignore the sound of Joe's chatter over his porridge close by, and head straight for where I know Asha keeps her rifle, her room. She'll kill me six different ways if she catches me, but I have bigger enemies to worry about. One of them is practically on my doorstep.

Asha's room is sparse, but larger than the other rooms. Her bed is enormous, and I wonder, not for the first time, what her husband was like. She is barely older than me, and already a widow. I reach under the bed and pull out the Martini-Henry rifle her husband left her. It's extremely heavy, but I think I can use it if I need to, especially if Luke makes me mad enough. Dad taught me to shoot years ago, or years *from* now, I forget. Sometime in my past, but not the world's past, anyway.

Asha's room has a large picture window, one that is more like a door than a window. It's almost romantic somehow, and I wonder again about her husband. If this were a more modern era it would lead to a patio or a swimming pool, but Asha's only leads to wilderness behind the boarding house. I leave through this window instead of sneaking out through the house. It's difficult enough to sneak without lugging around the world's heaviest firearm.

Boris comes squawking up to me, his ugly eyes looking mean as ever. "Get away from me, you smelly bugger," I threaten, brandishing the rifle. "I have eaten plenty of rooster pudding in my time, and I am not above eating it again." Such a culinary oddity was one of Prue's specialties, along with squirrel pie and alligator gumbo. These memories make me realize how much I miss her, and cause a sharp pang. I'd give anything to smell her strange pastries and bizarre stews again.

Leaving her behind in London was difficult, but necessary. Lost herself, she may travel on her own, but it was a better alternative than traipsing about countries with our pursued and endangered family. Also, once the Lost get old enough their traveling whittles down to nothing if they aren't near any other Lost to get pulled into their journeys. I can only hope she lives out her final days, in culinary bliss, at Sir Halloway's house.

Asha has a shed out back, past the chickens, the well, and the garden. I am drawn in that direction, and I'm already annoyed with myself. If I do indeed find Luke there, it will mean we are still drawn to one another in a way. The last human I would want to think like is Luke. I don't want to have anything in common with that traitor. I traipse through the mud angrily. I know I am bungling this. I never should have gone to sleep without telling someone about Luke and how he's found us. If I couldn't get the guts to tell Israel, I should have told Dad. Dad would only be mildly upset, in his typical gloomy fashion. Iz, on the other hand, is going to kill me.

Maybe neither of them needs to find out. I can just shoot Luke and then feed his remains to Boris. Good idea! I see no flaw in it at all and instantly feel cheered.

I make no sneaky ceremony of jiggling the shed door, creeping up quietly, or softly calling his name. Instead, feeling rather like a vigilante, I shoulder my rifle, take off the safety, and then kick the door in with all fury and strength I can muster. The door bursts open. I aim directly for the shadowy figure that I knew would be inside, but he doesn't even do me the courtesy of jumping to his feet, or shouting out in surprise. His long legs are folded up as he sits on an overturned bucket. He regards me with something like amusement, and he takes the time to grind out his cigarette before he speaks.

"Hullo, Gray. You're looking...tan," Luke said.

"And you're looking like a murdering piece of scum," I reply. "What the hell do you want?"

"Language, language," Luke tsks. "I admit, we didn't part on good terms, but you could act a bit more polite. I am your brother-in-law, you know."

I can't help but feel taken aback, though I try not to show it. Luke and Rose, married? "No, I didn't know. The invitation must have gotten lost in the mail." I keep the rifle shouldered, though my arms ache. I wouldn't lower it for a million dollars. "You two married ... there's a thought that makes my stomach turn."

"Why? Don't you want someone to take care of your sister?" He pauses waiting for me to answer, but I'm silent. "Obviously, you've given up on her yourself." His voice is laced with disapproval, and more than that; disappointment?

His words hurt, but I stuff the hurt down inside to deal with it later. "You'll make a lovely pair, I'm sure. Now, you have twenty seconds to tell me why you're here and what your plan is for leaving again. Is Rose here?"

"Three questions, and only twenty seconds to answer them? You've gotten impatient, Gray. It doesn't suit you. No, Rose is not here. She's in 1931, in Bedlam." He examines his cuff sleeve as if curious about it suddenly, like he's acting more casual than he really feels. Typically, Luke is an exceptional actor, so this bit of careful nonchalance is out of place. He must be feeling more uncomfortable than usual. I look at his cuff as well. His clothes are fairly common for the Lost to travel in. He wears characteristic nondescript black trousers and a white button down shirt. I'm far from a fashion expert, but I'd say they're expensive and well made. Almost as if he came straight here from some wealthy party. Somehow I'm not surprised. There's a lot of playboy in Luke Dawes.

"Why? Why did you leave her behind?" I'm surprised. I'm certainly not sad she isn't here. In fact, I feel my shoulders relax a bit, but I'm stunned he would jump eras without her. That's risky.

"She doesn't know me," he replies, flatly. "Not as me, anyway. She doesn't even know herself. If you thought Rose was," his voice cracks, and I know he's having a hard time saying the words, "insane before, back in London when last you saw her, she's much worse now." Luke runs his hand through his sandy-colored hair, the way he does when he's tired or thinking deeply. It's gotten so long that he could probably gather it into a messy ponytail. Combine his hair with his five o'clock shadow, and he'd look like a twenty-first century movie star. His looks were always a little distracting.

I roll my eyes. I'm having a hard time imagining Rose being any worse. Is she boiling kittens in her spare time now? Setting orphanages on fire?

"She's sick, Gray. Her illness has forced her into a place inside herself where she has built up an elaborate world. She doesn't even know herself, calls herself Lizzie. She calls me Sam. Come on now, you've been a part of the modern world. You've heard of multiple and split personalities, or dissociative personality disorder?" He waits for my response.

"What's your point?" I sigh. There's no hope for it. I can't keep aiming this rifle. I lower it slowly, and my arms thank me by deciding not to fall off in a heap by my shaky legs. "Sounds like a great thing actually. Only you would ever miss Rose Gray anyway."

"Because she can't travel." Luke's voice is monotone. His eyes search me and keep talking even when his voice stops. *She's stuck,* his eyes communicate to me. *Stuck in time.*

I get a chill. "So, she's stranded in Bedlam? And, what? You're upset because eventually you'll travel without her, is that it? Ah." Again, his mouth stays shut, but his anguished eyes speak volumes. "Well, that does put a kink in your relationship."

"Have a heart, Gray. I need to get her back before it's too late. What if her memory comes back, and I'm not there to keep her stable? If I'm gone centuries in the past or in the future?"

"You've done such a lovely job up until now keeping her stable," I scowl. "She's probably better off without you enabling her anyway."

"I see your point, but believe me, she's much worse on her own. Think of all the damage she could do without me. She knows Jack. She knows how to steer her journeys. She found you once, and she'll do it again." His smooth voice is a threat now. "If you help me bring her back to herself, I'll keep her away from you. I swear it."

I laugh without any humor. "Your word means nothing to me, less than nothing actually, and there are a couple problems with your master plan. One, I can't get myself to 1931 even if I wanted to, and for another, how could I help? If I was even willing to, which I assure you, I am not." I must be missing something. He had to have known I wouldn't join forces with him. I frown, searching my memory, looking for the missing piece.

"Don't you see? I'm hoping that seeing you will trigger something in her. Like it or not, you're the biggest thing in her life. She's been obsessed with you for years. She knows you. It's my only shot. I'm desperate."

"And the other thing, genius? Wait..." My eyes narrow when a thought occurs to me. "How did you even get here if you've been to 1931 with her?" My thoughts are swirling, and I don't like where they're going. There is a certain kind of smugness to Luke's handsome face now that worries me. He shouldn't have been able to get to me intentionally if Rose truly isn't with him, unless she's taught him how to navigate. Merciful heavens, that's all the world needs, Luke Dawes hopping through time, on purpose. I shoulder the rifle again, but Luke only looks mildly annoyed.

"For God's sake, Gray, don't trip or anything. We both know you aren't going to shoot me on purpose."

"You underestimate the depths of my hatred for you," I respond, "and I'm not going to trip. If I shoot you, you can damn sure bet it was because I intended to. Just so you know dear brother-in-law, I'm not aiming at your heart." I lower the rifle about a foot to make my point. Predictably, his mild annoyance shoots up a notch to slightly nervous.

He puts up his hands in a surrendered stance. "Okay, okay. I got here because I brought someone with me, someone else who knows how to get where she wants, your grandmother Nora."

"What?" It's all I can say. My tongue is tied in knots.

"Did Noah ever tell you about her?"

Did my father ever tell me about my grandmother? Not until recently, when he remembered to mention that she too, knew how to find her way through time. I hadn't thought too much of it, especially because he said she was a bit batty. Evidently, madness and supreme cosmic powers run in my family. All I got was the ice blue eyes. Nice.

"He mentioned her." I tread carefully. "What do you mean? She's here with you? She brought you here?" My voice threatens to squeak, which for me is odd. I have a deep, throaty voice for a girl.

"She did, indeed, so if you'd like to meet her, you probably shouldn't murder me."

"It isn't murder when the victim is a dirt bag. It's public service." I get no further because I see Luke's eyebrows shoot straight up into his hair the way they do when he's surprised by something, and that something is behind me. I whirl, and am met by a string of profanity in at least seven different languages, including some Gypsy curses. The hair-rising expletives are followed by some very specific promises directed to the man next to me in the shed.

"Israel, I can explain." I swallow, but the rifle is already out of my hands before I can stop him, and Israel pushes me behind him with a force that I know is not entirely necessary.

"Later," he growls, and I dread later already. "Dawes."

BANG! He shoots the wall a scant inch beside Luke's head. Luke doesn't flinch, but his eyebrows haven't returned to their normal resting spot either.

"Come on, let the girl explain." Luke's hands go up in a submissive gesture that only serves to irritate Israel further.

BANG! Israel blows another hole on the other side of Luke's face. The expression on his face doesn't change, but Luke's eyebrows have completely vanished into his hairline now.

"He has my grandmother!" I shout. I probably don't need to yell, seeing as how I'm only inches from his ear, but adrenaline has kicked in with the force of a hurricane. I may have just deafened my love. Getting a hold of myself, I lower my voice to continue. "I don't much care if you kill him four ways from Sunday"

"Gee thanks, Gray," Luke interrupts.

"In fact, I'll help, but can we do it after we learn why he's here and where he's stashed my grandmother?"

"What?" Israel glares. "Prue is here?"

"No, not Prue, my biological grandmother, Nora. My mother's mother."

Israel sighs with enough passion and emotion to win him an Academy Award. I remember watching the show on the television with Harry and Matthias a couple of years ago. "This is not how I planned to spend my weekend." I can literally hear his teeth grinding together in frustration. It sounds painful.

"Well, plans change, old boy." Luke's eyebrows return to their rightful spot above his beautiful eyes, and I know that he knows that he's won, at least temporarily. "Can we get out of here, please? It wasn't the world's most comfortable bedroom last night. I swear to God, I think I heard a lion prowling around, and I hate to be crude, but I really need to pee."

"That was a rooster, moron, and I'm in charge here. You aren't going to take a step, a breath, or a piss until I tell you you can." Iz growls.

"Alright if I blink?"

"I wouldn't."

"How about one eye at a time?"

"Alright, girls! Enough already!" I am back to shouting. One boy at a time, that's my limit. Put these two together, and I feel like a drunken referee. I am hoping Luke's story can be told incredibly swiftly, and he can either be sent on his merry way or put six feet under. Honestly, I cannot take the two of them much longer. Heaven help me if he sticks around.

Chapter 3

We march back to the boarding house with Luke a few feet ahead of us, his arms held high the way Israel demands, the rifle aimed squarely between his shoulder blades. When Luke complains, Iz threatens to make him dance like a ballerina instead. I consider staying in the quiet of the shed, and maybe finding Luke's stash of cigarettes. I've never smoked a day in my life, but now seems like a good time to start.

"Hey, Mr. Dawes!" Joe waves cheerfully as he bounds out of the boarding house. Since Luke's hands are held high, Joe jumps to the logical conclusion if you're a man-child, and makes a show of leaping as tall as possible, trying for a high-five.

"Hey, scamp!" Luke replies cheerfully. I want to kill him right then, I really do. He's responsible in part for Joe's mom's murder, and he is acting like he forgot about that detail? Joe doesn't know, obviously, and he always liked Luke. So did I – at first.

"Get away from him," I shoo Joe away. "He's a bad man, and you aren't to talk to him." My auntie tactics and creed involve mainly handing him excessive amounts of sugar and tickling him, so my words have the opposite effect. Joe sticks his tongue out at me and runs off. I have a headache.

"Sit down." Israel motions to the furniture on the porch after we all climb the steps. Luke obediently sits and watches us, expectantly.

"Well?" he drawls. "What's it to be? Torture first, and then breakfast, or maybe a light brunch followed by some suffering? Hot pokers? The Wheel? Thumbscrews? *The Brady Bunch* reruns on a continuous loop? I've been around, you know. I'm pretty familiar with torture. Is there a flow chart for our activities or something?"

"I really, really hate him," Iz growls to me. He's done nothing but growl syllables for the last little while. I'm concerned for his throat. Will I have to feed him hot broth for the rest of our natural lives?

"I know. Me too." I kiss his cheek, lingeringly, and get the satisfaction of seeing a disgusted look on Luke's face.

"Gross. Can we skip ahead to the water boarding?"

"Shut up. I hated him back before we knew the truth, and I hate him now." Israel's voice seems less growly now. "Now what's all this about your grandmother, Sonny?"

"I don't know yet." I drop down in a chair, the farthest one from Luke, and push back my straggling hair. It's hot already, and the stray hair that has escaped its hair-tie are limp and beginning to frizz. Twenty-first century hair products are #72 of the things I miss. "He said she brought him here on purpose. He wants me to go back with him or forward, to 1931." I look to Luke for confirmation, and he nods cheerful.

"Well, that's not going to happen. Can I shoot him now?" Israel's arm hasn't wavered. I'm impressed by his strength. I bet Luke's arm would be shaky by now if it were him.

"Soon," I promise. "Rose is stuck there. Evidently, she doesn't know who she is, or who Luke is. Oh, and they're married."

"My condolences. I'm sure you'll make a hellish couple." Israel seems to shudder. I see goose bumps emerge on his brown bicep.

"Thanks, bro." Luke grins. My heart used to do a flip-flop when he grinned like that. Now it just makes me want to smack him upside the head with a brick.

The screen door to the boarding house opens, and out steps beautiful Asha. She doesn't break stride, but takes in our little tableau on her way down the steps and out into the yard. "I'm going out. Bea is watching the front desk." Her voice is as smooth as honey. "Don't get blood on my porch."

We watch her leave in silence. "Interesting dame," Luke muses. "Can we take a bathroom break soon? I hate to break up our heart to heart, but I'm not kidding. I really have to go."

"Just take him," I sigh.

Israel looks at me like I have three eyes. "What? Are you crazy?"

"Well, I'm certainly not taking him!"

"I'm perfectly capable of going by my" Luke interjects.

"Shut up!" we both yell simultaneously.

"No one is taking anyone." Israel is back to growling. "You're a big boy. Hold it. Now, will someone please tell me why we are still listening to this nonsense and why I can't shoot him yet?"

Luke raises his hand like a schoolboy. "Pick me," he says. "I know the answer! Because Nora is a very old and frail lady, and if you'd like to meet her, you'll keep me alive. Also, no matter how much Sonnet denies it, she still cares for her sister and hopes there can be some healing or cure for Rose's issues."

"Issues," Iz snorts.

Luke ignores him and continues. "Also, this plotting your course through time? Seems to run in the family, if you know what I mean. I think Sonnet can be taught. If she can be taught, just think of where and when she could go. Think of it, Gray! Where would you go first? To save your mother? To save Emme?" His gaze is sly.

"That's not fair." My voice trembles, and I speak softly. I'm not sure anyone hears me. There's a buzzing sound in my ears, like I'm surrounded by invisible mosquitoes.

"You're a manipulative little bastard," Israel mutters.

"I know," he agrees with no tone of irony or smugness. Just stating a fact. "At first I thought Rose's ability was due to her lobotomy. We both did." Luke crosses his hands behind his head.

I shiver. Rose had a lobotomy?

"But then we learned about Nora from Prue. By the way, she sends her love."

"You saw Prue?" I am not speaking softly this time, and I leap to my feet. "What did you do to her? If you hurt her ..."

Luke scowls at me. "Of course I didn't hurt her. What kind of monster do you think I am? She's fine, but it's Nora we're talking about, remember? When I heard she could do it too, I got to thinking. The Grays must be special. Well, not the Grays exactly, since your dad is useless, and Nora is Carolina's mother, not his. What is it about the women in your family? Haven't you ever wondered if you could do it, too?"

"Do what? Navigate?"

He nods solemnly. "Haven't you imagined it?"

"Not really."

"Oh, come on, Gray! You've never thought about where you would go first? What time, what place?"

Well, yes, I had sort of, with Emme. We used to play Best and Worst: the best and worst times and places in which to wake up. I remember the last time we played, on the day we shopped for Joe's birthday gifts. It was cold and windy, and we were walking. I had recently stolen Israel's car for a little joyriding to the laundromat, and was forbidden from ever setting foot in it again. That wasn't the only reason we were walking though, Emme was terrified of cars and avoided them completely.

"Best: Cancun," Emme said. "Worst: The Black Death."

"Best: discovering America," I had said. "Worst: Marie Antoinette's court!"

"Best: abolition of slavery. Worst: on board the Titanic!"

"Best: the nativity in Bethlehem. Worst: The Trail of Tears."

"Best: The Wright Brothers' airplane. Worst: Vietnam in the sixties."

"Best: you know that scene in every Robin Hood movie? Where they're gnawing on turkey legs? That! Worst: The Great Depression."

"Yeah, I've had those turkey legs, and they weren't so great," Emme said. "It was like gnawing on shoe leather, not poultry."

"Please tell me you didn't actually meet Robin Hood!" I had stopped in my tracks.

Emme had laughed. "Pretty sure he's a fictional character, genius. I did meet a lot of friars back then, though, and maidens in long frocks. Castles aren't nearly as romantic as they look, let me tell you. Bloody cold and full of rats."

I am jarred out of my memories by the screen door slamming again. I guess we should have stayed in the shed if we wanted privacy. It's my dad.

"You have got to be kidding me." He stops dead in front of Luke, who smiles politely. "What is he doing here? Where's my daughter? Where's Rose?"

"She isn't here, Dad," I sigh. "Sit down, and we'll start at the beginning. Again." I fill him in quickly. He seems most surprised at the thought of seeing his mother-in-law again. He confirms that it was sometime in 1915 or so that they had left her behind in a small mental hospital; it wasn't Bedlam, but they could have transferred her years later. Blast it. Luke's story is checking out. Well, of course it is. Luke was always a man with a plan, with a vindictive mad woman behind the plan.

"Don't you understand?" Luke leans forward and stares straight into my soul. "Don't you see? You can undo all the bad. You can save your mother. You can save Emme. You can stop Jack, reunite with Harry and Matthias if you want. I don't much care what you do. Just come with me to 1931 first. Think of it, Gray!"

Dad looks skeptical, and Israel still looks angry, but I am already thinking of it. Damn him. I am already thinking of it. "You have Nora, you don't need me to get back."

"I need you to bring Rose back to me, and as a reward, she and Nora can teach you."

"What would stop Nora from teaching me herself? I don't need Rose."

"You've always needed Rose," Luke argues. "You know it. Nora won't help you without my say-so. We've been through a lot lately. She likes me."

"She always had terrible taste in men," Dad mutters, and I smile. "I feel much better now, since she always disliked me. She used to call me a waste of skin." He strokes his whiskered chin, remembering.

This is such a bizarre conversation. It feels surreal sitting here on Asha's porch, talking about time travel with my enemy. Once upon a time, he wasn't my enemy, or at least I didn't know it. I remember a date we had to an art show that Emme helped me dress up for. Lord, she helped gussy me up for someone who would later have a hand in her murder. Luke and I had flirted and played at being grown-ups, and afterward he had taken me to look for Rose. Of course, this was before I knew Luke already knew where she was and that he was in love with her. He was deceiving me then, and I don't trust him now. I was too easily taken in the first time. I won't make that mistake again.

Yet, I can't deny that the possibility of undoing all of Rose's damage is tempting. I can accept that Rose will never change, but if I could change what she did? What if it is possible to go back and change everything that has happened? Could I hold the key? What if Joe doesn't have to grow up without his real mother, after all, and Bea could get her daughter back? What if I could have my mother back, all those years, like they never happened without her in the first place?

"Dad." I settle down at his knee and speak softly. "Do you think it's possible to change history? You're the scholar, the historical nut. You have to have thought of this. Can history be altered or will there be some sort of horrible side effect?"

Dad pats my head and gives me a wobbly smile. "Honestly, all I have to go on are episodes of Star Trek. Usually didn't go too well for them. Paradoxes and whatnot, one small ripple causing a huge tidal wave later. That sort of thing."

"I'm not going to make my decision based on an episode of Star Wars," I snap.

"Star Trek," he corrects.

"Whatever!"

"Come on," Luke interjects. "We could go back and see if the Klingon and Federation Peace Treaty really happened. No Worf. Tasha Yar could still be alive. It'd be epic!"

I simply stare at him. Had everyone found time for television during our stay in modern centuries except me? Oh, right. I actually had a job.

"I rest my case. It never turns out well," Dad replies. "Remember 'The City on the Edge of Forever'?"

"Of course, and that had a very happy ending."

"Kirk sacrificing Edith to the car accident in order to let her die so the Nazi's wouldn't win the war?" Dad is incredulous.

"No, earlier, when the Nazi's won. That was my happy ending."

"I'm going to scream," I announce, calmly.

"I'll join you," Israel mutters. "Come on, traitor. Up!"

"Where are we going?" Luke stands. "Are you going to lock me in a closet again, because honestly, it's a little predictable at this point."

"Shut up." Iz motions to me to open the screen door. I do, and all three of us traipse inside. "Noah, would you do the honor?" He tips his head to the large closet nearby.

"Really?" I murmur, after Luke is securely put inside and Israel makes a show of dragging a heavy sideboard from the dining room and placing it in front of the door.

"What?" Iz growls.

"Nothing," I smile brightly. "It's just...it is a little predictable, that's all. I think we need to brush up on what to do with captured villains or something."

"You got a better idea?" He removes the bullets from the rifle. "I don't want this loaded with Joe around. Here, you take them."

I place them obediently in my pants pocket. They are heavy and make my men's pants sag, which they were doing already. I hike them back up and wish I had a belt instead of these suspenders. "No, not really. We should all talk about this without his big mouth around."

"Exactly," Iz responds. "You can start. Start by explaining to me why you were in that shed with him and Asha's rifle."

I swallow. That isn't exactly the part I want to talk about.

"Yes, I'm surprised you didn't tell Lover Boy about our rendezvous, Gray." Luke's muffled voice comes from inside the closet. "You mean he didn't know I was here? Wow. You two have some trust issues." He whistles.

I wish the bullets were still inside the rifle where I could make good use of them. "Shut up!" I snap angrily. I pull Israel's arm and practically drag him away to the next room. His whole body seems to be made of iron, really, really irritated iron.

"Look, I found a note from him late last night. Remember, you were asking what was wrong?"

"Yeah. I thought you were being shy about being alone with me. I didn't think you were planning on meeting him." Israel's dark eyes are even darker now.

"I wasn't. I tore the note up."

"What'd it say exactly?"

"Something about life or death and that he needed to see me about Rose. I was shocked that he was here, and I didn't really know what to do." My voice sounds as miserable as I feel.

"Really? Because it seems very obvious what you should have done. You should have told me."

"I know. I'm sorry. I just knew you two would get into it, probably fight, maybe kill each other."

"That's no excuse. You should have trusted me, Sonnet. I can't believe this. You knew he was here, roaming around, a *murderer*, and you didn't mention it?" Israel's hands are clenched at his side, and I fear for the wall next to him. He looks like he could punch holes in it anytime. Asha would definitely blame me.

"I said I was sorry," I answer weakly. I reach for him, but he shoots me a look of disgust.

"I really need to get away for a little while. If you let him out of that closet, I swear to God, Sonnet..."

He doesn't need to finish his threat. I already know what was unspoken. He and I would be finished.

Chapter 4

"It won't do us any good to fight about it," I say albeit a bit weakly. "I am sorry, I really am, but you know about it now, and we have to figure out what to do. We can't just leave my elderly grandmother in whatever hole he's stuck her in. She has to be our first priority."

"If she's really here at all," Israel points out. I can tell he is still angry. Well, anyone with eyes could tell. His voice is flat, and he won't look at me.

"She must be. He couldn't have gotten here without her. He can't have grandma-napped just anyone. Dad will recognize her, even after all these years. People don't change that much."

"Don't they?" Israel looks at me then and breaks my heart a little. Point taken.

I bite my lower lip and blink back tears. I don't want to fight with him. Sometimes it feels like he is all I've got. He's always been my rock, and I've chipped him, put a dent in him, cracked him a little. If we spend all our life together like I think I want, will I continue to chip away at him until there's nothing left but a sliver of the man he used to be? What if I'm no good for him?

"What am I supposed to tell Bea? He's starting to bang around in there." Dad sticks his head around the corner and into the room. His bowtie catches on the door and turns topsy-turvy. No matter what era we end up in, Dad manages to fashion a bowtie somehow. He thinks they're timeless, and I'm not sure I'd recognize him without one. This one is made of African batik fabric. He raises an eyebrow at me, waiting for an answer. "Well?"

"Tell her the truth." Israel shrugs. "She can handle it. She's tougher than we give her credit for."

I'm not so sure, but the last thing I'm going to do is pick another argument. If he wanted to serve Luke's head on a silver platter to Bea, I'd defer to his judgment. Heck, I'd put the apple in his mouth, like a Christmas ham. When did I get so blood thirsty? Inwardly, I chide myself, but it's halfhearted.

"Speaking of tough," Dad continues, straightening his tie. "Nora is a tough old bird as well, but she is elderly. I do suggest we find her quickly."

"I have a feeling Luke will give her up for a price." I sigh. I already know what he's charging for the release of one grandmother, my presence in 1931. "Why don't you fill Bea in, Dad? She should be a part of this."

"Good morning," says a voice in Chinese. Lu is awake, it seems. This is becoming a regular party.

We all smile like our lives depend on it. The Lost are very good liars, but somehow our best casual faces appear slightly ridiculous. We look like kids caught in a sticky situation. Everyone chirps a good morning, slightly too loudly. Then we all grin like banshees. Lu stares at us for a moment, squints, and then leaves out a side door.

"Really," I say, "we need to get out of here. The guests in the house are stirring, and who knows where Dr. Smythe is. I'm about out of excuses for why we're lugging around firearms and why it sounds like we are holding a wildcat in the closet. Let's get him up to our room. If he knows what's good for him, he'll be quiet, and we can figure out what to do."

Israel frowns, but I'm not sure if it's at my plan or just aimed at life in general...maybe just me in general.

* * *

It's been several hours, and we aren't getting anywhere with Luke Dawes, in spite of allowing him one quick outhouse break. He's infuriating, calm, resolved, stubborn, and not giving Nora up without my cooperation. Israel is about to completely lose his cool, and I feel like I'm coming apart at the seams, like my old white nightgown, the one that got left behind in 2012. I'm frayed.

We tried talking nicely. We tried leaving him tied up on the floor for a while, and we left. We tried talking some more. We tried intimidation, or rather, Iz did. I leave for a few minutes and when I come back, Luke has a split lip and a bloody nose. I raise my eyebrows at Iz, and he looks at me innocent-like and shrugs.

"Tell him he shouldn't smack around an unarmed prisoner." Luke spits out some blood and what I hope is not a tooth. "Definitely not hero behavior."

"Oh, shut up. You deserved that, and much worse." Israel cracks his knuckles.

"I'm just saying the good guys are supposed to be above that kind of thing, morally speaking. There's a code, you know. You're a cheater. I think my nose is broken."

"Good. Well, what's it going to be? Something has to give. I'm tired of this back and forth. Just tell me where my grandmother is before I have Iz set your broken nose so I can break it again." I glare at him.

"Jeez, Gray. I missed your sweetness." He makes a gargling sound that sounds like he swallowed some blood.

"The Gray girls aren't really sweet. You should know that being married to my sister."

"Rose can be very sweet." He glares. "You should have seen how happy she was at our wedding. You should have been there, the maid of honor or something. Aren't sisters supposed to be there for each other?"

"Oh, please. That would have worked out well. She would have stabbed me with the cake knife, and you know it."

"She would not have." He looks insulted, as if I'm making up lies about his precious wife. As if she wouldn't slice and dice me, cheerfully and singing the whole time. "I'd happily tell you where Nora is, but I want your word. Just come with me to 1931. Just show yourself to Rose, that's all I'm asking. If it doesn't work, have Nora bring you back here, or to wherever you want to go. I don't care."

"And if it does work?" I swallow. "If seeing me does bring her back, then what? You stand by while she smothers me or beats me to death or something lovely like that? Because I don't exactly trust you to save my life."

"She's half your size. I hardly think she could overpower you. Cross my heart and hope to die. Stick a needle in my eye if I lie."

"I will," I vow. "Several times at least, and she's not *half* my size." I find myself trying to appear shorter, more petite. Cracks about my height and weight are uncalled for. It's not my fault Rose is the size of a ten-year-old boy. Doesn't mean I'm abnormally large...

"Are you seriously considering this?" Israel hisses in my ear, whirling me around to face him. "Have you lost your mind?"

"What am I supposed to do?" I hiss back. "He's not going to budge on this. We aren't going to break him. I don't care if you go all rogue interrogation tactics on him, he's not going to talk. He's been in prison and Bedlam, what can *we* do to him?" I pause, but Iz doesn't reply, just glares. Maybe there are a few things he could do to him. "I don't think he really wants anything to do with us anyway, he just wants his wife back."

Luke interrupts. "I know what you're thinking, Rhode. You agree just to get Nora to safety, and then go back on your word, right? Won't work. I told you, Nora likes me. She trusts me. She isn't going to trust you so easily, especially with this nice shiner I've got working." He works his jaw, and a look of pain crosses his face. "I still can't believe you hit me with a chair."

I can't help raising my eyebrows in surprise. "Really Iz, a chair?"

The corners of Israel's mouth twitch. "Seemed like a good idea at the time."

I look down at the floor. The chair has a broken leg. Great. Another thing Asha will blame me for. I give up.

"Okay." I stare at Luke, who is trying to rub blood from his chin onto his shoulder. Some of it is dried already, and he looks terrible, like we really have spent hours torturing him.

He stops rubbing. "Okay, what? You'll come with me?"

"We'll come with you," I correct. I hold out my hand to Israel, hoping against hope. Have I asked too much this time? He was always frustrated with my independence, and how I didn't ask him for help before. When I went searching for Rose and was locked in that old house for days, he was upset that I had gone alone in the first place. When I had my crazy tea party with her, he was angry I hadn't taken him with me. Am I making the right choice now?

Because he has to know, if he knows me at all, that I'm doing this.

I'm going back.

*　*　*

After what feels like an eternity of my heart alternating between pounding loudly and being strangely silent, I feel Israel's fingers lace through mine. I let out the breath I'd been holding for forever. I haven't blown my chance with Iz. My relief is palpable. Then I make the mistake of looking at him. He has storm clouds brewing in his eyes, and he glares at me with a passion that makes me cringe.

"I hate this," he says, through clenched teeth, enunciating very clearly. "If we live through this, I'm going to make your life miserable in every way possible, Sonnet. I am not kidding around."

"Great!" Luke grins. "Let's go."

Finding Nora involves traipsing around the outskirts of the village for what seems like hours. Luke, Iz, Dad and me, are silent the whole way. Sometimes I open my mouth to ask a question or make a comment, but there's nothing really to say, and I shut it again with a force that makes my teeth clack together. In the beginning, I feel uncertain, but the further we get the more complicated our route becomes, and the more secure I am in my decision. We wouldn't have found her on our own. Luke knew what he was doing, as usual. I watch him as he walks in front of us, saunters is more like it. He has his confidence back, though it seems a bit diminished in some strange way. He has a slower gait, his shoulders hunched just a bit, and that light in his eyes is not as bright as it was the last time I saw him. I don't think it's just from being hit with a chair. I wonder what these months away from us have done to him? Has it been even longer on his end? A marriage, and then the sudden loss of his wife. I don't feel sorry for him, but I wonder how it's changed him. He certainly takes his vows seriously; I'll give him that. In sickness and in health, he had to have known what he was getting into. Rose has never been in good health, at least not mentally.

At dusk, we finally arrive at Luke's hideout. My first glimpse of my grandmother is of a sleeping old woman, huddled with her arms around her for warmth. Her back is up against a cave, her gray hair plastered around a withered face wearing nothing but a threadbare gown. I'm so angry at her condition, pathetic and feeble, that I shove Luke up against the wall of the cave. I search my memory for some of Israel's curses, but my blind fury has eradicated my powers of speech.

"You are a horrible person!" I finally manage to choke out. I'd like to crush his windpipe. Never have I had such cheerful, giddy thoughts of murder. "How could you leave an old woman in this place with no food, no water, no help for two days?"

Somehow, he manages to speak around my hands on his neck. "I didn't."
His eyes are leveled at me, and they are cold. "You did."

I can't crush his windpipe; my hands aren't strong enough. I settle for the
next best thing, and knee him as hard as I can where it counts. He lets out
a whoosh of stunned air and collapses on the ground. I step over him to
get to my grandmother.

She is as still as the dead.

Chapter 5

Getting Nora back to the boarding house is tricky. First of all, we have to wait for Luke to quit rocking in the fetal position and threatening to vomit. I don't feel bad for causing his agony. When we are ready to leave, Israel carries Nora, and though she's probably light as a feather to him, it still slows us down. It's dark, and the lantern I swing is somewhat dim. Dad walks at one side, stroking his mustache thoughtfully. Luke is at the other, walking funny. He doesn't stray too close to me. He can probably feel the hate coming off me, like a cocooning rage. I would have preferred to leave him there in that dank cave, but he only would have found his way back and then what? Also, I gave him my word. If I broke it, wouldn't I be like them, like Rose and Luke? I may lie, but only about the little things. This isn't little.

My grandmother has not awoken from her dehydrated slumber. Israel assured us she isn't dead, though I'm starting to feel skeptical. She doesn't look like she's living; her skin is as thin as tissue paper. Her veins are blue beneath it, and her hair stringy, white, and greasy. I wonder about her life in mental hospitals. Dad said she was happy enough in her madness, not violent or prone to anger, and he thought she'd be taken care of. He'd never expected to see her again. I've heard enough of Bedlam and its dark practices from my sister and her time there. Had she really been taken care of? What of being reunited with Rose, her lunatic granddaughter? Had they plotted against me?

The thought gives me shivers, and the lantern trembles in my hand. The shadows jump out at me, and the light only flickers at them, like a kitten pawing at a mouse, or a snake. It's not a match for the darkness, not my little lantern.

Not me.

* * *

Bea is grateful for something to do, and she snaps to attention the way I haven't seen her do in months and months. She pulls the sheets and blankets back from her own bed and readies water, towels, a fresh nightgown, a heating pad, strips of cloth, everything in anticipation of what Israel, the doctor, might need. I realize she'd make a good nurse. I see that Israel is thinking the same thing. He smiles at her warmly, and she beams back at him. It does my heart good to see her have a moment of happiness, but I'm too scared for my grandmother's health to allow the moment to live long.

"Will she come through?" I murmur to Israel, as Bea and I struggle with getting off the soiled hospital gown. It is stuck to her in places (God, I hope not with blood), that we must cut it off with scissors. Underneath, she is frail and white as bone, and I avert my eyes with respect for whatever dignity she may have left. Dad has gone to be with Joe and to tell tall tales to Asha. If her lack of concern for Luke earlier is to be believed, she won't mind that we are coaxing the half dead back to life in her boarding house. Maybe I should give Asha more credit. She may not like me, but as boarding house mistresses go, she's a peach.

I don't need Israel to tell me Nora has a fever. Her skin is dry and hot. It isn't blood that makes her clothing stick, thankfully, but dried sweat and urine. Which I suppose is better, but which angers me further against Luke. How dare he leave a feeble woman in the wilderness with no hope for survival? He really would do *anything* to help Rose, even become a monster, if he wasn't one already. I used to think Rose was pulling the strings in their twisted relationship, but now I'm not so sure. This is all Luke, no Rose necessary. Maybe he was the mastermind all along.

"There's nothing to do but wait," Israel tells me, when Nora is clean and settled. "She doesn't appear to have injuries, not that I can tell, no broken bones or bruising, but there are other symptoms we should be concerned about. Fever, this deep sleep, shaking chills..." He doesn't finish, but he doesn't have to. I know where this is leading. I've been a doctor's in-name-only wife in Africa for long enough.

Malaria.

I feel suddenly very sick and as though I need air. I cannot be cooped up with Luke Dawes, husband of the woman who murdered my mother and my best friend, and the man who has now, most likely, killed my grandmother. I don't care what Israel does to him while I'm not here to intervene. There are several chairs in this room, good strong, steady chairs. Mahogany, I think. They could do a lot of damage.

Down on the first floor, Lu is playing checkers with Joe. Joe, I had almost forgotten him entirely. He is fresh-faced as usual, with ruddy cheeks and messed up red hair, so very like Emme that my heart skips a beat. Little Fairy Fay.

What if I go with Luke to 1931, Iz and I, and something happens? What if we can't get back? I'd never see Joe or my father again. The thought makes me groan aloud, and I sink into a chair at the table. Joe moves the board game in an annoyed fashion as I plunk my elbows on the table.

"Good," Lu says in Chinese. "You take over. I'm too old for this." She is gone in a flash. "He has no morals!" She shouts a warning from the other room.

Joe loves games, he also hates to lose and loves to cheat. The combination of all those makes him a fiend to play with. He'll go for hours with no mercy for his bored/irritated/hungry playmates. Without much thought, I move a checker, and he crows triumphantly.

"Dumb move, Auntie!" he chortles. "King me!" He has something sticky on his face and something dubious stuck to his nostril.

Obediently, I plop a checker into place. "Joe, I have a pickle, and I need your help."

He wrinkles his nose at me. "I don't like pickles. They're slimy."

"Well, no pickle, but a problem. I need advice."

"Okay," he responds, slowly. He begins to pick at a scab on his skinny knee. "Like you want me to tell you what to do?"

"Yes! I want you to tell me what to do. Exactly. Now." I eye him carefully and put on my best serious face, which isn't all that difficult because I kind of want to cry anyway. "I think there's a chance I could do some very good things in this world, but it's only a chance, a small chance, a dangerous chance."

Joe's eyes light up. "Dangerous is good!"

"Yes, well, you might change your mind once you get older. So, it's very dangerous, and I'd be risking a lot."

"Will there be dragons?"

"What? No. No dragons. Different dangers."

"Ohhhhh. Like, bad guys?" His voice has dropped to a dramatic whisper.

"Yes." My heart does a flip in my chest. "Like bad guys." And girls. Oh, so bad.

"Well, Auntie," he says, in a very grown up voice, "if no one stops the bad guys, they just get badder and badder. Did you know that?" He flicks his scab across the table.

"Do they?" I sigh. "And please don't do that. It's gross."

"Yep. They get badder and badder, and it's your turn! You don't pay attention."

"I do, too. For instance, I saw you hide that checker a moment ago. Now give it here, you little monster." I return the piece to the board. This is probably a teachable moment for Joe, but I'm too tired and sad to preach to him about the perils of corrupt gaming techniques. As long as he doesn't grow up to be a killer, I'll be happy. My standards are so very low.

I probably shouldn't procreate. "So, you think I should stop the bad guys?"

"You?" Joe looks incredulous, his favorite word. "No way! You're a girl! I'll stop them!" He puffs out his tiny chest magnificently. "You just ... just ..."

"Stay home and keep your dinner hot?" I purse my lips, thoughtfully.

He looks appalled. "No way! Your cooking stinks! Okay, you can come, but you have to stay out of the way when I'm fighting and stuff. You can like, I dunno, hold my sword or something."

"Fabulous. Well, it's settled then, Big Man. Please don't pick your nose. We're a crime fighting duo, fit for the nineteenth century! Or wherever we end up next!" I toast him by solemnly holding up my checker.

"Cheers!" He squashes my finger with his checker, and then palms it. "I win!"

"Well, that's debatable, but we'll go with it. Hold still." I lick my finger and try to swipe the sticky substance off his cheek. I'm not going near the crusty one on his nostril though. There are places Auntie won't go.

"Gross! Stop it!" Joe ducks and slides to the floor in an impressive maneuver.

"When was the last time you took a bath?" I demand peering under the table. For goodness sake, not taking his schooling in hand is bad enough, but forgetting to bathe the kid is unforgivable.

"Very soon ago!" He replies in his typical bad English grammar fashion. "I need a Band-Aid! My knee is bleeding!"

"They haven't been invented yet. Want me to kiss it?"

I hear a disgusted noise and then some scuttling and scooting. The next thing I know, the kitchen door to the outside world is slammed, and Joe's escaped.

I sigh. I barely have the energy and gumption to groom a small man child. How am I supposed to change the world? One step at a time, I suppose, one sleep at a time, one travel at a time. The thought of seeing Rose again gives me the shivers, though. I do love her madly, and against my will, but I'd be happy to never set eyes on her again. My dreams of redeeming her sanity are gone with the wind. It's obvious Luke hasn't given up on her though, not yet. He's either more committed and has more follow-through than me, or he's simply off his rocker, too.

Well, he did do time in Bedlam, didn't he?

My, I do know how to pick them.

Chapter 6

It has been four days, and there's no change in Nora, none that matters, and that's all that matters, isn't it? Sometimes she stirs a bit, mumbles things. Occasionally her eyes open, and her milky blue gaze settles on something, but she has not come back to us and Israel's opinion is she never will. Luke has as good as killed her, and the malaria will finish the job. I'd want revenge for this, but nothing I could do could make Luke more miserable, and desperate than he already is.

Without Nora, he can't get back to Rose.

I'd feel a momentary sense of satisfaction, but it isn't as though I want to keep him either.

For the first couple of days after finding Nora, we kept Luke at arm's length or, more specifically, at rifle's length. Gradually, as he slipped into a quiet place of despair, we nearly forgot about him. Now he never leaves Nora's room, like a dedicated son or grandson. He simply watches her, wills her to wake and be lucid. I think there is a small part of him that is sorry, not only for himself, but for her as well. Maybe I'm being too kind, he probably only mourns his ticket back to Rose. Bea and Joe have moved into another room. I tried to get them to move into ours, due to Israel's frosty coldness since this whole debacle started, but they didn't. I'm nearly freezing to death in my own bed. It's funny, depending on eras, there are so many social rules about love. Sleeping together in most eras without really being married can get you in a lot of trouble, but if this were a hundred years from now, I'd be made fun of for sharing my room but not sharing my bed. There's a certain relief in obeying the rules of the day. I love him, but I'm not ready to show it.

We have another problem now, as if there weren't enough already. The train to Nairobi hadn't arrived on the day Luke and Nora mysteriously appeared. There had been no travelers on the road, no horses, nothing. The villagers are becoming ever suspicious, and with suspicion comes hatred and fear. This lanky man with the dark look about him had been seen in the boarding house and outside with me. This ill old woman could hardly have walked here. Where did they come from? The whispers are becoming louder and louder. I am nervous to leave the boarding house without Dad or Israel. Bea has forbidden Joe to play outside, because she doesn't like the way some of the men are watching us. Israel and Asha are both dreadfully quiet, which bothers me immensely. It's as if they are keeping something from me, not conspiring, but not telling either. It is possible Israel isn't talking because he's mad at me, and Asha isn't talking because she'd rather muck out the chicken coop than talk to me.

Unbelievably, I find myself bringing Luke a tray of food. The boy I knew used to eat enormous amounts of food, but this Luke hasn't touched anything other than cigarettes since early yesterday when Israel confirmed the malaria diagnosis, and added that in his opinion, she wasn't going to live. I remember another time when I brought Luke food, at my house in the twenty-first century. I'd piled it high with Prue's leftovers and brought it to him, while he and Israel glared at each other, they'd never liked one another.

"No squirrel pie, I'm afraid," I say lightly, and sit down on the floor by Nora's bed. She hasn't moved a muscle since this morning when I was last here. I cough and make a show of opening the window to get rid of the cigarette smoke, but Luke doesn't seem to notice.

"What?" Luke looks at me, but not really. He looks through me, like I'm not even here, like I'm a ghost of someone he used to know. I kind of am, but so is he.

All of this seems so surreal, and it strikes me that it probably feels so to him too.

"Never mind. For what it's worth, I'm sorry this is happening. Even though you're the cause, I'm actually sorry it's affecting you, too." When I say it, I realize I am. I really am sorry for this worthless piece of irritating boy who's lost the only link to his mentally ill wife. He deserves it, yes, but somehow I feel very nearly bad for him. The fleeting thought of returning to other times to undo the damage he and Rose have wrought is gone too.

A small part of me is mourning that, as well, though I hadn't really wanted to attempt it in the first place.

"Thank you." I'm not sure if he means for the food or for the consolation I'm offering. Either way, he seems sincere. "Gray?"

"Hmm?" I reach up to the bed and stroke my grandmother's motionless hand. What a tragedy I never got to know her. She could have told me stories of my mother, yet another woman I never knew.

"What do you think about when you're falling asleep?"

"What?" I make a face. "What kind of question is that?"

"Have you ever missed a place so much, wished to be somewhere so much...never mind." He shakes his head and then runs his fingers through his hair.

It dawns on me then. "You still think I can do it? Control, steer, navigate, whatever you want to call it?" I snort in an unladylike fashion. "Don't you think I would have done it by now if I could? It can't possibly be that easy, this imagining and focusing on where you want to be!"

"Why not?" Luke leans forward, and for the first time I see some sparkle come back into his eyes. "How often do you think of locations, and really focus on them as you're falling asleep? Come on! You know you're thinking of what to eat for breakfast or whether or not your dad made it home safe or boys or the state of your hair or a million other things! Religion, politics, weather, millions of things!"

"Boys?" I roll my eyes. "I'm not twelve."

"Sure, boys, especially with your raffle prize snoring next to you. Have you ever wanted to be somewhere specific so badly that it just consumed your whole head as you're drifting off?"

"I don't want to talk about this." I stand. Impulsively, I lean over and kiss Nora. Her cheek feels like tissue paper beneath my lips.

"Why? Because you have or because you haven't?" Luke pushes. His eyes really are sparkling now, and I'd like to smack him.

"Because...I don't know. Maybe I haven't, but not because I'm boy crazy. I've just always had a lot on my mind in my life, more important things than where I live. When you're Lost, you accept it. What's the point of building dreams for yourself in other places? You know that." I dare him to argue.

"Sure. I get that, but it proves my point."

"Which is?" I sigh.

"That you haven't tried it, not really. You're a Gray woman. I really believe you can do what Rose and Nora can." His voice is so sickeningly sincere I want to be ill.

"And risk my sanity?" I reply drolly.

Luke looks momentarily offended, which makes sense since I've just insulted the state of his girl, but he waves his hand. "Unrelated, I'm sure."

He's probably right, but I'm not sure it's a chance I'm willing to take. Dad says Rose was always off, even as a tiny child, long before she knew how powerful she was. Still...

"I'm sure *you're* sure, but I'm not. I don't need to mess around with the state of my grey matter, thank you very much."

"Really? Even if it meant saving Emme? Your mother? Rose? And come on, people mess with their grey matter all the time. For God's sake, you've spent time in the twenty-first century. People pop brain-altering drugs like candy. What's the big deal? Live a little, Gray. Don't be so boring!"

"I'm not boring!" I know I'm falling into his trap, but I am completely insulted, probably because it's true. I am boring. He used to tease me that the most exciting thing I'd ever done was send an email.

"Yes, you are. Some of the things Rose and I have done together would curl your hair, Miss Goody-Two-Shoes. That's *life* Gray, and it's beautiful, and it's wonderful, and it's dangerous, and you shouldn't miss it because you're busy being boring!"

There is silence for a long while as we stare at one another, him with a satisfied smirk, and me with an angry glare.

"If you think you can back me into a corner by daring me, like some petty, spoiled child on the playground..." I sputter.

"I dare you." Luke's voice is calm and low and soft and very sincere. "Oh indeed, I dare you."

I can feel my teeth grinding and my face flushing. I will my voice to be as frustratingly calm and icy as his was a moment ago. "Fine," I grind out. "I'm in."

*　*　*

Nora passes away within the week. She never did become lucid, never knew Luke or my dad, and never even spoke intelligible words. I feel dreadful for the old woman who finished her life in such a way, though I suppose death in Bedlam would not have been any sweeter. At least here she had her family.

Such as we are.

As I expected, Dad and Bea are hardly down with the plan of going forward to 1931. Israel isn't even talking to me, though I'm pretty sure he's still coming with me. I hope. I have no intention of leaving without him, so he'd better be on board. Whenever I bring it up, he shoots daggers at me with his dark eyes, and I murmur something about checking on Joe. I'm not much for conflict. I want to talk to him about it and see how deep his wounds are, but every time I try, I lose my nerve, and the words get lost right along with it.

The noise and fuss among the villagers is only escalating, so it's probably good that Luke disappears soon. One old man accused Asha of harboring a demon, another woman who used to do business with the boarding house refused to set foot inside anymore, and Asha herself makes Israel look like a teddy bear. I keep a wide berth around Asha on the day we bury Nora.

The Lost come to grips and adapt quickly when it comes to the customs of different centuries and different cultures, and death is just one of those things. In Victorian England we had to abide by their burial customs for Emme, including burying her in an unmarked grave outside the cemetery because of her questionable line of work and our lack of extensive funding.

In my twenty years of life I have seen burials, burnings, blessings, embalming, shrouds, eulogies, tears, and the forbidding of tears. I have seen Saxons cut off the feet of the dead to assure they won't walk around haunting us, and I have seen Aborigines cut off heads to assure that the body will be so busy looking for it, it won't have time to haunt them. I have seen mazes built around tombs so that the ghosts will get lost trying to get out. I once met a Sin-Eater whose job it was to eat the sins of the dead, thereby freeing them from their guilt and shame. He ate his bread and salt and drank his beer in a solemn, sad way, and he was an outcast in his time, a vagabond that everyone needed but everyone feared. So, when all they want to do with my poor dead grandmother is simply bury the body and sing a bit, I am rather relieved.

To avoid the nosy eyes of my neighbors, we keep Luke inside and keep the process very quick and simple. Dad officiates, since he is the only one who knew her at all, and Bea leads us in a hymn. Joe has ants in his pants and misbehaves. He's hungry since no one remembered to feed him a proper meal today, and he has to go to the bathroom, a malady he loudly whispers to anyone willing not to hush him. Dr. Smythe and Lu are respectful and polite, but they haven't been their normal selves since Nora and Luke's mysterious arrival.

Lu, of course, remembers Luke, and not fondly. She'd nearly knocked him senseless the day he almost killed me and Is, so she's hardly understanding. I can't blame her, and there's no explanation I could offer as to how he got here. I came up with a lame excuse and blabbered something about how they got off the train in Ethiopia by mistake and wandered around, trying to find us. It was pathetic, and she saw through me instantly.

Add Lu to the long list of people upset at me. The longer I live, the longer that list gets. Sometimes I wonder if it'd be best if I traveled alone with no one to upset, and no one to disappoint. My old uncle, the loner, may have had it right.

Don't form attachments. Don't love too much. Then there's nothing to break, is there?

Chapter 7

We pack our things quickly, Luke and Iz and me. Well, pack is an overstatement. We gather some blankets, our nightclothes, and some food. Just a few days' worth, in case it takes longer than one night to perfect my (I believe nonexistent) skills. We can't try with Dad, Bea, and Joe too close to us, or we'll pull them in with us, so we are taking the train and then a boat to Zanzibar. An island should be far enough away, we think. We've never actually *tried* to leave anyone behind before. It's a peculiar thing.

Luke got a funny look on his face when I mentioned island living. He hasn't said much since Nora's death. His expensive clothes are rumpled, though Asha reluctantly cleaned them for him. He hasn't shaved, and he still isn't eating much. He looks like a stereotypical pirate.

Bea is worried for me, I know. When I embrace her fondly, she holds on tightly for a moment and then cups my face. Her eyes are filled with regret and anxiety. I'm not sure her eyes have dried yet from Emme's death. They are perpetually wet, and her lashes dark with salt water.

"If I can get there, then I can get back," I promise with more bravado than I actually feel. "In fact, I could get back to right now, five seconds from now. You won't even have time to miss me!"

"So, if you aren't back in five seconds I know to start worrying?"

"That's not precisely what I meant. Take care of Dad?" I look over to him. I smelled liquor on him this morning and know he has fallen off the wagon again.

"Of course. He'll be fine. He always is. Say goodbye to Auntie Sonnet, Joey." Bea grabs him by the shirt collar and spins him to face me.

"Why? Where are you going?" Joe demands never stopping the attempt to break free. He's been told at least five times in the past ten minutes, but when it comes to paying attention to uninteresting bits of news, Joe doesn't retain the knowledge long.

"Just away for a bit. We'll be right back." I sternly will myself not to cry. I will not cry in front of Joe. I will not.

"Okay. Bring me something!" He's nearly out of his shirt. I can see his belly button. It's dirty.

"Like, candy?"

"Or a Nintendo!"

"Um, sure thing, captain. Give me a kiss?" I bend down, and he starts squirming in earnest.

"Gross! No way! Mom!" He appeals for help, but Bea has the hands of a professional wrestler with seven years of practice, more than that, if Emme was like Joe, and I'm willing to bet she was.

I plant an especially juicy one right on his mouth, though it goes a bit awry, and I get a nose in my eye for my trouble. At least my tears aren't out of place now.

Dad is even tougher to say goodbye to, though what I had said to Bea was true. If I can get us there, I can get us back, so really it isn't that big of a deal. Unless of course, Rose manages to kill me, but no one is talking about that concern. No, it's the worry about me being forty years in the future that has everyone worked up. I've never been anywhere without my dad, not a single over-night ever, no summer camps as a teenager, no sleepovers with friends as a child. No business trips for him. It's funny, but though I think of him as being completely and utterly unreliable, he isn't really. He's always been there for me, present and accounted for, drunk yes, but physically by my side.

"What's the date again?" I tease.

"Very funny, Sonny," Dad tugs my hair. "October 14, 1888. Kenya. Don't forget!" His bowtie is twisted, and I straighten it, needing something to do with my shaky hands.

"I won't. You'll hardly know we're gone."

"And, Sonny?"

"Hmm?"

"Be careful." The alcohol on his breath nearly makes me feel tipsy too, but his words are sober enough. "Don't trust Luke, and don't trust..." He can't bring himself to say Rose's name, but I know who he means. "Her."

And we're gone. What a crazy trio we make, too. If I'd have known a week ago that I'd be traveling with Luke Dawes, of my own free will, I would never have believed it. I almost laugh aloud, but Israel's stone face removes the desire.

*　*　*

The train ride is uneventful and dull. Normally I would enjoy it, as we're traveling at a speedy clip, the way I like to travel, instead of at the speed of my own feet, but the tension is so thick between the three of us, there's no room for pleasure. What odd company we make. I hope we can part ways quickly, and that thought leads me to ponder what lies ahead and seeing Rose again. Will she know me, as Luke thinks she will? If she does, what will her reaction be? She could ask me in for tea, or she could try to push me out a window. It's impossible to predict. There was a time I thought she could be helped or worse yet, I thought I was the one who would do the helping. Instead, I seem to make her worse. She has a vendetta against me that isn't getting any better with time.

Time: such an enemy with us.

"What if it doesn't work?" I muse aloud. I'm speaking to Luke, but Israel is so near me he's practically in my pocket. He tends to completely invade any personal space I might have when Luke is around. "I mean, let's pretend that I can get us all to 1931, what if seeing me doesn't change Rose at all? What if she stays Lizzie forever?"

"Lizzie isn't so bad." Luke shrugs. "I could live with that, except of course, I don't have a choice. If she remains Lizzie, I'll be forced to leave without her, unless you've been working on that anti-time travel potion in your spare time?"

"I've been otherwise occupied, and you know I hate that term." Time travel. Ugh. So cheesy.

"Sorry." Luke rolls his eyes. "Time Skippers. Time Journey-ers. Time Jumpers."

"Shut up," Israel growls. "Just answer the question."

"Sorry, old chap." Luke winks at me. He's back to being his old self, nearly, now that Nora is gone and he's wrestled with whatever demons were getting under his skin. That pesky conscience, maybe. It must annoy him. "What was the question again? Ah, yes. What happens if it doesn't work? Well, I suppose you can go wherever you like, back here I presume, and I'll be left to my life of crime and hope I don't wake up in Transylvania circa 1887. Hey! Before you go though, we should check that out."

"What?" I make a face. "Transylvania?"

"Sure! Supposed to be happening right now, Dracula and all. Very exciting. Didn't you have that on your bucket list, Gray?"

Now it's my turn to roll my eyes. "Don't think so. Vampires are not high in my priorities. Now, let's backtrack a minute. What if I can't even get us there in the first place?"

"Transylvania?"

"No, dummy, 1931. How many nights do we have to...," I said, pausing to search for the words. "Have to..."

"Sleep together?" Luke intercedes smugly. "Settle down, Rhode! I'm just kidding around." He reaches up and touches his nose, gently, probably remembering the last time Israel lost his temper with him. "I told you, we'll give it a few tries."

"And if I can't? Will you just forget about her?" I know as soon as I've said it that it is a dumb question. He looks at me like I've sprouted wings. "Okay, sorry. I'm sure you won't, but what will you do?"

"Worried about me, Gray?" Luke crosses his hands behind his head and regards me with amusement. I feel Iz stiffen next to me. The boy is like cuddling with granite these days.

"No!" I shoot back irritated. "Just can't wait to get rid of you for good. That's all."

"I'll think of something." Now the amusement is gone, and the only thing left is stone cold resolve. "I'll have to."

The train jerks to a stop, and I grab the small bag that holds my nightgown, money, and some bread and fruit. It's strange, I guess, but the Lost don't travel much intentionally. In America, I loved Israel's car that we affectionately named The Blue Beast, but I've never flown on an airplane, and I've only been on a train a couple of times. I've actually never been on a boat the size of the one we'll use to get to Zanzibar, so I have a flutter of anticipation in my belly.

* * *

I was wrong about the boat. My hopes of a large passenger boat, or a comfortable ferry, or even a small but luxurious yacht type are dashed when I see our options. We either pay every last cent we have to get a ride on a lovely looking English boat carrying spices, mainly cloves, or pay substantially less for a ride with a German individual also carrying spices, but in a distinctly less sophisticated fashion. Israel stays rather mum as we survey our options a black man even in a black nation has its disadvantages, slavery being one of them, and Luke refuses to open his mouth.

"I may or may not be wanted in the Great Lakes region," is Luke's explanation. "Probably best if I stay out of the conversations." He pulls his hat lower over his eyes and turns his collar up. He's been very cranky the past hour, and he says it's because he is down to his last cigarette. I'm not sure which personality I prefer, full of nicotine and cheerful or full of the shakes and persnickety.

"Here and now? You're wanted in this day and age? 1888?" I am dubious. I purse my lips in a skeptical face.

"I get around." He shrugs, and settles lower into his collar.

I stare. "You look ridiculous."

"Says the woman wearing men's pants."

So it's left to me to do the negotiating. The spice boat, the lovely one, isn't budging on the price. I don't speak Bantu, but I'm fluent in Portuguese, English, and German, so I can talk easily enough with nearly everyone in the port, but I'm not getting anywhere. Plus, the captain of the lovely boat wants passage there and back in advance, and I can't exactly come up with a reason why we only need it one way. *We plan on disappearing in our sleep. Don't worry about us* isn't the best justification for why I want to pay half the asking price. So, I move on to the German fellow, who is eyeing me with almost visible dollar signs in his eyes. I sigh, and tell him in his language that we'll buy three one-way spots on his uncertain looking, floating pile of wood. At least I hope it floats. I have my doubts.

The German's name is Conrad, and he has a cinnamon-colored mustache that looks like a small, well-trained pet, maybe a ferret. I just know I've seen smaller cats. He is very fond of his facial ferret and strokes it lovingly as we struggle on board. I wedge myself between some crates, and when I sit down, I can't even see Luke or Israel. It's as though we are in tiny little cubbies, packed in tight, like sardines in a can. I can't even stretch my legs out, and I feel a cramp coming on already. If this thing sinks, I'm not sure my legs will adjust to swimming quickly enough, and I just may drown. Just my luck.

"She's a very fine boat. Is she not?" Conrad bellows. Since neither Iz nor Luke reply, it's up to me.

"Indeed!" I shout back in German towards the vicinity of his voice. "All yours?"

"Certainly! Worth every bit I spent on her, she is. You see, my dear girl, the Germans will one day own this island, and I plan to know every bit of it when that day arrives. I will be invaluable to my country, Elodie and I!"

"Elodie is your wife?" I steady myself as the boat rocks out to sea. I find myself holding my breath as though we will topple into the water any second now.

"My wife? No, no, you're sitting on Elodie, you are! Didn't you see the bow? Painted the name on myself, I did. Named after my sainted mother."

"Oh, yes, of course. Are these crates steady?" I put my hand up to still the one to my right. The boat is rocking only slightly, but the crates are stacked so willy-nilly I'm afraid for the state of my head should one topple. They smell of spices and remind me of Prue. She used to make an Indian corn pudding with fresh nutmeg and cloves. If I close my eyes, I can taste it, heavy and spicy on my tongue. Mmm, that combination would make a lovely latte, as well. I add the ingredients in my head.

"Naturally, they are, young lady. I'm no amateur! Been sailing since the day I was born, and I've done this trip longer than most, longer than those fancy English over there." Conrad sounds disgusted.

The fancy English seem to be passing us right now, if Conrad's raised voice is any indication. Sure enough, from my cocoon of boxes, I can hear jeering back from somewhere out on the water.

"Careful, old man!" A British voice calls. "You seem to have lost your boat and accidentally set your trash afloat!"

"Oh, bugger off, you cry baby!" Conrad bellows. I wonder if they even understand one another since neither is switching from their native tongue. Perhaps insults are a universal language, and all you really need is tone. I can hear Luke chuckling from somewhere to my left.

"Ignore those blights on humanity, my dear," Conrad continues speaking to me. At least I assume he speaking to me, since I still can't see him. "English people will be the death of me. I apologize if that is your ill-gotten race. I cannot quite place your accent."

I smile. "No, no. No offense taken. I'm not English. I'm…" I pause, "of mixed nationalities, I'm afraid."

"Ah. An adventurer! Good for you, my dear, good for you. We only get this one life, and we must take every opportunity to seek adventure!" His voice is rather proud now, as if he can take credit for my gypsy-like ways.

I'd prefer not to seek adventure actually, but regardless, it seems to find me. I don't tell Conrad that though, since I rather liked the proud note in his speaking. My father is rarely proud of me, or if he is, he forgets to mention it. I suppose if it's a race between my sister and me in the pursuit of our father's love. I'd come out ahead, but it isn't much of a competition when your competitor is chronically insane.

"Do you need us to tow you to shore, old man?" comes the British man's shout once more.

"I'm not half the old man your mother is!" Conrad retorts, and his ferret quivers with rage.

"Did I just hear a yo mama joke?" Luke asks. He sounds delighted. His German is impeccable, though I'm not entirely sure what he's talking about.

Conrad grunts loudly. "Ignore the English brats. They'll never be as civilized and genteel as the Germans. A meek and humble race we are."

I hear Luke chuckle.

"What do you plan to do on the island of Zanzibar, if you don't mind my asking?" Conrad leans up against a crate and watches me, curiously. "I don't mind a little friendly competition on the spice trade, but I warn you, it's a bit crowded these days. Especially if you aren't blessed enough to have an Elodie." He pats the crate, fondly, though it isn't really part of Elodie, or maybe it is. Maybe it's the crates holding her together. My legs brace themselves for swimming once more.

"No, no spices. Just visiting." My explanation is lame and vague, and when I get no reply, I keep talking. "My aunt owns a plantation there." The lie slips smoothly off my tongue, and I sound confident.

"Ah! The illustrious Mrs. Fairfield, I presume?"

"Um, sure. That is, yes. Distant aunt. Once removed. Not sure she'll remember me." I had better cover my bases if Conrad knows this island as well as he says, though it doesn't really matter whether or not the sailor believes me. It isn't likely I'll ever see him again.

The floating Elodie finally makes it to shore, and we part ways with Conrad. He is kind enough to offer to take us back when our visit with my "aunt" is over. Of course, the only way we'll need that is if we fail, which is a distinct possibility. On second thought, I make sure to thank him and not burn any bridges.

We trudge along through the ankle deep water to get to shore, as Conrad declined our help to bring Elodie in. Israel is still quiet, and I am feeling nervous. Luke is craning his neck, trying to look everywhere at once. He seems enchanted by the island. When the sand goes from wet to dry and Iz and I drop down to put our shoes back on. Luke tosses his bag aside and lifts his arms up and crows. I pause in the lacing of my boots to cock an eyebrow at his exuberance.

"Tell me again why we're doing this?" Israel mutters.

"I forget, but I'm pretty sure I had a reason."

* * *

It is an hour later, and we've found a place to sleep, not a good place, not a comfortable place, but a place. It's a church, an English style church, but a tiny one, rather dusty, and empty. Either the parishioners aren't much for housekeeping or they're really into the whole minimalist thing. Perhaps they've abandoned this place for the shinier model down the street a ways. It had been easy work to jimmy the door, and now I know why. There's absolutely nothing to steal unless you are in the market for a pew or two.

"I think it's the slave church," Israel explains. I don't ask him how he knows, but I save the question for a later date.

"It's like camping," Luke says, stretching out on a pew. "This will be fun!"

"Sure. Fun." I gingerly plump up my wrinkled nightgown as a pillow. I'm going to sleep in my clothes. I can't seem to find the wherewithal to wear my old fashioned nightgown in front of Luke. He'd probably make fun of me, call me a librarian or Laura Ingalls or something. "We can tell scary stories and braid each other's hair."

"I know a few stories," Luke muses. "They'd turn your hair white though."

"Oh, knock it off. You're just a two-bit criminal, and you know it." Israel is still not amused by anything, especially Luke's nonstop talking.

"Am I?" Luke drawls in rebuttal.

"Don't start," I warn. I break up the fruit in my pack into three piles. One is substantially smaller, and I cheerfully put that one aside for Luke. "I'm supposed to be thinking of 1931, remember? Not breaking up you two every three seconds."

"He started it." Luke's cheerful tone is back. "What'd you bring to eat? I'm starving."

"Tacos."

"Really?" He sits up and rubs his hands together.

"No. Now eat your tamarind, and shut up." I push it over to him. It's dark now, and there's no lighting in the church, but even if there were, we wouldn't risk it. I can barely make out Luke's outline as he reaches for his portion. Grudgingly, I add a piece of Asha's bread to his other hand. "Now, tell me about 1931."

"Ever been?"

"Would I ask if I had?" I sigh.

"Probably. I know you like the melodious sound of my voice. Let's see, London, April 20th, 1931. It's raining, of course. That goes without saying. Bethlem Hospital, Bedlam, has moved locations by the way. Whatever you do, don't send us all to the old one. Wouldn't be a fun place to wake up. The memories..." He shudders. "Anyway, picture the sign that says Bethlem Royal Hospital, the wrought iron fence around the place. There will be cars, old fashioned ones of course. I drive a Rolls-Royce. You would love it, Gray."

I probably would, but I don't reply. I'm thinking of London, how it looked when we left it, months ago. Picturing it with cars moving down the streets instead of carriages and horses. Would Whitechapel still be there? Be as it was when I last saw it, when Emme died? Would the Thames still smell like cabbages and steam?

Luke continues speaking. "It's between the World Wars, naturally. Too many orphans running around. Things are depressed, but getting better, at least for now." He snorts. "Then comes the second World War, but there's no telling them that. Anyway, what else can I tell you that will help?"

"I don't know," I snap. "Besides, I'm still eating, not sleeping."

"Well, I'm sleepy, so hurry up!" He pulls his hat down over his face as he lies on the pew. "Don't want me traveling without you, you know."

"Don't we?" I mutter.

"Don't be petty. So, anyway, it's an odd mixture when it comes to the people. There's the very wealthy, positively dripping with jewels and sophistication, and then there's the poor, dripping with exhaustion and hopelessness."

"You've become rather poetic." I chew on my bread.

"I've always been. You've just never noticed. Did I mention the date enough?" I hear a match, and I see he's smoking his last cigarette. No wonder he sounds more cheerful.

"Yes," I sigh at the same time Israel groans. It's the first sound he's made in a while, and I scoot closer to him and lay my head down in his lap. After a moment's hesitation, he strokes my hair. Progress. I instantly feel warmer and more content. Wherever we are when we wake up, my rock will be by my side.

Luke keeps talking and smoking, and all I really want to do is ignore him. It's all so odd and surreal, this plot. Luke goes on and on about the date, about the feel, the smells, the look of London, April 20, 1931. He talks about a skinny woman who roams the halls of Bedlam, and he talks about Lizzie as though she is someone entirely different from Rose. He mentions his Rolls-Royce Phantom in detail, and how he left it parked outside the hospital. Daffodils and magnolias are beginning to blossom, he says, and there's a scraggly magnolia tree near his car. There are velvety red tulips planted outside the front steps, and one has been trod upon.

I pay no attention to most of this. I ignore everything to do with the hospital. I am thinking instead of the Thames and a bake shop I went into with Emme. I am thinking of Sir Halloway's house, though he would be dead and gone in 1931. I retrace every step I can from my walk with Emme that day, from the bake shop to the mansion, and back again. I remember every detail I possibly can.

Because though I may want to go to London, I have no intention of traveling to Bedlam to see my sister.

*   *   *

I am cold in my bed. When I open my eyes, I can see the outline of the room I am in. There's a hard wooden chair and a cold metal table. There's a window that's open, and an icy wind blows through. There are bars on the window and locks on the door. I know even if I can't see them. My blanket is insufficient and scratchy. It feels as though there are thousands of tiny cruel insects rubbing their millions of prickly, spiky legs against my body. Spiders with needles for legs. I want to push them off, push off the blanket, but my arms are held down by something. I look down and see cold metal bracelets that strap me to the bed and prevent me from even brushing my hair out of my eyes. I shake like a cornered, frightened dog.

Rose comes and sits on the bed. She smiles fondly and pats my head like I'm her pet. I shrink away, but there's nowhere for me to go.

"It gets better," she whispers. "You'll get used to it. Welcome home."

"No!" I want to say, but I can't open my mouth. I want to thrash, but I cannot. I am paralyzed. "This isn't my home!" I want to shout, but my lips won't even part. I am as silent as the tomb.

"Welcome home, sister." She tucks my hair behind my ear for me gently. I'm terrified, so very terrified. "Welcome home."

Bedlam isn't my home. This can't be. I'm not insane! I'm not! I'm not! She's replaced herself with me. What has she done?

"Welcome home." Rose's hand moved down the dreadful blanket, past the manacle around my wrist, and winds her small fingers around mine. "Welcome home."

I come awake with a gasp, clammy and cold. It's so dark I can't make out the shapes of anything, not even myself. I will my heart to settle down from the panicked thumping it is performing in my chest and even out my shallow breaths. I want to rub my wrists from the imaginary iron that had held them down in my dream, in what I knew had to be a dream. There is something warm nestled in my hand, another hand.

Another hand.

My heart seems as though it will burst or stop, or both. Whose hand have I been holding?

It seems to take me a long moment to think rationally. I have a moment of terror that Rose has found me, but I am finally able to pull my hand away. It isn't Rose. It's Luke. I smell his spicy aftershave and the lingering scent of his cigarettes. He probably thought I was Rose, his wife, and moved closer in his sleep. Finally breathing normally, I give him an irritated shove and go back to sleep, thinking once again of 1931.

Chapter 8

I smell the Thames before I even open my eyes. I'm suddenly scared to death that it worked, that I did this. I made us travel. I tell my stomach to stop flipping and allow myself a silent and figurative pat on the back. My emotions are tethered somewhere between excitement of my abilities and what it means, and feeling as though I'm going to be sick. I finally open my eyes.

Israel is staring at me in fascination. "You really did it." His sounds awed.

"I really did it," I echo. I sit up and rub my sore arms. Sleeping on the ground gets less thrilling the older I get. When I was ten, I didn't care. When I was fourteen, I was preoccupied with being caught in my nightgown. Now that I'm twenty, I long for a nice featherbed to wake up in. I glance around. It's barely sunrise, and we're alone in nearly the same place we woke up before, so long ago.

"Where is our talkative companion?" I narrow my eyes, searching for Luke.

Israel shrugs. "I'll give you three guesses and the first two don't count."

"Bedlam?"

"Took off like a bat out of hell about an hour ago." Israel looks happier than I've seen him in the past couple of weeks. Our couple of years in the twenty-first century has taught him quite a few modern expressions, this being one of them. I have absolutely no idea what he's talking about. Bats? Hell? Of course, I've been accused of speaking like someone out of an Austen novel. "I don't think he was too happy with your deviation from his plan."

I yawn and stretch. "Well, he'll come to terms with it. He expected to wake up inside the hospital."

"Did I mention? Well done!"

"You did not, as a matter of fact." I can't help but smile, a bit smugly.

"Well done, Sonny. I married a witch," he adds wonderingly.

"I'm not a witch, and you didn't actually marry me," I point out. I smile, having a flashback to Emme calling me fondly a "time traveling witch."

"Well, I've been meaning to talk to you about that..." He winks at me, and I know he's teasing, "when you're ready to talk about it." Suddenly, I'm not so sure he's teasing. I feel butterflies in my stomach. "Anyway, let's face it. He'll be back."

"Who?" I'm confused. My mind ground to a halt when we started talking about marriage. The butterflies float away. I can't decide whether to chase them or let them go.

"Luke. He'll be back to get us, you specifically. I'm surprised he wasn't in a piece of mind to take you with him now, but I think he was so happy to be back in the same era as Rose, he didn't want to waste time. He definitely owes you."

"Well, he's a devoted husband. I'll give him that." I stand and offer my hand. "Shall we? I know an excellent bakery down the way. If they're still there, I'll shoplift you a sticky bun."

"Speaking of romantic..." He flashes his white teeth as he smiles at me, and I'm suddenly very happy that he's happy.

I remember being found on this street with Emme. A bobby, a policeman, named Walter Andrews had loomed large over me when I woke. He had an impressive handlebar mustache that I recall quite vividly. He and Conrad would have kept hair pomade in business between the two of them. So much had happened on this street. A conversation with Rose when I found out she was insane, Israel proposing his madcap marriage scheme, munching on biscuits with Emme and Joe, and running into

Luke when I thought he had been lost to me forever. This was the street we all woke up on, though in different locations. It takes me a minute, but I find the right building that Rose and Luke had moved into temporarily. I had had a crazy tea party there on the day I found out he betrayed me. How can one street that I only lived on for a few weeks have so many memories?

"Do you think the year is right? Do you think it is 1931?" Israel asks, intertwining his fingers through mine as we stroll.

"Only one way to find out," I muse. "Oh, look! Newsies!" I can't keep the delight out of my voice. A small lad with a cap sees me pointing and crosses the street eagerly.

"Two pence. On sale for the pretty ladies." The boy beams at me, handing out his prize.

"Let me see the headlines first, if you please." I adopt my most upper class British accent, which comes in handy at the oddest of times. I scan them briefly as the boy obeys: *Spain Becomes a Republic, American Capture of Al Capone, The Yellow River Flooding in China.* Here it is, as if it weren't anything monumental at all: April 20, 1931.

I really had done it.

"No, thank you," I murmur to the boy, this time in my regular, hodgepodge of accents. "Not today."

He leaves, disappointed and scowling.

"Now what?" Israel asks. His thumb caresses my wrist. The butterflies flutter back as though they had never left.

"I'm not entirely sure," I confess. "I didn't really expect to get this far."

"I thought you had some master plan!"

"Not really, no." I know I sound sheepish, because I am. "I mean, long-term plan, sure. But here and now? Not exactly confident on how to proceed. We could just go back to Dad and Bea?"

"Then what was the point of coming at all?" Israel stops rubbing my wrist, and once again it's like holding hands with a granite statue. The last butterfly crashes abruptly.

"To get rid of Luke!" I reply cheerfully. "He couldn't get back to Rose without me, not now that Nora is gone."

"Speaking of Rose..."

"Yes?" I proceed cautiously.

"You have no plans to see her?" Iz seems surprised. Not upset, just surprised. Why wouldn't he be? I've been obsessed with my little sister for as long as he's known me. "Are you really giving up?"

"I gave up when Emme died. You know that." I pull my shirt closer around my arms. It's chilly in London in April, breezy and wet in the air. Even with my chemise under my men's shirt, I need a jacket. The thought makes me nervous. I'm not fond of shoplifting, but I don't have any money.

"I was only thinking if she isn't Rose any longer. I mean, if she remains Lizzie, maybe that would give you some closure?"

I stop short and stare at him blankly. "What are you going on about?"

"Closure. You know?"

"Twenty-first century mumbo jumbo? That kind of closure? I don't know, Dr. Rhode." When I feel trapped, I tend to use sarcasm to cope.

"I mean it, Sonny. Listen. You need to say goodbye, or good riddance, or whatever it takes to let the past go. The way it all ended in London before… That was no way to put everything to rest. I don't want you to be haunted by all the could haves, would haves, and might have beens. This whole thing needs to end, one way or the other. I don't want to always feel like we're watching our backs all the time. I plan to be around for the rest of your life, you know."

"Of course, you do. You'd be lost without the full-time responsibility of being driven batty by me." I tease.

"I'm being serious." He leans over and kisses the top of my head. I self-consciously tuck my mussed hair behind my ears. "I'll do whatever it takes to make the best of this situation."

"Short of being pushed off a cliff?" I ask wryly.

"Short of that, and short of letting that happen to you, either."

"There's something you haven't thought of though," I continue.

"Yes?"

"I have absolutely no desire to see Rose," I say flatly.

"I didn't say it would be fun. I just said it might be necessary." He widens his eyes, which makes his forehead wrinkle. He has these deep lines from smiling and from thinking. I love them. They're like life lines in his face. He's going to be wrinkled as a raisin when he's old.

"Ugh. Why do you have to be so, so," I struggle for the word, "smart?"

"Med school."

"You didn't even go to med school," I laugh.

"Sure, I did. I attended two semesters of Anatomy and Physiology at a community college in Kentucky in 1982."

I laugh again. "You are so not ever operating on me should the need arise!"

"Heck, no!" He grins. "I hate blood, especially when it's coming out of someone I love."

We walk in silence for a while. The bakery is no longer where I recall, and we walk on with no destination in mind. His words, though meant to be lighthearted, chill me a bit. Rose may very well try to kill me, and I'd prefer to keep my blood on the inside of my body as well, now that he mentions it.

"Besides," Israel sighs, "Luke will only come back for us. He knows this town better than we do."

"But if Rose is Rose, he won't need us anymore," I argue, "and if she isn't Rose, if she's still Lizzie, he can't get back to 1888, which is where we're headed, remember?"

"You're giving me a headache."

"Tell me about it."

"So, what do you think?" He stops walking and pulls me in close to study me. Sometimes I feel like a specimen in Israel's personal laboratory. It isn't an uncomfortable feeling to be so scrutinized, but it is unsettling at times.

"I'll think about it," I promise. "That's the best I can do, but there's something I want to do first."

Chapter 9

"It's been forty years, Sonny. What are the odds that any of the Halloways will still be here, in this house?"

We stand, looking up at the same looming mansion I had stared up at with Emme by my side, so long ago. Forty years, but not really. Not to me. To me it's only been a few months.

"It's worth a shot. Come on." I tug on Israel's hand, but his feet stay planted firmly on the ground. I sigh. "What?"

"Nothing. Just come here." Israel smooths my hair back and pulls out a leaf. "You look like you've been sleeping on the ground all night," he teases.

"Hey, be nice! I've traveled forty years in the future just recently. I'm bound to look a little haggard."

"You don't look haggard. You look beautiful." He leans in to kiss me.

"Thank you," I murmur against his mouth. He swallows my words and they become a part of him. "I love you."

"I love you back."

The I-love-yous are new to us. Still fresh, out of the box, kind of amazing sort of thing. Like a shy present, we give each other. It drifts around us, and encircles us in a warmth that makes me feel giddy. He hasn't said it since Luke arrived in Africa, and it's so nice hearing it come from him again. I feel like a weight has lifted off my tired shoulders. I can finally breathe again, deep, gulping breaths full of oxygen and hope. I hadn't realized I'd been slowly asphyxiating, suffocating in my own worries and emotions.

"Seriously," Israel chuckles, softly. "If Prue answers that door, I'm going to drop dead. Even she can't possibly live to be that old."

I laugh too, partly because I know Prue would have laughed, as well. Laughed and then probably smacked both of us. "She's been 92 and holding for what seems like half my life, so you never know. I would not be surprised. Maybe she sold her soul to Satan for his recipes in exchange for immortality."

"Well, go on then." Israel gives my bottom a smack, and I yelp. "Ring the bell. I'll hang back here."

So I do, and stand there for a small eternity, biting my nails. I stop when I remember that's what Rose does, bites them down to the quick, until her fingers drip blood. I stop immediately and will myself to never bite my nails again, not ever. I'm picturing my future, long, perfectly groomed nail beds when the door swings open.

It is an old lady, but not my old lady. Of course, Prue wouldn't be alive, but I still get a little drop in my stomach of disappointment. If anyone could live forever, it would be Prue.

"Hello." The lady standing at the door seems rather upper class, so I hurriedly drop a curtsy, suddenly forgetting altogether which century I'm in and not knowing what in the world would be appropriate. "Are you the lady of the house, ma'am?"

"I am." She regards me rather coldly. She is very old, though not as old as Prue the last time I saw her. Her gray hair is pulled back from a face that was once severe, but is now only tired. Her face is surprisingly wrinkle-free for the most part, and I wonder if she had not done much laughing in her time. When I'm old, I want to be dreadfully wrinkled around my eyes and mouth so that Israel and I can be raisins together. That and gorgeous nail beds are really my only goals in life. "Who are you? If you're selling something, I'm not purchasing it." She glances at my clothing with barely concealed condescension.

"No, ma'am. I was only curious, ma'am, as to who lives here now. You see, my," I fumble a bit, searching for an appropriate lie, "grandparents lived near here, many years ago, and I've always wanted to see the part of London they used to walk, you see. My grandfather was a servant in this house many years ago. His name was Oliver. Ollie? He was a young boy. There was a cook named Gertie he used to talk about, and then later, a cook named Prue?" I nearly hold my breath.

I remember Ollie fondly, the little scamp. My math is off a bit, but the thought of him being my grandfather makes me smile. He wouldn't be quite old enough to be my grandfather, but I'm hoping she doesn't catch that. I should have said he was my father. I also hope my smile makes me look harmless and innocent and curious, and not full of malarkey.

"Ollie? Let me see." The old lady purses her lips together as she thinks. "This is tiresome, making an old woman think."

"Forgive me, ma'am." I drop another curtsy since she seems appeased by the first one.

"I remember Ollie. My husband had him employed when I arrived. I had been gone a while during those years, you see."

Lady Halloway? This is Lady Halloway? The adulteress wife whose clothes I had once stolen? I school my face to not betray my thoughts. She had come back to Sir Halloway then.

"I don't recall a Gertie, but Prue was our cook for many years. Ollie was a mischievous lad. I do hope he grew into a respectable member of society?"

Had she ever missed her dress? And shoes? Those shoes had never fit me. I feel guilty for taking them, and my toes clench and curl inside my boots.

"Oh, yes, ma'am. Indeed he did, ma'am. And what of the cook, Prue? He spoke so fondly of her, my grandfather did."

"She passed away many years ago. My husband was very fond of her. I wanted to let her go as she got on in years and hire someone younger, but he disagreed with me as usual, and she worked until the day she died."

"Was it peaceful? Her death, I mean." I feel tears pricking my eyes but blink them back rapidly. I'm so glad she stayed here until the end, and didn't travel somewhere on her own. With the very old, that's usually how it goes. They just stop being Lost somehow, and that's how they know their end is almost near, when they wake up day after day in the same place. I'm glad this place was here.

"She wasn't sick if that's what you mean. Just ancient. She must have been one hundred if she was a day. Now, if that's all you wanted, I'm afraid I need to say goodbye. I can't be standing here in the doorway all day while you gab about the dead. Give my regards to your grandfather."

"Yes, ma'am. Thank you, ma'am." I curtsy once more.

I hurry back to Israel, who is waiting patiently though with a curious look on his face.

"Prue stayed here. She passed away." I smile, though a bit tremulously. It's weird, this jumping throughout time, finding things out in the wrong order. Especially now that I know I can go when and where I like, what kinds of things can I discover? The thought is mind boggling. Mentally, I check myself for signs of trauma, forgetfulness, and anything that could tell me I'm having side effects like Rose does. I don't feel particularly crazy. Yet.

"That's good." Israel smiles too, but I catch the waver. We're the only family Iz has. He loved her, too. "Now what?"

I make a face. "Well, since a bubble bath is out of the question, I'll settle for breakfast."

Israel peers back at the Halloway's house. "The back may be unlocked."

I make another face. "I feel bad for stealing her shoes forty years ago. I don't want to add to my crimes here."

He laughs. "It isn't any less bad to spread your stealing around, Sonny."

"Yes, it is," I disagree piously. "We should spread the thievery, like Robin Hood. Only, he was giving it back, and we're taking it, but you get the idea. Also, I need different clothes."

"Why? You look cute. I like those pants."

"Oh, hush. I need whatever girls are wearing these days so I can blend in."

"You want to dress up to go to a mental institution?" Israel's nostrils flare like he's holding in laughter.

"Yes." I draw myself up to my full height, thereby making myself feel more grown up. "I can't concentrate and relax if I'm worried about everyone looking funny at me."

"Well, you're getting high maintenance on me, I'll tell you that much. First breakfast, now a new set of clothes?" he teases. "I never pegged you for one of those material types."

"First of all, smarty, wanting breakfast does not make me high maintenance, nor does wanting a decent dress, or skirt, or whatever it is they're sporting for fashion in this time period. But if you make me choose, I choose breakfast every time."

"That's my girl. Since we're looking at petty thievery or pick-pocketing, I'm afraid it's going to fall mostly on you today."

"What? Why?" I stop walking, dismayed. I much prefer to have my sins committed by others, namely Israel or Dad. They're like my personal hired thugs. I'm sure it isn't fair, but then again, they don't seem to mind so much, morally speaking. The last person I stole from nearly caught me trying to give him back change.

"Look around." Israel gestures.

I stop and stare. The few people nearby are women. I steal a sideways glance at my companion, an oddly dressed and ridiculously tall black man. Yep, there is no way he would be able to get anywhere near these ladies without alerting half the population. Unfair!

I groan pathetically. "Come on! Can't you just break and enter somewhere or something?"

"While you hang out nearby, sitting pretty?"

"Pretty much. Yes. That's my favorite plan."

"Nope." Israel crosses his arms over his expansive chest and stares at me. "It is so your turn. It's been your turn for about three years actually."

"Meanie."

"Baby."

I glare. "Fine. But don't say I didn't offer to do this a different way." I take a deep breath and push him with all my might, which is still only half the might I use to start screaming. "Oh my God! Help me! Help! He's stolen my money! Let go of me! Someone help! Stop him!"

Israel's eyes widen in alarm but only for a second. With a muttered curse under his breath, he takes off at a run.

Everything happens the way I knew it would. The women in hearing range flock to me and don't try to chase him, predictable. I do see a man I hadn't noticed before, and like a true gentleman he obligingly begins running off after my supposed predator. Since he is twice Israel's age and double his weight, I'm not too concerned. Then I see a much younger and fitter man behind them both and realize Israel is going to have his work cut out for him getting off scot free. Serves him right.

"Oh, my gracious! What did he take?" A blonde girl in a short dress gasps dramatically. "Your money? Oh my gracious! Oh, honey!"

I school my face to one of upset sorrow. "Just my spending money, but oh, what a shock I had!" I gulp fanning myself. "I can't believe...He was just so quick I never even saw or never did suspect. Oh girls, check your belongings, do!"

Ever unsurprising in their reaction, my gaggle of new friends instantly begin looking through their bags, pockets, and hidden folds in their skirts. Each giving away the locations of their valuables, and sighing with relief as they discover nothing is missing. One girl impulsively embraces me.

"Oh, honey!" she says. "I'm so sorry for you, I really am. What a nasty turn of events for you, and you just...just..." she falters. "What exactly are you doing dressed like that?"

"I'm an actress," I lie. "Well, just an extra really." I conjure up some false modesty. "Hollywood is doing a film about archeologists and science and all that. I play a woman who digs up mummies." I should be disturbed at how quickly and easily I lie. I hitch up my pants, sheepishly.

"Oooh! Is it the new Lillian Gish one? I heard she was in town!" A raven haired beauty pipes up.

"Yes, yes, that's the one. Well, anyway, I'd better be getting back. Thanks for helping a sister in need. So sorry to have alarmed you." I pat the arm of the blonde, and lean in for a quick peck on the cheek by the brunette.

"You must report him!" Another blonde sternly tells me, and I give her a quick hug of thankfulness.

"Yes, do!" they chorus.

"I will," I promise, "and you all be careful on your way home now." They swear they will and all disperse, waving cheerily at one another, and holding their now mostly empty handbags tightly.

Chapter 10

"Really?" Israel scowls at me, when I finally catch up to him several blocks later. He had yanked me into an alley and nearly given me a heart attack, which he firmly claims is my own fault. "Really? Was that necessary?"

I swallow my smirk and settle for a hangdog look. "It worked, didn't it? You wanted me to take care of breakfast, didn't you? Well, here's enough for breakfast, lunch, and dinner. And accessories to go out to dinner, to boot." I hold up a gold necklace and a diamond tennis bracelet. I'm pretty sure I deserve a kiss, but I settle for a light punch in the shoulder.

"Alright," Iz sighs begrudgingly. "Not bad, I'll admit. Though I'm going to have to resign myself to back alleys and dark nights, thanks to you. They all got a good look at me."

"Well, if they're smarter than the average they'll be looking for me too once they realize how much I lightened their purses. Oh well, we won't be here too long, will we?" I force myself to sound cheerful. In truth, I'm more than a bit nervous about meeting Rose again, and I'm not entirely sold on the whole idea. I have a better one actually, but I don't think Iz will compromise.

"Come on, you little thief," he says looping his arm through mine. "Let's find something to eat and get some clothes."

We hasten along, trying to look inconspicuous, which is simply ridiculous, a black man with a young woman dressed as a man. Thank goodness, we aren't still in Victorian England, but with the stares we are beginning to attract, I'm not sure 1931 is much better.

"Why do you have to be so dark?" I grumble.

"Why do you have to be so pale?" he counters sounding just as grumpy as I feel. This isn't the first time our relationship has elicited odd looks and muttered words. I know I'm being naïve if I think we could ever wake up anywhere where our skin wouldn't matter, wouldn't cause suspicion, or even hatred. Is there such a place? I've yet to see it, and I think I can safely say I've been around more than most.

My thoughts make me even more sullen, but also rebellious and stubborn, so I intertwine my fingers through Israel's and walk boldly. I look down and see how they fit, his large and black, and mine small and peach-colored. Our hands look like a braided rug with two different shades of yarn.

"Come on," Israel nudges me to the side, and takes my thoughts out of where they were lingering. "This looks good to get something to wear. I want one of those fedoras."

I look where he's focused his attention and see a small shop selling men's clothes right next to another selling women's. With similar signs in lettering and paint, they seem to be owned by the same entrepreneur. The men's offers jaunty hats and suit coats, while the women's flaunts crepe dresses and pleated skirts that are shorter in the front and dip a bit lower in the back. There is even a hat on a mannequin made to look like an ice cream cone, and I can't help but giggle. I won't be buying that.

"Meet me out front in a half hour!" Israel gives me a quick peck on the cheek. "And Sonny?"

"Mm?" I'm pocketing my stolen money again and trying to look presentable. I lick my palm and smooth my hair behind my ears.

"Get the short one." He gestures to a fancy evening gown which looks positively scandalous for this day and age, and I roll my eyes.

"I'm getting something comfortable," I retort, as I open the door to a cheerful jingle. "Prayerfully, overalls."

Fashion has never been my specialty, and I'm woefully out of my league once inside. An overeager sales girl tries to outfit me from head to toe, but

I decline firmly and end up with a sensible wool skirt, a tweed jacket, and shoes that are only five times more uncomfortable than they look. I would have thought oxfords would be in style nowadays, but evidently I'm mistaken. Either that or this particular shop doesn't sell them, and the shortest heel they have make me feel like a giant.

The sales girl also is determined, with the fierce fortitude of a style soldier, that I purchase nylon hosiery. Though polite, it's a battle I am resolved to win. I leave bare-legged and probably scandalous, while the sales girl tries to soothe the temper of a spoiled teenager who is determined to spend more cash than her mother wants to.

The mother wrings her hands and looks embarrassed, and momentarily I want to slap the girl silly. Her face is blotched from tears, and she is only humiliating herself. I look at her and want to say, *Don't you know what you have? A mother to take shopping? A mother AT ALL?*, but I know she would mouth off and hate me and think me woefully stupid.

Israel waits for me, casual and looking rather striking in a grey suit and the much sought after fedora. Darn man looks handsome and dashing in every era. I'm not sure how he does it. Clothes just hang on him properly, and he always looks at ease. I always feel like my clothes are wearing me, not the other way around, and I pull at my skirt as I walk to meet him.

"Ah, you did go with something short," he says, approvingly.

"Not really." I tug it down, self-consciously. "I'm just tall. It was longer on the mannequin. The woman in back offered to let it out for me, but my stomach was growling so loudly I could barely hear her. Breakfast?" I don't like talking about my appearance. I never know when I'm being complimented or the victim of polite small talk, though, of course, Iz doesn't do small talk, and he is hardly ever polite.

He agrees, and we make short work of a stack of griddle cakes in the nearest restaurant we find. Griddle cakes make me think of cake, which make me think of Rose, which makes me pensive company. Maybe Israel is right, maybe I do need closure, but what if that closure comes with a price? Like, death? I stab my last bite ferociously.

"I think it was dead already," Israel raises his eyebrows at me from across the little bistro style table. "Nervous?"

"Wouldn't you be?" I toss my fork down, and it skitters across the table and comes to rest against my orange juice. "Aren't you? I feel sick. I keep replaying everything from the last year in my mind. Did I do everything wrong?"

"What? Love your sister? Try to help her? Come on, Sonny."

"Just, just." I splay my hands and sigh. "Just everything. Iz, I've been thinking. I mean, I suppose a miracle could happen, and maybe we can get this closure thing and never hear from Rose or Luke again, but if not? If it goes poorly, like I imagine it will, then I have to do something else."

"I get the feeling I'm not going to like this idea." Israel narrows his dark eyes at me, and I look away.

I continue as if I haven't heard him. "Well, the thing is, you're right. We will be watching our backs all our lives, and I don't want that for us either. But what if I could change it all? Go back? Now that I know I can, I can go anywhere. I can go back and fix it from the beginning. Fix Rose."

"How?"

I stare at him pointedly. "By going back where it all started. The night we left her behind."

Israel sighs, a deep, overly dramatic sigh in my opinion. "Sonny," he drawls.

I scowl at him. "You had to know I was thinking about it."

"I did, but I was hoping I was wrong. I was hoping," his voice gets a bit louder, "you weren't as harebrained and halfcocked as I thought. I was hoping you were smarter."

I stick my tongue out. "Well, you overestimated my intelligence then, I'm afraid. Are you in, or are you out?"

He glares down at me. Suddenly, he seems huge, a proverbial giant of a man. He looks very capable of swinging me over his shoulder and dragging me off somewhere, probably to beat some sense into my harebrained head. "Don't give me ultimatums, Sonny," he growls. Back to growling again, and he doesn't promise anything.

*　*　*

"I hate this place," I mutter. Bethlem Royal Hospital is cold and gray. I had nearly turned back three separate times just while going up the walkway. I hold Israel's hand as if my life depends on it, and his grip on mine isn't exactly slack either. I think we're both a bit frightened, though his face is only grim. I wonder what mine looks like. White as a sheet, probably. I feel like scampering off into the hedges in my best rabbit impression.

We pass the scraggly magnolia tree with Luke's Rolls-Royce Phantom car parked sideways beneath it. It chills me for some reason, like he had foretold the future, only it wasn't the future. It was the past, his past. There's nothing supernatural about it. Well, of course there is, but nothing I'm not used to, I mean. Still, it makes my blood run cold.

The red tulips decorate the path up to the looming front door of the hospital, and though I don't want them to, my eyes roam ahead, looking for the trod upon petals that Luke said would be there. They are, strewn about like velvet skirts on a girl's bedroom floor. I feel like screaming somehow.

I don't even realize I've stopped walking until Israel begins pulling me along once again. "Come on," he says gently. "It's the safest place to meet her, you know."

"Is it?" I mutter. Bedlam may be Rose's prison, but she typically has no problems finding her way out whenever she feels like it. I have doubts about the staff's ability to protect me, or their own selves for that matter. Do they have any idea who they are dealing with?

Before I lose what's left of my nerve, Israel has led me up the stairs to the front door and pushed it open. It moves silently, the massive thing, as if on freshly oiled hinges. We are met almost instantly by a pretty young woman around my age in a nurse's headscarf and shoes that are exactly like mine. She has a friendly, though business-like smile, and dark eyes with pretty flecks of gold and green in them like confetti at a party.

"May I help you?" Her accent is all London, born and raised, though it's the upper class variety, like the one I like to adopt when I'm pretending to be someone else. Pristine. "I'm Mina Dobson."

"Hello, Miss Dobson. I'm here to see..." I falter. If I say Rose, will this girl know who I'm speaking of? Who did Rose think she was in this day and age?

"Lizzie." Israel finishes my request.

Miss Dobson looks distinctly uncomfortable. "Um." She hesitates. "That is, Lizzie isn't, well, she's..."

"Is Rose Gray here, then?" I take her out of her apparent misery and get right to the point. The sooner I can get this meeting over with, the better. Might as well get on with it.

Miss Dobson looks surprised. Very surprised. "And you are?" She frowns.

"I'm Rose's sister. Sonnet Gray."

Now she looks as though I could knock her over with a feather. "You are?" She stares blankly. "That is, I'm sorry. This is quite a shock."

"I agree." I smile albeit bleakly. "She's here then?"

"Well," Miss Dobson straightens her skirt, which is already immaculate and pressed within an inch of its life, "she is, yes, but I don't know if she is up to receiving visitors today."

"Could you ask her husband?" I press. "It's rather important that I see her. It may be the last time, you see. We're," I stumble over my words and look to Israel for reassurance, "we're going away."

"Oh," she murmurs almost silently. "Well, please have a seat in the waiting room here. I'll just speak to Mr. Connelly, I mean Mr. Dawes, and also to Miss Helmes. Excuse me."

Miss Dobson leaves, and while Iz settles down in a stiff backed chair, I pace the room nervously. The hospital has an odor to it, typical of hospitals, of disinfectant and medicines and too many people in one place. I breathe through my mouth. My new shoes pinch. I long to kick them off under the settee, but being barefoot would make me look too much like Rose in appearance, a resemblance I don't wish for in an insane asylum, no less. It wouldn't do to remind the staff of the inmates. My dream of being strapped down in a bed rushes back with a fearsome flash. Is that where Rose is now? Strapped down and cold, with needle legged spiders crawling up her legs?

"Well, this is a surprise." Luke suddenly fills the doorway. "Just when I think I know you, Gray, you do something that stuns me. What in the world made you come here?"

He looks happy, content, and refreshed. I know instantly that Rose is Rose again, and not Lizzie. He doesn't need me to help jog her memory. He probably wouldn't even have come after us again. We most likely should have disappeared while we had the chance. We've taken an unnecessary and foolish risk.

"Something Israel here calls closure," I grumble. "How is my sister?"

"Right as rain." Luke is wreathed in smiles. He looks devilishly handsome, even if he does need a change of clothes, a shave, and a haircut. "Back to perfection."

I hold in a snort, which would only make me look childish. I smooth my features to a disinterested and polite smile. "Well, that's nice. Do you think it would be harmful to her" *or me,* I silently add, "if I were to see her? Talk with her?" *Is she restrained?* is really what I want to know.

Luke looks even more taken aback, if possible. "Really? Truly? Well, this is nice." He makes a move that looks as though he's going to clap Israel on the back in a friendly kind of way but stops short when he sees Iz's face. He pockets his hands instead.

"Look," I reply firmly. "I'm not saying we should all go out for cheeseburgers or anything. I'd just like a chance to put things behind us. Even if she'll never change, and even if she'll hate me all her days. I'd like to say goodbye and say my piece, while I can and while there are witnesses." *Safety in numbers.*

"All right." I can't tell if the look on his face is bemused or just plain confused. "Well, she's resting a bit now. She had a difficult night. We thought we'd stay a night or two here to recover a bit from the past few months. Put Lizzie and Sam to rest, so to speak." He acts like the thought of that is the most common thing in the universe, as if we all had to do that once in a while, like airing out the mattresses, or being put on jury duty. *Let's just bury our alter egos and go back to our original identities for a bit, shall we?*

Putting split personalities to rest. When did my world get so crazy? I nod, as though it makes all the sense in the world. "It won't take long, and if it tires her, we'll leave."

Luke's face goes from happy to suddenly suspicious. "This isn't some sort of weird revenge plot, is it? You had plenty of time to just disappear, you know. I'm still surprised you chose to come here."

I think back to all the times before when I chose to run after my sister, and now all I want to do is run from her. I tried so hard to get her to love me. Is that what I'm still doing? Will I never learn?

"It's hard to move on when you're always looking over your shoulder," Israel interjects. "Is that so hard to understand, Dawes?"

Luke shrugs. "I suppose not. Though when it comes to looking over your shoulder, you get used to it, pal. Keeps you from being lonely. Anyway, right this way." He gestures into the hallway, and we begin to walk through the halls of Bedlam.

The antiseptic smell of drugs and medicines and cleaning supplies lingers everywhere. Breathing through my mouth doesn't help. I can taste the sterile air on my tongue, thick and heavy, like breathing a nasty thick medicine. The air in the hallway is too warm, or maybe I'm too warm, and I shrug off my tweed jacket as we walk. My blouse sticks to my back in no time at all. I glance at Israel beside me, and at Luke in front of us and they seem cool as cucumbers. It's just me, who is completely unraveling.

It's dreadful to be so callous, but I want to shut my eyes and have Iz lead me blindly through the halls. Hating myself for my cowardice, I open my eyes wider and determine to take in everything about this place.

My toes are nearly run over by an old man in a wheelchair, who slows down long enough to glare at me before careening down the hall. A young man, who doesn't appear to be an inmate but instead an orderly or something like that, tips his hat at me and winks. There's an odd wailing sort of sound coming from behind a closed door that gives me pause, or rather it causes my feet to move even more quickly past it.

There's a girl, no more than twenty or so, sitting in the hallway. Her feet are bare, and she wears only a hospital gown, and for a moment I falter, but it isn't Rose. This girl's hair is brown. Her knees are folded up to her chest, and her chin rests on them. Feeling a nervous chill, and then once again despising myself for my spinelessness, I compel myself to not insult her by walking by too quickly or by refusing to meet her eyes. I pass in what feels like slow motion, and notice that she has very strange eyes, but then again, so do I.

Where mine are oddly light blue, hers are dark as night, and they pierce right through me. At first, they seem vacant, empty, like she doesn't actually see me through the chocolate-colored lens. Then they light up like too much life is behind them. Luke has passed by her without a glance, but my feet feel like lead. I hold her strange gaze, and she doesn't blink.

"Help me, mum?" she murmurs, and to my horror her hand reaches out and grabs my skirt as I brush by. I stifle the urge to scream, though I should feel nothing but sadness and compassion for the poor thing.

"I – I can't," I whisper, frantically. *Please God, make her let go.* The softness in her eyes turns abruptly to hatred, but she lets go of my skirt. I grasp Israel's hand more tightly, and we keep walking, giving a backwards glance to the dark haired girl. I had an absurd, creeping feeling that somehow she was following us on silent, ghostly feet, but there she still sits in her spot in the hallway.

How long has she sat there? How long will she sit there?

Chapter 11

Rose looks like an angel, or a fairy tale princess. She lays sprawled on her bed with no restraints, her yellow hair splayed around her like the Lady of Shalott. Innocent as the day is long, my sister is, or appears to be. She doesn't even look her full age, which should be nearly nineteen or thereabouts, but instead looks more like a sweet, little, napping girl. She isn't wearing a hospital gown, but what appears to be a nurse's smock, the same type of apron as Miss Dobson wears.

"I'm surprised you're letting her sleep without you," I comment to Luke, then realize that could have a double entendre that I hadn't intended, and I'm just innocent enough to blush. "I mean–"

"I know what you mean, Gray. She isn't asleep though." Luke smiles.

Rose's eyes, so like mine, are open now, and she blinks sleepily at me. "Fancy seeing you here," she murmurs.

I very nearly laugh, but it would be a nervous, fragile kind of laughter, and I swallow it back. I make myself take another step towards the bed to show I'm not afraid. "Hello, Rose. How are you feeling?"

"Better. I suppose you've heard about my life here? Luke." she looks at him in disapproval. "You didn't need to bring her here. You didn't need to tell on me." Her voice has always been higher than my throaty own, an angelic type of lilt that matches her exterior, if not her behavior. When she's angry though, it can rise to shrill.

"I didn't, love, not exactly. Sonnet came on her own. Wasn't that nice?" I can tell his tone is a bit anxious. He doesn't want to start anything between all of us, it seems. How nice, and out of character.

"Did you bring our father?" Rose asks me.

"No."

"Why are you here?" She seems genuinely curious, and she sits up in her bed and tucks her feet beneath her. Her hair streams down her back, a bit tangled and in need of washing and brushing, but still beautiful. "I don't know what to do with you here." She wrinkles her button nose like she finds me distasteful. What kind of maniacal villainesses have button noses anyway?

"I know. It's because we need to end things, Rose. We both need to let go. I think if you're being reasonable, you'll agree." My palms are sweaty, but I stifle the urge to wipe them on my skirt. I won't show any weakness in front of her.

She laughs, and it's a real laugh, full of mirth and authentic enjoyment, not her frightening, mad laugh. She seems delighted in my words. "Aren't you a funny thing?" She claps her hands together. "Luke, isn't she funny?"

"Always made me laugh." Luke winks at me.

Israel is stiff beside me, and suddenly I realize why, he's never actually been in the presence of my sister. My words and tales of our short times together hadn't done justice to her persona. Is he repulsed, or does he think her more normal and sane than I know her to be?

"So, Sonnet," Rose continues. She picks at the ends of her hair, pulling out a snarl. "What exactly are you looking for here, huh? You want me to make a truce? I stop looking for you and you stop obsessing over me? Is that it?"

"Something like that."

"I'm supposed to just forgive and forget that you left me behind? That I grew up without my family?" She yanks her hair hard, and I see several strands pull out in her hand. Nearly a handful. I wince; I can't help it. Sympathy for her scalp or no, I object to her words.

"I was four years old!" I burst out. "Stop blaming me. It wasn't anyone's fault that night! No one has regretted it more than me, except maybe Dad. What do you want from us?"

Rose's blue eyes narrow. "Don't be angry with me. Don't you dare. I'm the one who was abandoned, remember?"

"I *remember* you killed our mother, and I *remember* you arranged to have Emme murdered, so yes, Rose, I *remember* a lot of things. You wanted your revenge, and you've had it, and now it needs to stop." The words are out before I can stop them, like a flood. So much for easing into the hard part of the conversation.

Rose twirls the now tangle free lock of hair around her fingers. Her finger nails aren't so short anymore, aren't caked with blood. Lizzie must not have bitten her nails. I wonder if she'll start back up now that she's put Lizzie to rest. She looks at me, craftily. "But why? Weren't we having fun? *We* were having fun, weren't we, darling?" She turns her attention to Luke, who smiles fondly.

"Well, perhaps, but I don't think Sonnet was." He shrugs at me as if to say that's the best he can do.

Suddenly, Israel decides to say something. His voice is strong and sure, the one he uses in a professional capacity when he is counseling his patients, and just hearing it relaxes me a bit. "Rose, I know you haven't had much cause to trust doctors, but I'd like you to trust me. We're never going to be friends, but it's important for everyone if you can cooperate and focus on what Sonnet is here to say. Can you do that?"

"Can I do that?" Rose purses her lips, as if in thought, but I know she's pretending. "Can I do that, oh esteemed Dr. Rhode? Can I trust you?" She taps her finger against her rosebud lips, contemplating. "The man who never went to medical school? Who never went to any school actually? You, who call yourself a surgeon? Can you even hold a knife steady, Israel Rhode?" She leans in closer and speaks very softly. "Because *I* can."

"Visiting hours are over." The sudden announcement comes in a woman's voice from the doorway. The skinny woman is all hard and pointy angles except for her chest, which is pillowy and large. She frowns at us. "The patients here aren't accustomed to long visits, especially unannounced. When you make an appointment, they can be properly told ahead of time how to be hospitable. It isn't good to surprise the ill. You can come back on Wednesday."

"Oh, Miss Helmes, don't be such a ninny!" Rose tosses her head. "I won't be here on Wednesday myself. I was only staying until I was all rested up and recovered from your little experiment." She glares at Miss Helmes, and I see Miss Helmes blanch. So Miss Helmes was keeping Lizzie's identity secret, too. What a tangled web they weaved. Foolish. Had they thought their plan through? Will they live to regret it?

"It's all right. I think we're done here," I address the pointy Miss Helmes. "We'll show ourselves out. Rose," I pause and turn my head and force myself to look into her eyes, those eyes are so much like mine. "I'm sorry. I just want to say that before we leave one another. I forgive you, and I hope you forgive me."

I know my voice is shaky and on the verge of cracking, but I've gotten the words out and that's what matters. Not poetic, not perfect, not the flawless speech I wanted to give, but good enough. It will have to be good enough, because I plan on those words being the last I ever speak to my sister. Rose cocks her head and regards me.

She says nothing.

*   *   *

Outside, I gulp in large swallows of fresh air. Bedlam made me feel as though I was stifling to death, slowly. Do the inmates feel that way, too? Casualties of oppression and helpful staff? I imagine a horrid cemetery with tombstones reading, *Interfered With to Death, Murdered by Poisoned Air, Smothered by False Kindnesses, Drugged Until I Died.* In my imagination, the girl in the hallway, leans up against one, staring at me, sorrowfully, and the stone that belongs to her reads *Ignored.*

When we had left the building, the girl named Mina had reached out and touched my hand as I put my tweed jacket back on.

"Don't give up on her," she had murmured. "She's my friend."

I had said nothing. There was nothing I could think to say. *No, she isn't,* seemed cruel. Was she? Did Rose have a friend? Why did I feel jealous? Was it because I missed Emme, my only friend? She was gone forever, unless of course, I traveled to the past. I suppose in some ways, the Lost are somewhat lucky since it is possible goodbye isn't permanent for us. Would I meet a little red-haired girl someday with Joe's freckles, and know it's Emme? I'll never meet her as an old woman though, that much is certain. Was I jealous because Mina had gotten closer to Rose, even if she was Lizzie then, than I ever had accomplished? I glance back at the asylum.

"This is ridiculous," I mutter to Israel. I gesture over to Luke and Rose, who had only been a few maddening steps behind us as we left those halls. Apparently, they had changed their minds about staying for a rest. Luke waves. I glare. "They didn't need to ruin our exit. I've only been planning it for forever."

Iz chuckles. "I know. They really are obnoxious. This whole situation is absurd. Tell me again why we came?"

I glare harder, this time in his direction. "Funny, funny man. Tell me again why I put up with you?"

"You're shallow, and you're with me for my looks, especially in this fedora." He offers me his hand, and I take it gratefully. "Keep walking, and don't look behind you."

"What? Why?" Of course, I look. It's the Rolls-Royce, driving at a snail's pace, following us. "Oh, for goodness sake! This has left ridiculous and absurd and is bordering on insane."

"You think?" Iz replies drily. "Did you expect sane behavior from those two?"

Frustrated, I throw up my hands, a difficult endeavor as I am still holding onto Israel's. His goes flying up into the air, as well, and the look on his face would be comical if I weren't in such a bad mood. "What I wouldn't give for the Blue Beast," I grumble. "We'd give them a run for it. What are they doing anyway?"

The Rolls-Royce continues to drive along. If it were a person, it'd be an old man, shuffling along, strolling, meandering. I want to pelt it with rocks. I whirl and march up to it, my heels clicking angrily. I trod upon another innocent tulip.

Luke lowers his window and smiles at me as though I'm an old friend he has just happened to run into at the market or some such thing. "Gray?"

"If you're going to run us down, could you speed it up?" I seethe, through my teeth. "Otherwise, go away!"

"We have a flat up the road a bit. Didn't want to speed by you, seemed rude with all the puddles." He tips his hat toward the ground. "Go ahead. We aren't in a hurry."

I want to kill him, really and truly. How did I ever think I might be falling in love with this Neanderthal? I know Rose is mentally incompetent, but really. I'm starting to think even she could do better.

"After you," I grind out. Israel has caught up with me and puts his arm around my waist. I'm too tense and riddled with rage to relax against him.

"See you around, Gray," Luke answers. "Rhode. Say goodbye, honey," he direct Rose, next to him in the passenger seat. She turns her head towards us.

"Bye!" she chirps cheerfully.

"Oh, and," Luke pauses, looking pained, "I don't know how to say this, but–"

"What?" Israel sighs.

"Do you two have some place to go? Of course, you don't," he answers himself. "Well, you're welcome at the flat. I suppose you'll think that's odd, but I just wanted to put it out there. You know, with bygones being bygones and all that? They are bygones, aren't they?"

I think a small eternity goes by. Birds sing and leaves fall. Grass grows. I age. I am an old woman now.

"You must be joking." It's all I can finally come up with.

"Well, just think about it. That's all. Don't say we didn't offer." Luke tips his hat again. Where did he get that hat, anyway? I suppose it must have been left behind in Rose's asylum room when he and Nora traveled to Africa to find me. It looks like Israel's, only more expensive. He's smoking again, too. Must have had a stash there as well. The luxurious car drives away, a bit faster this time. It turns a corner, and it is gone. My sister is in that car, and in some small way, I feel as though part of me is too.

But it isn't a part I mourn anymore.

Chapter 12

We secure a room at the Savoy after springing for a cab to get there. We probably could have walked, but I couldn't shake the feeling of being stalked by a certain Rolls-Royce, and the cab was faster. I've missed automobiles. I had rolled the window down, though it was cold, and the cabbie looked at me as though I was bonkers. He did pick us up near Bedlam, so I guess I can hardly blame him. I twirled my fingers in the cold air and wished I could hang out my head like a spaniel. I wanted to feel the London air through my hair, though it would probably smell like the Thames afterward, so I refrained.

The Savoy is lavish. We have no business being here, of course, but I had managed to pocket a substantial amount of cash off the girls I stole from, and we won't be staying here long enough to spend it. Might as well enjoy it. At least that's Israel's side of things. I would normally argue we could give the rest back or distribute it among the poor like a proper Robin Hood, but I'm too tired. I feel a hundred years old. I'm the youngest old woman in history. I barely notice when Israel tells the man in charge that he and his wife will take one room for one night. I'm so used to being his not-wife that I would have broken in and objected if he had stated otherwise. Still, it does dawn on me, with a warm and comfortable glow that he hadn't needed to lie here, not here and now.

It must have crossed his mind, as well. "Sorry, force of habit," he whispers, as we follow the bellboy. Why do we need a bellboy? We have no luggage, which probably looks odd. I nearly say something about the airlines losing it when I realize what year we are in and conclude air travel is hardly common in this day and age. "I can ask for two rooms if you like."

"No way. I don't want to come running to your aid at 3 a.m. when you're screaming that you've found a spider in the tub," I reply, drily.

"Funny, funny girl. Why do I put up with you?"

"For my looks, of course, shallow man." I do a fancy two step up the stairs that makes the bellboy turn and smile and give me the once over. I'm getting the hang of these heels actually, though I'm not saying I'll miss them when they're gone.

We spend a few minutes in awe over our posh room, tip the bellboy even though he didn't really do anything, and I kick off my heels. I sit on the edge of the bed, rubbing my feet, while Israel pulls aside the draperies and stares out at the view of the Thames.

"She really is a mess, isn't she?" he finally speaks.

I yawn and topple backward onto a fluffy, divine stack of pillows. "I tried to tell you, and she wasn't even nearly at her worst. You should see her lose her temper." I raise my palms up to stare at them; the scars of shattered teacups and saucers had been crisscrossed there until recently. Rose had thrown them at me in one of her fits, and I had picked them all up so she wouldn't step on them in her forever bare feet. The healed scars, the disappeared calluses from my old guitar, and my nibbled upon nails. My hands have as many story lines as Israel's face. A forensic scientist could tell my whole sad tale with only the remains of my hands someday. "Or when she suddenly doesn't know what's going on or who you are anymore. That's frightening."

"That's what Luke's been living with, I guess."

"I guess." We are silent for a bit. Are we supposed to feel sorry for Luke Dawes? He couldn't have had it easy these past few months, but still. He earned what he got. "I wonder if she'll slip back again."

"He'll have to convince her to stop controlling their traveling. No telling if that's really what makes her worse, but he shouldn't take any chances." There's a hidden, not so subtle, hinting to his words that I pick up on.

"Don't worry." I stretch out on the bed. "I'm not going to control it either. Much."

"Sonnet."

"Once or twice. That's all I'm asking, Iz." I yawn again and roll over. "Come take a nap with me? I feel like I could sack out forever."

"Is this a trick?" Israel grumbles as he plops his large self on the bed and nearly bounces me right off the other side. "Am I going to wake up somewhere I don't want to be?"

I hit him with a pillow just moments before I succumb and fall asleep.

*　*　*

We sleep for hours, which is a terrible thing to do in the late afternoon. We wake past a decent supper time, ravished because we skipped lunch, and knowing we will have a hard time getting back to sleep tonight, especially if we plan on traveling.

"I've always wanted to call room service!" I feel positively gleeful as I peruse the menu the bellboy had pointed out to us. "Mm, maple meringues, petit fours, ice cream!"

"Are you going straight to desserts?" Iz chuckles from his blanket cave he's made in the bed.

"Yes, I am. What's a Dubonnet?"

"It's a drink. A grown up drink."

"I'm a grown up."

He snorts. "You're not that grown up. And you're not getting drunk and then making me travel someplace weird. You're falling asleep stone cold sober tonight, Sonny."

I stick my tongue out at the back of his head, which totally belies my earlier comment about being a grown up. "Cream puffs, Banoffee Pie, Treacle Tart..."

"I want roast beef."

"Don't interrupt. Custard, Shrewsbury Cake..."

"With horseradish."

"Yuck. I'm getting two of everything on the dessert menu. How much money do we have left?" I pick up the telephone, an old fashioned looking thing. Then I realize how long it's been since I've seen a telephone, period, so I laugh. The sound makes Israel chuckle, even though he doesn't know what is so funny, and the moment feels nice. I can't help wishing we were here under better circumstances. Where we could really relax and enjoy everything. I finish ordering – my sensible side forces me to order a sandwich to go with my three desserts, after all – and wait for it to arrive, my stomach growling and grumbling so loudly, I'm very nearly embarrassed.

I'm delighted when our bounty comes through the door, all wrapped up and presented in luxurious fashion. A gleaming silver lid covers Israel's roast beef (which does smell delicious), and my Treacle Tart looks even more amazing than my imagination had painted it. I reach for it as Israel tips the waiter, and my heart does a funny flipping thing in my chest when something else on the wheeled table catches my eye. A single rose in a bud vase, but isn't the sight of the rose that causes my breath to catch. It's the creamy white petals marred by something ugly: ashes. Caught between each and every velvety petal of the flower, a repulsive invader in an otherwise flawless piece of beauty, is a tiny thimbleful of ash. A gray rose.

*   *   *

Questioning the waiter is fruitless. He apologizes profusely for the state of the rose, but he hardly knows why I am so upset. He offers to bring another though I can tell he thinks I'm ridiculous, probably a spoiled, petty, socialite brat like he's used to dealing with, but I dismiss him.

I shove a bite of Treacle Tart in my mouth, angrily.

"Really?" Israel smiles a little. "You're going to eat?"

"I'm stifling the cussing," I retort around the dessert.

"But what if she's poisoned it?" Iz pokes around his roast beef.

I nearly choke. "I hadn't thought of that. Now you tell me." I eye the remaining tart suspiciously. "Well, now you have to eat yours."

Iz widens his black eyes. "Says who?"

"Says me! If I'm poisoned, you're coming with me!"

He continues to stare at his roast beef.

"You are the worst Romeo ever," I mutter, stabbing a forkful and eating it defiantly.

"I was going to eat it..." He trails off and watches me closely for signs of pending doom. When nothing happens besides my glare intensifying, he settles into his supper cheerfully.

"She was just letting you know she knows where we are," he tells me conversationally. "Classic really. Has to have the last word. Characteristic behavior when it comes to psychopaths."

"Did you just call my sister a psychopath?" I tuck into my sandwich. Poisoned or starved to death, we all have to go sometime, and I'd rather die with a full belly.

"Um, I'm sorry?"

I wave him off. "No offense taken. Just hadn't thought of... labeling her. That's all. Mina, the nurse, doesn't want me to give up on her. She says they're friends. Can psychopaths have friends?"

"I suppose. I mean, basically they are crying out for attention, same as everyone else. Well, *not* the same as everyone else, but the basic reason is the same. I'm sure they get very lonely, but that doesn't mean Mina shouldn't watch her back."

"Amen." We finish eating in silence. Poisoned or not, everything is perfectly delicious. "Come on. Let's go walk all this off." I stand and stretch. My stomach is happy now, if a bit too full. The petit fours were especially wonderful. I do have a weakness for anything frosted. I slip my heels back on with a sigh. "I miss sneakers," I complain. "What is taking them so long to be invented, anyway?"

Outside, in the streets of London, it's twilight. It's a pretty time, all lavender hued and full of watercolor edges. Like we're strolling through a portrait. Outside the frame of our picture is another young couple in love, strolling hand in hand through a museum where my life hangs in oils and pastels. A nice, romantic thought. I take Israel's hand as we turn towards the Thames.

"We can't be too close to them tonight, or we'll end up taking them with us to Africa, you know. If they aren't going to keep their distance, then we'll have to leave the Savoy." I feel irritated that Rose and Luke are putting us in this position. I had really hoped my little tête-à-tête at Bedlam had put some of our animosity to rest, but I should have known it wouldn't be so easy. Nothing with Rose is ever easy. Will I be doing this dance with her for the rest of our lives if I can't get away? Until one of us dies?

"Well, you're right, but let's figure it out tomorrow. I'm not passing up that wonderful bed for the cobblestone streets of London. I still have a crick in my neck from the last time we slept there months ago."

We wander a long while, no destination in mind. Briefly, we discuss trying to locate Prue's grave and saying hello, but the process seems so daunting. I hope they gave her a decent funeral. Prue would have wanted everyone's attention and plenty of carrying on. She was a dramatic old thing. I smile, remembering.

What would have become of me without Prue, with only Dad for most of my life? He probably would have forgotten my existence, or wandered off in a drunken haze, or just given up altogether without her orneriness and stick-to-itiveness to keep him on the straight and narrow. I'd be thin as a rail without her cooking. I wouldn't have learned my numbers without learning the fine art of pricing her food items and automatically adding 5% for her tips.

She taught me to sew and how to braid hair; how many times had I combed through her coarse salt and pepper hair, braided it and wound it around her head with the same old silver pins she'd had since I had known her? Countless. She corrected my Portuguese with an impatient berating of my accent and let out my skirts for me that summer I grew five inches.

Her skin smelled of herbs and olive oil, and her fingertips always smelled of garlic. I know because I recall the way they would brush my forehead and eyebrows when I was sick or having trouble sleeping. I wish I had her favorite apron to keep with me, but it's so hard to keep anything when you're Lost. I can sew tiny things into the hem of my nightgown, but all it holds right now are several different varieties of coins and money. Nothing sentimental. Nothing real. Nothing that matters. Just cold metal discs and crackling paper that press against my ankles and annoy me when I sleep.

I'm so lost in thought and Israel must be as well, because suddenly we nearly bump into a crowd. The people here, in 1931, look so drastically different that it keeps startling me. I am used to these streets of London being full of Victorian inhabitants, so when I see a dark man in a top hat, black cape, and walking cane, looking as though he stepped out of a

Dickens novel, at first I am not surprised, but then I am, because he shouldn't be in the here and now.

In a deep voice that sends chills up my spine, he addresses the crowd of twenty or so. "Beware the nights of Whitechapel and those who wander here. The deeds that have been done in this dark place would keep the demons themselves up at night. Those of you who are not faint of heart, follow me." The dark man brandishes a lantern and vanishes in an alley.

My feet seemed glued to the cobblestones. I hear a soft crying, like the mewing of a kitten, and realize faintly that it is me. What had we wandered into? I turn to Israel for reassurance, but he isn't looking towards the dark man, his eyes have focused on something else. As the little crowd follows the man into the alley, someone is left behind. Leaning against a building, looking as though she belongs there, like she belongs anywhere, in her favorite red calico dress, is Rose.

She stares at us, but tosses something back and forth between her hands. It looks like a pocket watch. She watches me without a sign of anything on her face, no recognition, dismay, or taunting. The watch transfers from hand to hand, the moon light and streetlights glinting off it. She then loops the chain through her fingers and lets it sway back and forth.

"Tic tock," she says, softly.

Chapter 13

Almost like *How do you do? Pleased to meet you. Isn't it a lovely night for a stroll?* But instead, *Tic tock.* In that bittersweet voice of hers. *Tic tock.* She spins the pocket watch in the air lightly and catches it without even looking at it. Her hands are quick and light, her fingers longed and tapered. Somehow, I know that her nails have been bitten down to the quick, though I am not close enough in proximity to see.

"Let's get out of here," I murmur to Israel, and unbelievably, we melt into the crowd that had gone before us. Unbelievably, because I think we've just joined a tour of Jack the Ripper. Oh, not himself, of course, but still a tour. A tour, dramatizing and perhaps making light of what my Emme went through. Would we step on the ground where her blood had spilled? Seeped into the cracks of the cobblestones forty years ago, would there still be pieces of her dress or a strand of her red hair? I feel sick, but what's waiting behind me is sick too. My sister. I don't know which I feel capable of facing right now.

"It's alright, Sonny. Lean on me and ignore what he's saying. I think it's best we find the middle of the crowd and stay there." Israel sounds angry and somehow that instantly cheers me a bit. His temper feels like an anchor and a piece of something real and tangible in this moment of dreamy, surreal fantasy. "This is asinine. What happened to Dawes keeping her away from us? Wasn't that part of his master plan, seeing as how we reunited them?"

"We were fools for trusting him," I answer. A woman with harsh lipstick and unbearable perfume next to me hushes me in an annoyed fashion. I stifle the urge to give her a good talking to. How can this entertain people?

The dark man takes his place at the head of the crowd and speaks again in his overly dramatic fashion. "This is the very site where the first victim, Mary Ann Nichols, lost her pitiful life, torn apart by something from hell itself, they say. Why, even the bobbies were sick at the sight. Little did they know; the nightmare was only just beginning and Jack the Ripper was only getting started with his twisted crimes of passion and hatred."

"What about the other one, the other girl some say were his first victim, eh?" Some man from the crowd with a cockney accent raises his hand like a school boy. "What about Fairy Fay?"

The dark man wrinkles his nose, which causes his mustache to lean lopsided. "Fairy Fay is a legend, made up by a reporter trying to sell newspapers. No one takes her existence seriously."

"Well, rumors got to start somewhere, ain't they?" the man persists.

"Not always. There's no evidence of her existence and no grave either. She never lived, much less died. Now, let's save the rest of the questions for the end of the tour, shall we? Right this way, ladies and gentlemen, and we will see the very place that Annie Chapman, his second victim, died." He swings his lantern ahead of him, making strange shadows on the building as he moves. Our own shadows lurk along, like silent, faceless monsters creeping through the murky alley.

The crowd moves, and I feel sick, moving along with it. "She did live," I whisper to Israel, though it's me who suddenly needs convincing, "and she did die. At his hands, too."

"I know, Sonny. It's alright. Emme would find this whole thing amusing. Try to remember that." He rubs my shoulder, his arm around me. This never works, walking joined like this, but I like it anyway. We get a sort of crooked, loping, gait going, like we're in a three legged race or something. It's like have a limp, but I still want his arm around me, so I don't move out of his embrace.

"Would she? I think she'd be mad as a hornet. If her ghost is here, she's going to give that man a fright for claiming she was only legend." The thought makes me smile. "Emme would love to be a ghost."

Israel chuckles. "She would, but I'd prefer she doesn't jump out at me tonight. I'd likely have a heart attack."

I look nervously behind me, not for some specter of my former best friend, but for the very real presence of Rose, who frightens me much more than a phantom Emme. Ghost Emme would just berate me for not wearing stockings and try to do something with my unruly hair, God rest her soul. I don't see any sign of Rose. Perhaps she stayed out of the alley, though it seems a place she'd love to lurk. Does even Rose have fears and phobias? Did Lizzie?

The dark man speaks on, retelling grisly details of the murders of the prostitutes and the bafflement of Scotland Yard. All of London was terrified, he says, and I can't help but remember I did try to warn them. No one would listen to us. No one cared about Emme's murder or the letter I wrote to Inspector Andrews. It must have been lost, or discarded altogether, either that or it lies in a museum somewhere. A document of a strange and awful time in history. I don't listen to the man leading the tour, he in his silly Jack the Ripper getup, not while he's sensationalizing the deaths of innocents. Well, they may not have been innocents in every sense of the word, but they were real. Living, breathing girls and women with dreams, or dreams of the dreams they used to have. Emme wanted to live, and she wouldn't have given in to death without a fight, that's for sure. She had Joe, and Bea, and me, everything to live for. I wonder if the other girls had anything to live for.

The man with the top hat is now droning on about the long list of possible subjects for the identity of Jack. *I know someone who knows for sure,* I think, *and she's about a half a block away. Of course, half the time she forgets who she herself is, so you might not get a straight answer, but still. She knows. Rose knew Jack.*

"Aw, we all know it was that butcher, that one that killed all his wives!" The man with the cockney accent pipes up again.

"A very definite possibility," Top Hat Man agrees. He strokes his cane like a dog. His lantern is at his feet, the flame dancing merrily. "But George

Chapman's method of murder was poisoning. It would be odd for a killer to change his methods like that, would it not?"

"He had to have had medical knowledge." The woman with all the perfume speaks up. "To have sliced them up that way. He knew what he was doing."

I feel sick again. Emme hadn't been sliced up, not exactly, but the end result was the same.

"Ah! An excellent point, Madame." The man brandishes his cane towards her. "A most excellent piece of deducting on your end! It is widely believed that Jack may have had surgical knowledge and experience. At the very least, an interest in the anatomy of the human body, which might lead us to a gentleman, a scholar. What else, ladies and gentlemen? Other theories? Remarks? Suspects?"

"Weren't there some man from the crazy house? Some mad bloke?" Cockney again.

"Aye, indeed, sir. Indeed. Aaron Kosminksi, but he had a harmless reputation in the asylum."

"Reputations are often wrong," says a familiar voice from somewhere on the edge of the throng. I don't need to swivel my head in the direction. I'd know that cocky Australian voice anywhere. Luke is here.

"True," someone else in the multitude agrees with Luke. "And wasn't there a woman? Some lady out for revenge on childbearing women because she wasn't able to have them herself?"

"There was indeed." Top Hat Man nods sagely. "Sir John Williams' wife, Elizabeth, but could such dreadful murders, such appalling horrors, such unthinkable atrocities, be committed by a woman? I ask you."

"Be difficult without the upper body strength, I expect." Luke again. "Unless she was one large lady."

"Fair point."

"And does a woman need such womanly reasons? Can't she be motivated by the more masculine? Simple anger? Revenge? Lust? Money? Pleasure even? I ask you." Only I can hear that Luke is poking fun, impersonating the puffed up persona of the top hat man. To everyone else, he seems the very picture of a docile and eager audience member.

"Interesting! Interesting! Is it possible that our brutal killer be none other than a lady? Perhaps we will never know. Any other theories before we visit the site of Mary Jane Kelly's death?"

I turn to Israel, and I'm sure the desperation shows in my eyes. "I feel as though I'm stuck in a nightmare and can't wake up. Pinch me, please."

Instead, he pulls me in closer. He's become my jacket, my suit of armor. I don't feel as though it will be enough to shield me from what is coming, whatever it may be.

What do they want from me, I think, desperately. *Why can't they leave me alone? Why can't this be finished?*

"Will we get to see the letters?" the woman with all the perfume asks. My, but she is a bloodthirsty one. I presume she is talking of the letters from Jack, not the one from me.

"Ah, patience! Let's remember who is leading the tour, shall we?" Top Hat Man chuckles, good-naturedly. "Right this way, ladies and gentlemen! Stay close...these alleys are dangerous places at night..."

I remember Rose, playing with her pocket watch. He has no idea.

*   *   *

"Isn't there a twenty-first century joke about not wanting to meet so-and-so in a dark alley?" Israel whispers in my ear as we stop for yet another grisly recap of one of Jack's escapades. "Now we know where it originated. Hey, maybe it was us!"

"What?" I am too distracted to be paying close attention. I keep moving further from where I think Luke is in the crowd, like the opposite ends of a magnet we repel one another instead of attract. Once, I was attracted to him. If not falling in love with him exactly, I was at least intrigued by the scruffy photographer who could make me laugh. Drank coffee with him. Sang songs for him. Let him in my house. Wanted to spend time with him, wanted to fulfill items on the bucket list I made with him. Dratted man.

"Never mind." Israel nips my ear playfully, and I swat at him.

"Really? Here and now you have romance on your mind?"

"Here and now and forever," he replies cheerily, though I know he's only distracting me and his heart isn't in it. "After all, we could be dead tomorrow."

"Gee, you're comforting. Aren't you supposed to make me feel better?"

Some man in the crowd hushes me, and feeling petulant, I stick my tongue out at him when turns around once more.

"Don't make enemies, Sonny," Israel chuckles. "They have to watch our backs and let us stick close to them when we exit this god forsaken place. I'm affixing myself to that large woman over there. I can hide behind her skirts, and if that doesn't work, I'm pretty certain she can take both Rose and Luke for me."

"My hero. Where does that leave me?"

"Hasn't Joe taught you any survivor skills? Kung-fu or anything?"

"Yes, but I wasn't paying attention, and I think his exact words were, 'You suck at self defense, Auntie Sonnet.' We're definitely in for it. Toast."

Joking makes me feel a tad better, though I'm still cold to the touch, and my stomach hurts with anticipation. I haven't heard a peep from Luke in the past ten minutes at least, and that worries me.

What worries me even more is the lack of a visual on Rose. She's scary enough when I do have an eye on her. I don't like the idea of her wandering around back alleys, waiting, watching, with that blasted pocket watch. What kind of ridiculous prop was that anyway? Was it really necessary? Some poor bloke is without his dear heirloom pocket watch just because my dotty sister wanted to borrow it and turn it into a menacing toy to frighten me with. Isn't she supposed to be resting in Bedlam? Where does the girl get her murderous energy?

The crowd, bloodthirsty and full of excitement, moves along from the spot where we had all obediently stood as Top Hat Man related the tale of Catherine Eddowes. For goodness sake, just how many killings were there? I must have muttered it aloud, for the perfumed lady is back at my side, and she answers me swiftly in a hushed tone.

"The Canonical Five, of course, my dear. There are others who say more, but these five are most definitely Jack's: Catherine, Mary Ann, Annie, Elizabeth, and Mary Jane." She titters, positively titters, and at that moment I hate her very much, ticking them off her fingers like she was tallying up the guests at a garden party. *Oh, there's Elizabeth and Mary Jane, naturally... Don't forget Catherine and old Annie! Mustn't seat Mary Jane next to Elizabeth now... Catherine will have the beef, and Annie the fish...* I want to argue, there weren't five victims! There were six. I hate that Emme is gone and forgotten, though of course, I knew she would be; we all did. Now she's just a legend, and not even a well-known one. That would have annoyed her greatly, Emme did love a little recognition. She probably does haunt these streets. The thought makes me a smile a little, but it doesn't last. Luke is finally speaking up again.

"Was it the hatred of their profession that caused Jack to kill them?" Luke poses the question as though he is terribly interested in the opinion of Top Hat Man. "Or merely their sex?"

"We may never know. Certainly Whitechapel was crawling with–" The tour guide pauses delicately. "With ladies of a dubious vocation, but was that why they were chosen?"

"Or were they chosen? Perhaps they were random?"

"These kinds of savagery take a bit of forethought, my good man. A bit of planning." Top Hat Man smiles generously in the direction of Luke. His lantern casts a gloom across his face as he sweeps it through the audience.

"Do they?" Ah, finally, I can see the man behind the voice, thanks to spotting a glowing pinprick of smoke. Luke is dressed in dark colors, and his expensive hat is pulled low over his eyes, almost like when we were in Zanzibar, and didn't want to be recognized and arrested for some past sin. This time, though, his hair is neatly combed into a low, short tail beneath the rim of the hat. Somehow it suits him. He leans against the wall of the building nearest to him, casually smoking. He does not look at me. "Not to the insane, I assure you. They improvise and work in the moment, the here and now. To some people, planning and time are quite irrelevant. Time especially."

"But was Jack insane?" Cockney eagerly enters into the conversation again. "That's the question, isn't it?"

"No." Luke flicks ash on the ground. "That is not the question."

"It isn't really a question, because we already know the answer," says perfumed lady. "Of course, he was insane! Sane people don't go about, cutting women to shreds." She seems quite sure of her logic and equally proud of her deductions. Most of the crowd nods along with her.

"Of course, they do." Luke pushes off the wall, back to standing. "That's the rub, isn't it? We're all a bit mad, you know. Of course, you know. You're only pretending to be civilized, and so is he and so is he and so on. You're all pretenders. Jack was no crazier than anyone else, no crazier than you are, no crazier than I am, certainly."

"You speak as though you knew the man." Indulgently, Top Hat Man smiles. "Truly, a knowledgeable and erudite group I have tonight!"

The perfumed lady preens a bit next to me, though not before she shoots Luke an irritated glare at his debunking of her theory, and the crowd applauds. It seems we have reached the end of our tour. Thank God. I let go of Israel's hand and push through the crowd to get to the back of the alley, to Luke. Somehow with the dissipation of the tour and the macabre talk that it brought, I feel less stifled and afraid in the darkness of the alley. Now I just feel angry. I push past someone, several someones, a rustling of skirt, a large man, even a child. Lord, who would bring a child to this? I feel a pang of frustration when I hear Israel say my name tenderly from behind me where I left him.

"Just a minute," I call over my shoulder, pushing through the last person, who glares at my impudence.

"Sonny?" I hear it again, very gently, barely audible over the excited talk of the throng. Luke hasn't moved, and I am only feet from him now. He watches me with a wary look on his face. No, not wary but apologetic. Why is he remorseful now?

"Sonny?" Suddenly, I know why, and I whirl around. The crowd has moved as a swarm would, huddled where I had stood only moments before. So many people are saying it, that it sounds as one, "He's been stabbed! Get a doctor! He's been stabbed…"

I seem to cross the alley on angel's wings, so fast am I running. I shove through the throng with all my might, nearly wanting to hurt them in the process. They came for sensationalism and titillation, and they are getting them in spades, and I hate them for it. *Israel, no, no, no, no!* I think I am only thinking it, but I hear it escape my lips, a weird, eerie chanting, a prayer.

A prayer for the man in the fedora, sprawled in a pool of his own blood. My Israel.

Chapter 14

"Iz, I'm so sorry," I whisper. I press my tweed jacket to his chest, where a massive amount of blood is seeping out. God, there's so much blood, too much. I've been a not-doctor's not-wife for long enough to know there is far too much blood.

He doesn't answer, just keeps his eyes on me, though I can tell it's with an effort. Each blink seems more labored than the last, like a sleepy baby, like with the next one, they won't flicker back open again. The thought terrifies me, and I know there are tears running down my cheeks. Iz hates it when I cry. I swipe my face with my palm furiously. I don't have time to cry like a child. I push so hard on the tweed that Iz gasps a bit. Good, gasping might keep him from closing those eyes too long. I press again, knowing it's hurting him, but it's also killing me.

Someone has run for a doctor, and everyone else is huddled around us, looking helpful, frightened, and sick to their stomachs. I had looked back briefly, only to confirm what I already knew, Luke was gone. He had been only two feet from me when the knife had entered Israel's chest anyway, so I know who the attacker was, Rose. It had to be. I feel Israel's hand move up to cover mine, labored but heavy.

"Not safe here," he murmurs. It's the first thing he's said.

"I know," I whisper. "I'm sorry. I'm so sorry for bringing you here. I never should have, I didn't think..." I choke on my own tears. I wipe them away again and realize my face is wet not only from my eyes, but from his blood on my hands. I must look as though I've been attacked too.

"Not safe," he labors again. He does one of those slow motion blinks once more, and my breath hitches and my heart stalls in my chest, because I think, *this is it. This is when he dies.* "Run!"

I jerk my head up and look around. I don't see Rose or Luke, but that hardly means anything. "What? No. I'm not leaving you. We're going to get you to a hospital."

He still hasn't opened his eyes. "Run," he whispers. "Please, Sonny. Run."

So I do. God forgive me, but I do.

*   *   *

I run until I feel as though my heart will burst from its chest, and then I think of Israel's chest, gaping and bleeding, and I run some more. Plenty of people try to stop me, a bloody girl in nothing but a white blouse and skirt, in the cold London night, but I don't slow my feet until I collapse somewhere near the Thames. I want to sink into the cold, cold sludge, let it bury me alive, but I don't have the luxury of such thoughts and actions. I curl into myself, trying to piece back together the heaving and broken parts of my heart and lungs.

Do you even know how to use a knife, Doctor Rhode? I hear Rose's taunt in Bedlam's room. *Because I do.*

Because I do.

I do.

Why hadn't I listened? Israel may be dead at her hands, literally at her hands, her small, white hands, while I was busy wasting my time on Luke. What a fool I am, a stupid fool.

My breathing has slowed, and my thoughts come more clearly. With those thoughts, a revelation comes, it doesn't matter if Israel is dead, not really, because tonight won't happen. I lean over and splash water on my face, rubbing to get the blood off. It has crusted, and it hurts when I am savage in my attempts.

Tonight won't happen. I'm going to go back and take care of everything.

My resolve strengthened, I stand. Water drips down my face and onto my blouse. The stains of darkest red have softened a bit to pink, but it's still blood. Can't be mistaken for anything else. I take a deep, shuddering breath and look around me. I'm not clear enough on London's geography, not at any time in history but certainly not in 1931, to know where in the city I am. It really doesn't matter anyway. I'm mostly looking for signs that Luke or Rose may have followed me. I don't think Rose could have kept up with my long legs, not with her tiny, undersized frame, but Luke certainly could have kept pace had he wanted to, or were they finally done with me? Had they finally done enough damage? They are slowly picking off my loved ones, one by one. Were they already on their way to Dad? Bea and Joe? Soon, I will have no one left at all. I'll get my awful, dreadful wish, the one that I'll have no one left to hurt.

That horrifying thought only angers me more, and I begin to walk. I know exactly what I am looking for, an apothecary, a drugstore, or whatever they might call it in this century. I need to sleep, and I won't be able to sleep without help, not tonight of all nights. I don't have any Nightfall pills on me, and I doubt they'd be strong enough anyway. I need something serious, and I know exactly what.

I have to walk for what feels like a small eternity. I am determined not to think of the pain Israel is feeling, or worse yet, the pain he might not be feeling. I cannot think of him dead, not that large boy I love so much. The one who could make me feel safe, make me laugh, and keep me in line. I remember how he growled at me, the way I always make him furious. No one makes him angrier than I do, and I can't help the way that makes me smile. He has done so much good in his life, saved so many. Someone has to save him now. If the doctors can't do it, then I will.

I keep walking. The heels have rubbed blisters on my feet, but the pain feels good, like a sacrificial punishment for my sins. I understand in a perverse sort of way why the monks of old would punish themselves physically or why people in anguish cut themselves. The pain is a reminder that I am alive when Iz might not be. The crowd would have him to a hospital by now, he'll be in a bed, and they'll be operating. Would they try their level best? For an unknown black man with a stab wound? Would they be busier with patients they deemed more worthy, more wealthy, more important? He had the jewelry on him, and whatever was left of our stolen money. I hope that upped his odds.

Finally, I find what I am looking for, a shop with a sign I can barely make out, *Quality Pharmacy Shop.* I don't even try the door to the quiet, empty shop, but instead pick up the largest rock I can locate at my feet. I chuck it through the window with all the angst and fury I feel at Rose, and thank God that Swift alarms have not been invented yet. I scramble through the broken window with all the grace of an enraged rhino and cut my hand in the process, another bit of pain to soothe me. I wish I had Top Hat Man's lantern in the gloom, but I don't dare turn on a light. Though I've certainly not been silent, I do have the advantage of the dark night should someone be strolling by on a midnight walk. I decide I might risk a lighted match though, and I strike one when I find a packet near an old fashioned oil lamp. The flickering flame is nearly hopeless though, and it burns out before I can read more than ten labels on as many bottles of drugs. I remember Israel's words from a conversation months ago.

"It's a Mickey Finn, Sonny."

"A what?" I am watching him pour a finger of whiskey for a patient. He is terminally ill and in terrible pain with the cancer eating away at him. I think his name is James. Was James. He's been gone a long time now.

"Chloral hydrate liquid. Knock out drops. They've been around for centuries. Terribly addicting and mind numbing, but a powerful sleep aid when you combine them with alcohol. There's nothing more we can do for him, and this will help with the pain and allow him to sleep."

Knock out drops. That's what I'm looking for. Chloral hydrate. Keep looking, Sonnet. I strike another match and move on. Whatever filing system the pharmacist here keeps, it isn't alphabetical, and I am frustrated and in a hurry. I spill a bottle of something that smells sweet, and it splashes on my feet. I have gone through all the matches, save one, and I take a deep breath, determined not to waste it. If the chloral hydrate is here, it must be locked up somewhere or higher on the shelves. Israel said it was addicting, so it would make sense to keep it out of reach of addicts, or thieves, like me. I look up. There are more bottles there, but I will need something to stand on. A ladder, in the dark, with spilled drugs, and a lighted match. I'm feeling rather confident in this plan actually.

I push over a chair and kick off my heels. They might give me an extra two inches of height, but they also make me wobble and sway like a palm tree in a breeze. I light my last match and am rewarded for my efforts when I find the bottle I have been looking for.

Chloral hydrate liquid drops.

I scramble back down to the floor, feeling triumphant. I pocket my treasure and speak aloud, with a small laugh that sounds as desperate to my ears as I am. "I really, really need a drink."

* * *

The next part is more difficult. As much as I don't like stealing, I like bars and pubs even less. The one I find closest to the drugstore is quiet and depressing. I expected it to be more raucous and party like, but my experience is limited to what I saw on twenty-first century television a few times and being in an Irish pub as a child in 1602.

The only patrons here, at the Toad's Head, are male, and they all seem to be a miserable lot. I suppose happy, go-lucky men don't frequent sad little pubs in the wee hours of the morning, drowning their happiness. They look up when I enter, and since I've never been very good in situations where I feel like the object of someone's unwanted attention, I tell myself to take confident steps. I take a deep breath and rummage in my skirt pocket. Thankfully, I have a bit of change from the purchase of my clothing. The salesgirl would fret and bemoan the state of them if she could see me now, a scant few hours later. I am thankful I don't have to cozy up to a random stranger and beg for a drink. Flirting has never been my gift, something Emme used to tease me about as she was wholly adept at the art. Of course, it was her job. I shake off thoughts of her, and ask the bartender how much a whole bottle of scotch is. The last thing I want to do is fall asleep here, though I reason it doesn't matter much, not really. Still, I'd prefer to drug myself in relative solitude if at all possible, and I doubt I'm allowed to wander off with one of his good ale cups. I'd rather have beer, but figure it isn't strong enough to make my Mickey Finn work.

The bartender, a round bloke with a pocked face, takes my money and hands me my purchase in silence. I think he is being rude until I realize he is mute when he points to the label and raises his brows at me, as if to ask, *Is this the scotch you want?* As though I had the slightest knowledge of spirits, I smile and nod. He stares at my chest in a fascinated way, and I am about to be righteously angry and humiliated when I remember the blood. I guess I would stare too.

"It's nothing," I say hurriedly. "I butchered a rabbit." He only stares. No wonder the other men haven't offered to buy me a drink or asked me to dance, I must look like a killer or the near victim of one. Somehow my ego is soothed.

The scent of smoke and liquor follows me back out into the night.

I have no desire to find my way back to the Savoy, nor do I plan on deducing which hospital Israel has been taken to. I could never justify being tucked in cozy like in a fancy hotel with a proper bed and pillows, and if I find Israel again, I doubt I could muster up enough courage to leave him. I just want to sleep, and I don't care where. The sooner I can get back to the night we left Rose behind, the sooner I can right all these wrongs. I finger the chloral hydrate bottle that I stowed in my pocket earlier as I walk quickly away from the pub, the scotch in my other hand. I must look like a drunken mad girl already, weaving and stumbling along in the middle of the night, with blood on her clothes, but I don't slow. I head for any place that looks like it would be good for sleeping, undetected from the populace. Just a couple hours should be all I need, but I don't need any do-gooders waking me because I look like I've been gruesomely murdered in the streets.

I settle for a small covered port on the docks that houses a tiny boat. How early do fishermen arise? Would I still be curled up in the bottom when day breaks? I'll have to hope not. I remove the stopper from the bottle of knock out drops and take a sniff. I don't know why. If it had smelled of decay and stench, I still would consume it if that's what it takes to save Israel.

It doesn't have much of an odor at all though. The scotch, however, nearly burns my nasal cavities. I take a sip and immediately begin to cough, my eyes watering. I wish again for a beer or ale, wine, anything else. I drink some more, and this time I follow it with a sip of the chloral hydrate. Then I repeat. How much will it take? As keyed up as I am, maybe a lot? Maybe too much? Has anyone ever died from this particular cocktail? Has anyone ever slipped *themselves* a Mickey Finn? How ridiculous does that make me? I take one last small dose of the drops, and a healthy swig of the scotch. Once I get used to it, I quit coughing, but now I feel exceedingly warm. Roasting, really. I push my hair back from my face and lie down in the boat. It smells of fish, unwashed people, and rotting wood.

I close my eyes.

I think hard of everything I remember from that night fifteen years or so ago in my life, but so long ago.

1741.

August 4, 1741: the night we left Rose behind.

The country side of France. A cottage outside of Reims. An old woman named Old Babba, whose voice was like nails on a chalkboard to me. The table I used to hide under. My mother, what I recall of her. Yellow hair and eyes like mine. My father, but younger, and happier. He had a well-kept, pointy beard then, I remember. All pepper with no salt yet.

I remember the hearth they used to sit by, Dad whittling something and Mother knitting, and a smelly sheep kept out back that I didn't care for because he bit me once. The small shape of a crudely made doll that fit perfectly in the crook of my neck. Her dress was coarse and scratchy, but I used to suck on it sometimes, along with my thumb. I can still recall the taste and texture of that burlap dress on my tongue. A teapot with a chipped lid. It was blue, I remember, and the cup I was allowed to drink from was brown.

1741. August 4, 1741.

I sleep.

Chapter 15

It's humid. That's the first thing I notice, even before my eyes open. There is wind that blows my hair in my face, which is probably what wakes me. It's a tickling feeling on my cheeks and across my eyelids. I'm scared, but not of the wind or some unexplainable feeling. I'm scared of where I might not be. I don't want to be still in the boat.

I can't lie here forever with my eyes closed, so I finally open them. When I do, it's as if I hadn't. It's so dark that that I might as well be blind, but I feel dirt and rocks beneath me. My legs are cramped, and my hip is sore from a particularly large tree root that I can feel with my fingers. I'll be bruised tomorrow, whenever and wherever that mysterious day comes.

It's cold, but not winter cold, just midnight cold. My thin blouse, crusted with Israel's blood, is not sufficient clothing, and I'm pretty sure my short skirt isn't helping my war with bugs. I reach down and scratch my ankle where something has bitten me during the night. My head is pounding, whether from the aftereffects of the scotch or from traveling, I don't know.

I've never been a fan of the dark. Who is, really? It's also not my biggest phobia, and I am practical enough to know that it won't last forever. Normally, if this were any other travel, I would just stay put. Well, first I would account for my father and Israel and Bea and Joe, but of course, I am alone. This time I don't have the luxury of staying here and discovering my whereabouts until morning, not when this may be the very night that started it all. I pick myself up, my muscles groaning a bit, and steady myself on the tree I am apparently underneath. I'm lightheaded, like when you stand too quickly on an empty stomach. Dizzy, I sway and clutch at the bark on the tree.

I should have willed myself to wake inside the cottage, not in the general vicinity. Feeling upset at myself, I stub my toe instantly, with my very first step away from the tree. I mutter one of Israel's favorite curses, appropriately enough in French. I limp on, but to where, I have no idea.

Now that my eyes have accustomed themselves to the ebony night, I can make out just the slightest shapes of trees, bushes, nameless hulking things. What if I stumble around this place all night, and never find the cottage? I should have come to August 3rd and gotten my bearings. Of course, me showing up in daylight, their own grown daughter, would surely have been something of a shock to my parents. Though not half as surprising as me meeting my own four-year-old self. I smile bleakly at my scattered thoughts. Would I recognize myself? Would my pigtailed self, with my thumb in my mouth and my doll in the crook of my neck, recognize her twenty-year-old, tall, bloody self?

The going is maddeningly slow. I take small, mincing steps, my toe still throbbing, though not nearly as hard as my head. My hands are held out in front of me to take the impact of any tree branches or other obstacles that I can't quite see. I must look like a zombie, wandering the countryside. That picture will make Israel laugh, or Joe. *God, please let me see them again.* Where am I going? What if I'm walking in the opposite direction of the old cottage? Then I see it, a shape in the gloom.

The shape has a roof, that much I can tell. I nearly exclaim aloud, but clap my hands over my mouth just in time. I walk a bit faster but stop suddenly when I am overcome with the feeling that I am going to be sick. I retch onto the ground, and the lightheaded feeling possesses me once again when I stand. I hug my stomach and wobble forward. I've never been hung-over, but if that is what this is, I vow to never touch scotch again. My head continues to pound, and I continue to ignore it.

The building with the roof is now close enough to put more detail to. It is extremely small; too small I think. Although it would have seemed bigger to me as a four-year-old, wouldn't it have? So, perhaps this is right. Cautiously, I move closer, close enough to see the chimney and a pile of stacked wood by the door. The outline of the cottage isn't straight, it's bumpy and lumpy, and that makes me frown in confusion. Then I realize it's covered with ivy, making the edges look curvy and uneven. I take another step and once again feel violently ill.

Instead of being sick, however, I take in great, gulping swallows of the night air. It seems to work, or at least it helps. The feeling passes, at least for now, and I am able to take another step. I raise my hand to touch the door, but stop short just a few inches. Can I just walk in? What should I do? I hadn't really had time to think this far ahead. Should I simply tuck Rose in, somehow get her to sleep, or should I wake the others instead? Myself, Mother, and Father? I could just make a ruckus outside. That would wake them, but would they just travel the next night and still leave Rose behind?

What if I can't do it, can't change the past? I swallow another greedy amount of night air, and touch the door. The soft wood feels as though it will give me splinters should I press too hard. I slide my hand down carefully until it rests atop the latch and pause. I press down. The lever moves, but when I push softly on the door, it doesn't budge. I push a bit harder. Nothing. It's locked from the inside. Of course. It is the dead of night, and the Lost have a tendency to be distrustful of others. As they should be, seeing as how their older selves might come strolling into their bedrooms in the middle of the night.

I try once more, but the door is firm and secure. I'll have to get in through a window. I turn, feeling ill again, and maybe that's what has me distracted. Otherwise I surely would have felt the presence so near me, so near that I should have felt her breath, so near that when I take a single step I am face to face with her.

I scream, but it's as if I'm trapped in a paralyzing nightmare, because no sound escapes the O that my lips form.

"Wretched girl," comes a voice from my nightmares. Her eyes are luminescent in the night and almost seem to glow. Terrible eyes. Old Babba's eyes. They rove over me in a disinterested but thorough way. "I know you. Wretched girl."

I feel my heart calming down. At least my fear has erased my nausea. Now I'm only terrified instead of sick. "You know me?" I whisper. I can't think of anything else to say.

"I knew you'd be here." Her thin shoulders shrug. "I could feel you out here. Could feel something wasn't right tonight." Her eyes gleam.

"I'm trying to stop it."

"You won't."

I push my hair back, for it's blowing across my face again. "I have to try."

Old Babba pushes by me, though she seems as loathe to touch me as I am her. I hear her key scratch in the lock. "Your family is evil," she hisses before she enters her dreadful house. "Stay away from me, wretched girl."

"Please be kind to her," I say, but it's too late. The door is closed. If I fail tonight, that old woman will raise my sister. Is it any wonder Rose turned out the way she did? The hate practically radiated off her, like the heat that keeps her bony body warm.

I have to succeed.

*　*　*

I remember Old Babba's house is near enough to our own that I could throw a ball nearly to the door. Not that I would have, Old Babba scared me then just as she does now. My cottage must be close. I turn and scan the darkness. There! Another shape with a roof. I move towards it but am hit with another wave of nausea. My head still pounds, too. If this is a hangover, it's a wonder anyone in the world drinks to excess. I hold my hand to my forehead because it seems as though it will topple off my shoulders if I don't and walk carefully to the cottage.

Each step makes my head thump harder, and when I pull my hand away, it's clammy with sweat. Moisture trickles down my face, except it isn't just moisture from the humid night or from my sweat soaked skin. I lick my lips and taste blood. My nose is bleeding. That certainly isn't a symptom of excessive alcohol consumption.

I'm still a few feet away from the cottage of my childhood, but I stop. My head has gone from throbbing to that curious, out-of-body feeling you get when you are burning up with a high fever. I hear whispers and voices, all talking at once, filling my head. I know they aren't real, an audible hallucination, but they still give me pause. I shut my eyes tightly, but it doesn't help as golden specks dance in front of my eyelids. I can't make out the words ricocheting around in my brain, but every voice is frantic. My nose continues to bleed, and I tip my head backwards, which doesn't help the state of my dizziness and lightheadedness. It's only a few feet away, that front door, but it might as well be hundreds.

Still, I haven't come so far to sit down and give up now. I will my feet forward, and the shape of the cottage shifts and tumbles around in my vision. Something is wrong, very wrong, with me, but I can't take the time to deduce what. Maybe it's the effects of forcing a travel. If Rose goes through something like this each time, it's no small wonder she's mad. I feel a bit mad myself.

I lurch for what seems like the shape of a door, though it's difficult to tell since to me it appears to be oozing around in space. My hand makes contact with wood or is it stone? Though I don't want to barge right in, the weight of my body presses in spite of myself. I nearly fall against it, and it creaks open.

Had the door been lighter, I would have swung into the cottage with all the poise of a bull in a china shop, but the door is heavy, and I only open it a few inches though all my weight is pushed against it. Dimly, I remember this door now, as a toddler I couldn't even budge it. Oddly, Rose had slammed my fingers in it once. My left index finger winces, as if in the midst of its own painful memory.

The cottage is still and silent. At least, it seems to be, but it's very hard to tell seeing as how my head is still filled with shouting. I suppose the cottage could be filled with music, and I would not be able to hear it. I wipe my nose on the back of my hand again. I have quit bleeding, but there's a hideous metallic taste in my mouth now, like I've swallowed a lot of blood. My hand shakes like a leaf.

There are no bedrooms, save my parent's, in this little home. Rose and I had slept on pallets near the fire, and my eyes go instantly to that place. There are tiny, red embers that remind me of Luke's constant cigarette butts in the hearth, like a million tiny Lukes have set up residence there, all smoking. They give just the slightest glow, only the smallest blush of light, but it's enough to make out a small shape. The shape of a girl, or is it two?

For just a moment in time, my head quits its dreadful pounding and shouting. Is it Rose or myself, curled up by the fire, or both? It's too dim to see the color of hair. Is it dark like mine or yellow like Rose's? I step closer, but when I do, another wave of nausea hits, and it's all I can do to not be sick again. My vision swims, and I feel as though I am seeing everything from underwater. I trip over something on the dirt floor a toy, a footstool, a boot, I don't know what. I only know I fall, and it causes a noise. There must be a noise, because the huddled, sleeping child sits up, and only a scant breath later, the curled up figure next to her disappears, leaving nothing but a blanket.

I am on my knees, my stupid ankle turned like it has a propensity to do, and I look at her, this little girl. She pushes her long yellow hair away from her face, and watches me silently, with a sober look in her icy blue eyes. My perspective of her is watery and blurry, but this time it's not because of my impaired vision so much as it is because of my tears.

Because it was me all along.

I woke Rose that night.

Chapter 16

It may be that realization that does me in and not the symptoms of the travel. A wave of dizziness passes over me like a breaking wave, and I am prostrate on the floor, the cold, dirt floor of my old home. When it finally moves along, as waves must, I lift my weary head and find Rose, three-year-old Rose, staring at me silently. She twirls a lock of hair the way she did in the hospital. She doesn't seem scared of me, or alarmed, like a sensible child would. She only appears mildly curious and maybe just a little bit surprised.

Does grown Rose remember this moment? Is that why she hates me so?

"I'm sorry, honey," I whisper. "I tried to fix it."

"You can't." The voice is Rose's, but little Rose's mouth doesn't move.

Confused and feeling as though my head weighs as much as a wheelbarrow full of bricks, I turn very slowly. It is Rose, grown Rose, standing in the doorway that I stumbled through moments before.

"Don't you see?" She shakes her head as though to clear it. Her voice is slow and halting. "Don't you understand how many times I've tried?"

"You've come back before?" I stand. My legs are like a newborn foal's, wobbly and gangly and hardly able to hold up my own body. I should be scared of being surrounded by my two sisters, but I don't have the energy.

"Of course I have. Come on, we can't stay here. It will get worse." Grown Rose rubs her eyes, tiredly. Amazingly, she holds out her hand to me. What trickery is this? Once again, I'm too weary and sick to think straight, and I find myself moving forward enough to take her hand. It's chilly, and I know mine is clammy in hers. The pain in my ankle pulses, but it's the least of my problems.

I look back once at tiny Rose, still sitting by the hearth, the red embers of light flickering over her. She watches us.

"Can we take her?" I whisper.

"No. It's too late for her," Rose replies leading me through the door. "Besides, I'm here already, aren't I?"

"Will she remember this?" I lurch through the doorway and into the humid night air. I should have phrased it, *"Will you remember this?"* but it's too fantastical to think that she is her.

"A little. There have been so many of these nights. I won't remember what's real and what's not, what really happened and how many different ways it played out. I made it worse, coming back so many times." Rose sighs and steadies herself on the door frame. She's unnerved too, and feeling the effects, but not as badly it seems. "But I have to keep trying."

"It never works? You can't change it? We can't change it?" The breeze has cleared my head a little, and I now have the wherewithal to be frightened of being alone in the dark with my sister. If I scream, will my mother hear? That's a luxurious thought I haven't had the privilege of having for years and years. But no, she's gone already, moments before, the same instant the tiny version of myself left this place.

"Of course not. You can't change history, Sonnet. Even I know that." She pushes off the door frame with finality.

I feel put in my place, and yet, she was here too, trying to do the impossible. I've stepped into Wonderland, and it's a fearsome place. I have no friendly white rabbit to lead the way, just a mad woman and useless cosmic powers.

"What's happened the other times?" I ask as we continue to walk in the dark. Rose seems to know her way, blindfolded by the night. She's always been better in the dark than me, hasn't she? I cling to her hand even as my brain chants at me to let her go.

"Once, I tried to get close enough to wake you, too." She's silent for a moment as she lets that sink in. That possibility, had it succeeded, would have meant I would have stayed behind too. I would have been raised, at least for a few years, by Old Babba. I instantly feel sick again. That old woman had invaded my nightmares enough, and I had never even set foot in her cottage. "But you are one hard sleeper." I expect her voice to harden too, but surprisingly, she laughs. A tinkle of a laugh, like a music box or the trill of a flute. "I can never change the outcome. I can change the circumstances, but not the ending."

"We can change the battle, but not the war."

"Something like that. Oh, sometimes I blame you. Mostly, I blame you!" Rose admits wryly. "But I've been responsible just as many times. Once I knocked over the whole table. Once I nearly burnt the whole cottage down. No matter what I do, I wake up that night. Maybe I never fell asleep to begin with, or maybe I can delay one night, but it happens the next."

"Then why do you hate me?" I speak in a low voice, afraid of the answer and amazed I'm even asking, all at the same time. My nose has started to bleed again.

Rose shrugs. It's too dark to see it, but I can feel her shoulders go up and down, as my hand is held in hers. "I forget, or I remember."

Her reply shouldn't make sense to me, but it does. When she forgets, she hates me, and when she remembers, she still hates me. "I'm sorry that you can't love me," I say, and I mean it more than any other apology I've ever made in my life.

She squeezes my hand lightly, as hard as a tiny little bird can squeeze. "I'm sorry, too." She pulls me down to the ground, and if I wasn't so exhausted, emotionally, and physically, I would probably fight her. "But for what it's worth, sister, I don't hate you right now. Go to sleep."

"I don't feel well."

"I don't feel well either."

"I wish we could change it."

"I wish we could, too."

Eventually, I sleep, but for a while, with my sister curled up beside me on the cold French countryside, bugs biting me and the wind drying the blood on my face. I sleep worried for the fate of Israel, saddened by the girl in the cottage, and concerned for my own health, but I find a way to value this moment. I can't concentrate enough to recall where and when I need to get back to, so I just finally slip into oblivion.

Chapter 17

I am cold in my bed. When I open my eyes, I can see the outlines of the room I am in. There's a hard wooden chair and a cold metal table. There's a window that's open, and an icy wind blows through. There are bars on the window and locks on the door. I know even if I can't see them. My blanket is insufficient and scratchy, and it feels as though there are thousands of tiny cruel insects rubbing their millions of prickly, spiky legs against my body. Spiders with needles for legs. I want to push them off, push off the blanket, but my arms are held down by something, cold metal bracelets that strap me to the bed and prevent me from even brushing my hair out of my eyes. I shake like a cornered, frightened dog.

I scream, for it's my very nightmare from the other night. My scream jars me farther awake, and I realize the manacles I thought I felt are imaginary. I clap my hands to my face in relief and sit up in the sterile Bedlam bed. I swing my legs to the side but am met with another wave of nausea, like the vicious ones from last night, only more subdued. I lie back down slowly and get my bearings. I know this is Bedlam, that much is as clear as a slap in the face. From the antiseptic odor and the sterile environment to the bars on the windows, there's no mistaking my location, but when?

When has always been much more important than the where to me.

Rose is nowhere in this room. I must have been caught up in her journey last night, since she is always and forever pulled back to the asylum. I hadn't felt well enough to steer my own course. I press my palms to my eyes and take a deep breath. If I'm locked in here for life, I will surely scream. I have to get myself under control before I attempt to open that door. I have to get to Israel if I can. Rose would have wanted to come back here for Luke. She left him in 1931, the same day I lost Israel, so if she was clear headed enough last night, we should be back in the same year. I just have to get out of the hospital.

With any luck, no one will have noticed my sudden arrival here. I'm not dressed in a hospital gown. Thank heaven for small mercies. My blouse though, is crusted with Israel's blood, I've lost one heel somewhere, and I'm sure I look a fright. I don't think I'll pass for a visitor after all. If they allow me to leave the hospital, it will probably only be to enter Scotland Yard for interrogation. I look as though I've murdered someone, or several someones.

Mina Dobson. I need Mina Dobson. Friend of Rose's or not, she can get me out of here, because at least she knows some of what is going on in my life.

My mind made up, I stand gingerly. I still feel dizzy and discombobulated and out of sorts, but I dismiss the feelings to the best of my ability and walk on stiff legs to the door. I leave the lone heel behind like Cinderella, if Cinderella had been in a horror story and her prince had been stabbed by her wicked stepsister.

I can't help holding my breath when my hand cups the knob, and I think I pause just a second before I twist it. I know I sigh in relief when it turns, and I exit the cold room. The hallway seems long, practically endless. In the depths of my fears, I worry that it will go on forever, like an optical illusion, and I'll keep walking, never getting anywhere, walk all my life and never reach my destination. Worse, in reality, there is a huddled form on the floor several doors down, and I know it's the young woman who made me so nervous before. It's the way I must walk though, unless I want to just stand here and scream for help like a spoiled child, so walk I do.

The medicinal smell is thick out here, and I wonder how quickly it has seeped into the walls and doors of this awful place. Luke had said Bedlam had changed buildings and only recently, too. It didn't take long for the building to embrace the feeling and aura of a mental asylum, or am I just letting my imagination take over? If a flower shop had moved in instead, or a jolly restaurant, or a boarding school with giggling girls in uniforms, would I feel such a haunting oozing from the walls? I am near the huddled girl. She doesn't raise her head from her knees as I pass, but still, I have to force myself not to run.

What if Mina isn't even working today? What then? I glance down at my blouse. Do I claim I've been attacked by a patient? Could I duck into a room and steal someone else's clothes, maybe a uniform, like the ones Rose and Mina wear? There has to be a laundry around somewhere, but it could take me hours to find it, slinking around the hallways like a ghost, trying not to be seen, and avoiding the patients and orderlies.

I can't help wondering, though it seems a stinking sort of betrayal to be thinking about creature comforts at a time like this. Is our room at the Savoy is still mine and Iz's? The key is long gone whether in Israel's pocket or fallen out of mine... I can't be sure since I can't quite remember who had it last anyway, but the bellboy would certainly recall me. I had done my silly little two-step on the stairs, and he had smiled at me, in on my joyful bit of playfulness. How can I consider a hot bath and a change of clothes, though, when I don't know Israel's fate? Then again, I can hardly make rounds in nearby hospitals looking for him when I look as I do. I'm at war with myself.

Frustrated by my preposterous circumstances, I am suddenly aware of an odd squeaking and squealing noise behind me. Whirling as though I fear for my life, which I suppose I do in this place, I am forced to look downward to see what is chasing me. It's the old man in the wheelchair, from yesterday, the one who had frowned at me and rolled on down the hallway at an impressive clip. I feel a bit of relief. Surely I have nothing to fear from a disabled, elderly gentleman, even if he is mad.

His wiry, springy hair grows from his scalp and ears and even his nose, and it reminds me of the alfalfa sprouts Prue used to keep on the windowsill, like they'll bud tiny green leaves if only I stand here long enough and watch them.

"She's back, you know," he snaps at me. He has a raspy voice that makes me think of what Luke will sound like as an old man if he doesn't quit the cigarettes. "That one always comes back."

"Do you need anything?" I can't think of anything else to say, so my barista skills step in for me, and I offer to help. "A push somewhere?"

"Don't be threatening me, missy!" he barks.

"I wasn't – um, that is, I'm sorry. I'll just be on my way." I feel chastised and feeble. I begin walking again, though I sense his eyes boring holes in my back. The squeaking doesn't begin again, though, so I know he is still where I left him. I turn suddenly. "Wait. Who is back?"

But he's gone. Squeaking or no, the old, mad man gets around this place faster than I do, and I can't help but be annoyed at that fact. I nearly consider wheelchair high jacking, and the thought makes me smile. Now I really must appear crazy. I'm covered in blood and smiling. If I don't watch myself, they'll commit me. My true story is worse than any made up fiction. I'll just try telling them I simply woke up here after a bit of time traveling, that should go over well.

I speed up but slow down again when I turn a corner. Corners in this place make me nervous. You never know what you might run into around them. My bearings, such as they are, are all gone now. I have neither any idea where I am nor any clear inspiration as to which way is out, trapped in a sense, though only half of how trapped the others are in this place.

My empathy kicks in with a heavy heart. My ears strain for sounds, not the sounds of the mentally ill, but the sounds of efficient staff, or even better, the sound of the heavy front doors opening and closing. Then I recall how eerily silent they had been. No help there, then. Another hour in this place, and I will attempt to jump out a window just to escape, except of course, for the bars. They certainly have thought of everything.

I'm starting to feel a bit frantic now, and my heart rate is racing faster than the mad old man's wheelchair.

The skinny woman, I forget her name, startles me out of my thoughts. She seems to have materialized out of the wall, until I see the door behind her is simply painted the same dull white as the walls. She cocks a sparse brow at me and waits for me to initiate speaking. I recall her complicity in Luke's scheme with Lizzie, and hope that gives me something to hold over her, an edge, a little bit of blackmail, anything to keep her from escorting me back to my room. I stand up straighter and smile a bit, not so much as to seem friendly or suspicious, but enough to make her see I've recognized her. *I'm perfectly sane, thank you very much.* Even my thoughts are spoken through gritted teeth.

"Oh, hello!" My false tone grates on my threadbare nerves, but I keep it up and add brightness and bossiness as to my words as well. "I'm afraid I've forgotten your name, Miss –?"

"Agatha Helmes." She regards me coolly. If I have the upper hand, she doesn't seem to see it that way.

"Yes, of course, Miss Helmes. There's been an accident with Rose."

That catches her attention, she starts. She rubs her bony shoulders as though she suddenly has a chill. My sister has that effect on people. "What do you mean by accident?"

"Well, not an accident in the truest sense of the word, since I'm quite sure she had every intention of shanking my husband, but yes, there's been an incident. Have you seen her?" I straighten my blouse self-consciously but hope it comes across as business-like, like Mina's skirt, pleated and straight and hanging properly. "I believe she came back here."

"Oh." She doesn't seem the type of person to say *Oh, dear!* so she simply lets the *oh* hang in the air, unfinished, like a dangling icicle off the side of a house, sharp as a dagger and twice as cold. "I see. She is not a patient here, however, so her activities are not really our concern." Or responsibility, she may as well add, since we both know that's her true aim. She pauses and then finishes with, "I'm sorry about your husband." The apology seems as rusty coming out of her thin lips as a box of old nails on a chalkboard. I almost feel as though I should apologize for making her apologize, it seemed painful for her.

"Thank you. You haven't seen her then?"

"No. Not today, at any rate. Why ever would you think she would come back here?" It's a patronizing question that is probably rhetorical.

Curious. Miss Helmes must not be privy to everything. She must not know of the Lost. *Rose will never leave these walls,* I want to say, *not for long,* but that would make it seem as though madness runs in my family, and that association will not do.

Aloud, I simply murmur an explanation that seems to suffice, and then I get the courage up to ask her where the exit is. It's all I can do not to let my feet fly when she offers to escort me. I breathe easier with every door we pass, but only half as easily and deeply as I do when I've finally closed the large doors of Bedlam behind me with a satisfying thud, and enter the London air once again.

At first, since I don't know where to go, I just walk quickly, glad to be rid of the place. Eventually, I have to slow and take stock of where I am, which could be anywhere. I've had three people offer to help in the past five minutes alone, since I look like I've been savagely attacked by a bear, and I've crankily refused them all.

Now I'm rethinking that approach, since I have no other plan. I could have at least asked for directions to the nearest hospital, or the Savoy, where I have my only change of clothes stashed, my wide legged pants and shirt from Africa. When the Rolls-Royce pulls up alongside me, I am neither surprised nor upset at the sight. It's as though I knew he would come, something in me was expecting it.

"Get in, Gray," Luke says through the window.

"Where's Rose?" I demand.

"Haven't the foggiest. She comes and goes as she pleases, you know that. Get in."

I step on a particularly sharp bit of gravel and stifle a yell. "Fine, but if this is a kidnapping, I warn you, I'm in a foul mood."

"I don't have any interest in kidnapping you," Luke mutters, as I climb in. Heavens, the seats feel like butter. I sink in, grateful. If he's going to kill me, I'm going to go in comfort at least. "Believe it or not, I'd like you out of my life as much as you do. I'm simply having pangs of –what do you moral people call it?"

"Conscience? Guilt? Repentance?" Emotions I'm sure have never niggled him.

"Repentance is going a bit too far. But, yes, my conscience is bugging me a little. Especially, when you choose to walk down the streets of London in broad daylight, covered in blood, and looking so pathetic. You're like a hangdog puppy, Gray, and I can't seem to get rid of you." He sighs.

"Thanks."

"It wasn't a compliment. I suppose you're looking for the good doctor?"

I swallow hard. Is this it? Is this when he tells me that Israel is dead, that he hadn't even survived an hour after I ran away? I nearly cover my ears with my hands but sit on them instead. They feel icy cold beneath my skirt. I would think they feel dead, only I remember my grandmother Nora's hands weren't this cold when I held them last. "Yes."

"He's at the Royal Free Hospital in Hampstead, or at least, he was this morning when I stopped by to say hello."

"You stopped by to say hello?" I echo incredulously.

"That's what I said, isn't it?" Luke looks annoyed that I've caught him in the act of being nice. "Don't get all mushy on me, Gray. It's not as though I brought him flowers or we passionately embraced."

"I'd be happy with not attempting to throw chairs at or stab one another," I shoot back.

"He's half dead already. I don't kill old ladies or small animals or giants who can't get out of their own beds." He shoots me an annoyed look from his seat as if I've insulted him mightily.

"Half dead?" My voice is anxious. "Which half?"

He snorts. "Where have you been anyway? You took off last night in a hurry, didn't even wait to see if lover boy was going to pull through."

If he doesn't know where I was last night, he must not know Rose was with me either. There's no reason to keep it from him that I can think of, but I do anyway. Having any kind of an upper hand where Luke Dawes is concerned is a must. Why wouldn't Rose have told him, or hasn't he seen her yet this morning? Was she still wandering the halls of Bedlam? Mentally, though I can't stand the skinny woman, I wish Agatha Helmes an early lunch. "Where's the Royal Free Hospital?" I change the subject.

"We'll be there in a minute. Are you sure you want to go in looking like that? You look like the sixth canonical victim. We can swing by the flat, and you can borrow something from Rose if you like."

"Not bloody likely," I answer firmly. I can deal with fashion later. I have to see Iz.

"Oh, come on. She borrowed your stuff recently."

"What? What stuff?" My voice raises an octave.

"Oh, when we were looking for you, that's all. Stayed a few nights in your old place. She used up all your bubble bath, I think."

I stare at him, dumfounded. "What a revolting thing to do."

"Oh, come off it! Sisters share, so I'm told."

"We don't."

"Suit yourself, you little martyr. At least take this." Somehow, Luke manages to remove his jacket, while maneuvering around a woman with a pram and a runaway toddler in the street.

The thought of wearing Luke's jacket, which probably smells like spice, cigarettes, and the lovely aroma of deceit, gives me more than a little pause, but I end up accepting it. I suppose I don't need too much attention in the hospital. I don't feel particularly inclined to stop and answer a dozen orderlies' questions about the state of my health.

"How gallant of you. Can I have your shoes, too?" I flex my bare toes. They're filthy, and my sore ankle is swollen. Plus I've lost half a toenail somewhere along the way. I am positively grotesque. Israel will be so happy to see me.

"Not on your life. These are Italian leather. I love these shoes."

"How do you do it?" I raise my eyebrows wonderingly. "Find time to steal so much in so little time?"

"It's a gift," he replies, smugly. "God is in the details, you know, and I worship my details, especially the expensive details."

"I think the expression is, the devil is in the details. Especially when you're doing the talking." I sniff.

"Blah blah. Besides, if you always knew you'd be back in London every other travel, wouldn't you stash things here and there?"

"Stash what, where?" I try to remain flippant with my tone, but I'm a little intrigued with his process.

"Coins, trinkets, antiques, small items. I have spots all over London, I know this city like the back of my hand by now. There are plenty of hiding places if you know where to look."

"So, you don't steal things then?" I'm surprised.

"Of course I do. But then I hide them for a rainy day. Never let it be said I'm not prepared. Anyway, we're here, and Gray?"

"What?" I pause, my hand already on the doorknob, as the Rolls-Royce comes to stop.

"Let's make this our last meeting, shall we?"

I open the door and stare back at him, in disbelief. "*I'm* not the one constantly showing up, dragging around and killing *your* grandmother, marching *you* through time, and then knifing *your* loved ones, am I?"

Luke opens his mouth and then shuts it again, opens it once more. "I see your point. Fair enough. I'll try to control Rose better."

I snort again.

"I'll try harder to keep Rose away," he continues, "and you should try the whole disappearing thing again. Although..." he trails off again.

"What?" I bark. I'm getting impatient, and I'm ready to get out of the blasted car, butter seats or no butter seats.

"Do you plan on controlling it now?" Luke looks genuinely curious. "Will you steer yourself wherever you want, now that you know you can? You won't mess with Rose, will you? Some of us like her just the way she is and wouldn't want things to be different."

"Some of us, meaning you? No. No, I don't think I'll mess with Rose and her life, or lives, or however you look at it." I keep thinking of being in the same room with two Roses, and I shake my head, partly for emphasis to my negative answer, and partly to clear it. "Her life won't change because of me. I promise." Why am I comforting Luke, of all people, anyway?

Luke looks relieved. Was that why he picked me up, and why he went to see Israel, for reassurance?

I get out of the car finally, and lean back in for my parting shot. "You two live happily ever after. Thanks for the ride."

It's the nicest thing I can think to say.

Chapter 18

The last several times I've taken leave of my sister, her villainous husband, and that dreaded mental asylum we call Bedlam, I've thought it to be my last. I always think it's goodbye, and it never is. The thought feeds my anger and heavy heart as I practically fly up the stairs and into the Royal Free Hospital. Will I burst into Israel's room, only to be greeted by Rose with a bloody cleaver? Will I curl up next to him, fall asleep, and wake in that cold bed across town with Miss Helmes frowning at me? Now that I know for certain I can't change the past, can't change history, all I want to do is get to Israel and then get away.

If he isn't dead already.

"I need to see Israel Rhode!" I blurt out, breathless, when I reach the front desk. The nurse, or secretary, or whatever she calls herself, looks at me with disdain. She has a mass of fluffy blonde hair that looks like a blob of bleached cotton candy, the kind you can get at the fair that dissolves on your tongue into sugar crystals and turns your mouth the color of the candy. She flips over her appointment book, or maybe it's a record book, or a sales log, and blinks deliberately in my direction. It's clear I have handled her all wrong, and she's not going to do me any favors.

"What floor, please?" She sounds bored. Her nails click on the pages of her book.

"I don't know!" I grit my teeth and somehow manage to refrain from snatching the book from her annoying fingers. "He was brought in last night with a stab wound."

"Was he?" She snaps her gum in a haughty fashion, something I didn't know until now was even possible. "Unfortunate."

"Yes, quite." I change tactics. Outside, I'm all smiles, but inside I'm seething. "I'm sure you're very busy. I would so appreciate your help."

"Hmm. Let's see." The woman flips a few pages maddeningly slow. "Name?"

I stifle the urge to slam my head into her desk. "Israel Rhode." I enunciate carefully and try not to let my irritation show. "Last night. Stabbing."

"Hmm." She snaps her gum again, and I want to remove it from her mouth and smear it all over her fluffy hair. "No. No one here by that name." She closes her book as though that is that.

"What? No. No, I was told he was here! Check again, please!" I place my hands on the desk and lean in, partially as emphasis to my plea and partly to hold myself up. My legs feel weak, and despair is creeping in.

"I said there's no one here by that name. Next, please!" She looks around me pointedly, though there is no one else in line, and it's obvious she's only wishing to be rid of the barefooted, bloody girl in the man's jacket.

I snatch her book from the desk and flip through it frantically.

"You can't do that! Give it here!" Abruptly, her lower class accent comes through, and she makes a move as if to grab the papers back. "I'll call security. I will!"

"Go ahead," I mutter flipping and scanning the handwritten notes quickly. It's a log, that much is certain, and I go backwards until I find the times between eight and midnight last night. My eyes search the names and complaints hastily. I frown. She is right. There is no Israel Rhode listed. Had Luke lied to me then? Why? I toss the book back on the desk, and the candy haired woman shoots me such a glance that if hatred were laser beams, I'd be fried within an inch of my life.

"Is something wrong?" A man's voice seems to appear out of nowhere, although it's possible he's been standing here for some time. I haven't really been paying attention. "Can I help?"

I turn to him, a doctor, thank God. I open my mouth to plead for information from him, but the woman behind the desk beats me to the punch.

"She's a menace is what she is! Needs to be escorted out, Doctor. She stole my logbook, right from under my hands. Won't take no for an answer, and just look at her! She's a street person! Who does she think she is, the Queen o' Sheba, eh?" The woman gestures at me with contempt.

I can't quite count all the ways she's just insulted me, but I let all that go and direct my attention towards the doctor. He's young for a doctor, though not as young as Iz. He is also very handsome, though not so handsome as Iz. My eyes fill with tears, and though it isn't intentional, it serves me well. The doctor sees my distress and offers me his arm.

"Come along, my dear. Take a seat and tell what it is that's troubling you. I'll take care of this, Vivian. I apologize for the interruption." He smiles at the fluffy haired Vivian, and that seems to soothe her ruffled feathers, though she glares at me once more before going back to her precious logbook. Click, click go her fingernails on the desk as I walk away. Vivian, my foot. She's a Bertha if ever I saw one.

"Thank you," I say warmly as I let him guide me. He offers me a chair in the waiting area, out of sight of Vivian. I sink down into it, gratefully. My ankle is throbbing again. "I'm sorry to be a bother. I was told my husband was here, and now I can't find him." The tears well up again, and one particularly fat one threatens to spill over and roll down my face like raindrops on a dirty window.

"I'm dreadfully sorry, Mrs. –?"

"Rhode. Sonnet Rhode." The lie slips out easily enough. I've had enough practice, and sometimes it feels as though it is my name. I thought maybe it would be someday.

"Well, Mrs. Rhode, I'm sure he hasn't just disappeared into thin air." The doctor smiles kindly.

I nearly burst out laughing. Disappearing into thin air is distinctly possible with the Lost, and it's that very risk that has me so tied up in knots. We were only separated one night. Had he traveled without me, like I had without him? I swallow my hysterical laughter and try to smile back. "I'm not a street person," I say, lamely. I cross my dirty ankles and try to tuck them under the chair. "I've just had a very trying night, week… a very trying year." The laugh slips through then, and I sound a bit mad. "I've had a trying life, Doctor."

He pats my hand. "What did you say your husband is ill with?"

"Um, he's ill with multiple stab wounds." Is that an illness?

To my surprise, the doctor's handsome face lights up. "Is that so? You don't say? How wonderful!"

I narrow my eyes. "I'm afraid I don't see the cause for such jubilation."

"Don't you?" The doctor chuckles. "Well, I do. I believe I know the very man you're looking for!"

A wave of relief and utter happiness washes over me. I leap to my feet. "Oh, thank God! Will you take me to him, please?"

"Of course, you see, he hasn't said much, and I'm afraid we didn't even know his name. He had no identification on him. We assumed he'd been robbed of that during the altercation that left his shoulder cut up in ribbons." The doctor seems to realize he's been crude in his description, but since I live with that kind of casual morbidity, and no look of distaste settles on my face, he continues on. "He's doing well enough, but he isn't exactly a talkative fellow, is he?"

"No." I finally smile a genuine smile. My relief is overwhelming. "He isn't. He'll live then?"

"Oh, yes! It was an ugly cut, rather jagged and done with something a bit dull, so the pain was most likely intense, and the slashing was rather deep, causing excess blood loss, but your husband is lucky, Mrs. Rhode. No major arteries were harmed. You did say he was your husband?" The doctor coughs, a bit delicately. He's obviously taken aback by the relationship between a young white woman and a black man.

I glare at my feet. "Yes," I respond shortly.

"How... unusual. What modern times we live in..." the doctor muses. I can't tell if he's pleased with my lie, or disturbed.

We have begun to walk, and I match strides with his long legs easily enough. When we pass by Vivian again, she snaps her gum and pointedly ignores me. "I'm so glad you could identify him. I never like having mysterious patients. Makes things so very difficult. Of course, I'll be sure to tell Vivian our young man's name so there aren't any more mix-ups. In case of other visitors and such."

I don't want to argue with him, though there shouldn't be any other visitors. Unless– "Can I ask that there be no one else beside me? No other visitors?" I hurry to explain, as the doctor seems taken aback by my request. "It's just that the attack was not random, and I fear for his safety."

"Ah. Well, yes, yes, of course, but if there are other safety precautions you would like to take, I'm afraid that's Scotland Yard's department, and I'm not sure you can afford them." He looks me over, but it's in such a good natured, teasing sort of way that I don't take offense. "Now, on a serious note, just how much danger is he in?"

I don't answer, because we have reached our destination. The doctor's hand rests atop the door handle, and in my eagerness, I abandon all civility and rudely push his hand aside in order to enter first. It's a large room, and a common one, meaning that are several dozen beds, mostly filled. I scan them all quickly, and Israel's dark form is easy enough to spot against the white sheets. I race to his side. He looks quite dead, but since I know he isn't, I come very close to throwing myself on top of him.

"Good Lord, Sonnet!" His eyes fly open in alarm as my weight settles against him. "How did you –? Where did you come from?"

I kiss him soundly. "Never mind. I've never been so happy to see anyone in my whole life," I say fervently, "and the next time you get yourself stabbed and then tell me to run, I'm going to finish you off myself! How do you feel?" I kiss him once more. His lips are very dry and warm. "You look terrible."

"You look beautiful."

I laugh. "You're obviously drugged up. Really, how do you feel?" I touch his forehead tenderly. I think that must be a woman thing to do, check for fevers. It's the extent of my medical knowledge, but it makes me feel helpful. He is as cool as a babbling brook in the spring.

"I feel as though I've been hacked up like Prue's fricasseed chicken," Iz replies cheerfully, "and I was regretting the whole running away thing, myself. It seemed like a good idea at the time."

"It was a horrible idea." I wrinkle my nose and remember waking up in France. I scratch the bug bites on my legs. "I'll tell you all about it later. When can we get out of here?"

"Now is good." Israel sits up, but a wave of anguish passes over him, and he falls back against the thin hospital pillow. "Later is good, too."

"Doctor?" I turn my attention to the man I had so rudely passed by moments before. He had followed me to Israel's bedside, but hadn't said a word this whole time.

"Well, I think a longer stay is advisable under the circumstances," he says. "You are, of course, free to leave when you feel ready, but I would highly recommend a couple of days. Make sure that wound wasn't cut with anything that might cause infection, and I'd like to see the x-rays. I don't like how some of the tendons were cut. We want you to play football again as soon as possible."

I don't get the joke, but the doctor seems to find himself amusing and he chuckles. "There will be some pain, naturally, but we can set you up with some medicines for that," he continues. "You'll have to exercise it, but slowly. You'll find the muscles will be quite sore for some time, I'm afraid. Since the cost isn't an issue, you may as well stay where you are comfortable and taken care of."

"The cost?" I'm confused. The cost is an issue actually. Our room at the Savoy would be someone else's by now, and if there was any money left behind, I'd wager it's comfortably in our dear bellboy's pocket now.

"Yes, didn't I mention that earlier? The young man who came to see your husband earlier paid for his stay. A Good Samaritan, I suppose. Didn't even know Mr. Rhode here, but said he saw it happen and wanted to help."

"Oh, yes, the Good Samaritan," I echo drily, "panicking over his near brush with repentance."

"Who?" Israel asks looking confused.

"Luke."

"Ah. I thought I heard his voice at one point, but I thought I was having a nightmare. Oh, well, his money is as good as anyone's, and I'll take it. I suppose he didn't leave enough for a private room?"

"Ah, I'm afraid not quite. Young love... there's nothing like it." The doctor chuckles once more. I find myself blushing, though I'm not entirely sure why. There was something untoward in his look. A private room, indeed. Now I get it. I punch Israel's arm lightly.

"You really were worried, weren't you?" Israel reaches up and begins working a knot out of my hair.

"Of course I was. I thought you might be dead. Ouch."

"Your Scottish brogue comes through when you're upset."

"What? Does not! I don't even have a brogue." I frown.

He chuckles. "Yes, you do, but only when you forget yourself or get mad."

"That's ridiculous. I've never even lived in Scotland." I close my eyes as he continues to comb through my hair with his fingers. "At least, not that I recall."

"I think you get it from Noah. I almost didn't tell you because I'm pretty sure I'm the only one who has ever noticed. It's like a part of you that I get to claim because I'm the first to know it."

"Mmmhmm. You've definitely had too many painkillers, they're making you loopy. Oh!" I open my eyes, remembering. "Speaking of pain killers, I don't recommend a Mickey Finn. My head still hurts."

"What are you talking about?"

"Nothing." I smile. "I'll tell you later."

Chapter 19

Later will come when I've gone and done something about the state of my clothing, empty stomach, and filthy body. Short of tracking down Mina Dobson, or befriending the cranky Vivian, I have little options for borrowed clothes. I miss Emme for the hundredth time today.

I leave the hospital reluctantly, firmly telling Israel to rest, after feeling his forehead again, of course. I'm relieved beyond words naturally that he isn't mortally wounded, but directly following that relief is disappointment that he isn't well enough to leave London. I am so very ready to go anywhere else, back to Africa to see my dad and Bea and Joe, of course, though I am trying to ignore the knotty feeling in my stomach that warns me of controlling my journeys. Well, one more will have to do.

I can't just leave them there alone, and it isn't only because they miss me. I'm just far too selfish for that kind of sacrifice.

My heart feels much lighter as I exit the hospital, not light enough to skip merrily along, but some of that reluctance is due to my sore ankle and exhaustion. Since Luke has a tendency to come along whenever he pleases and at the least opportune times, I scan the streets for his fancy car, but nothing. He must be searching for Rose. I wonder if she'll tell him about France. How often does she go back? Did she know I would be there that time?

There are too many questions with no answers, and I shake my head to clear my thoughts. No use dwelling on the fantastic. Coming up with practical advice for my life seems pointless. Everything always veers off in directions unknown with weirdness and oddities waiting for me around each and every corner anyway. I might as well meet them with an innocent naiveté and as much surprise as everyone else.

Mind made up to ignore my mind, I scout my area. The thought of robbing someone makes me even more tired, and my bones feel like wet noodles in my body. I hardly know how they are supporting my skin and keeping me upright. I'm nearly as tired, as the time spent in that abandoned house Rose locked me into over a year ago. I had to stay awake for so long, for fear of traveling without my family. Exhaustion is a palpable thing, an insidious beast that creeps along the length and width of my body with chilly fingers. It demands my cooperation, no, my compliance, and an appetite for sleep.

I move along, not caring where I go, but taking pains to remember my paths and turns. I don't need to misplace the hospital, of all things, with Iz inside it. He'd better not nap too deeply while I'm gone. My feet move a little faster, and I re-button Luke's jacket when I glance down and realize it's fastened crooked. I'm not so far gone as to think it actually helps my facade though.

Ducking into a little patio on the front of a small bistro, I stop to rest my feet and rub my ankle. I should have iced it at the hospital, that would have been an intelligent thing to do. Harebrained and half-cocked as usual, I tell myself. Barely three minutes go by before I am shooed away, politely but firmly by a man in an apron, and I walk on. I'm starting to get too far away now, and I still haven't found a solution to my problem. Why didn't I just ask that nice doctor for a gown or something? Isn't there something in the medical creed that requires him to clothe me? I sigh.

If I were in a movie, or a children's book, I'd find a lovely clothesline with no one manning it. It would be full of starched skirts, billowing blouses, clean underpants, stockings, and maybe a jaunty hat. If this were a movie or a children's book, however, I'd hardly be wandering around London in the wrong era with blood on my chest. I'd be at a ball, or kissing a frog, or living happily ever after.

Strangely, feeling sorry for myself perks me up a bit, and when I do find a line of drying clothes, I laugh aloud. Though not as wonderful as the ones in my daydream, and though there is not a jaunty hat to be found, I am still in luck, and I make short work of snatching a couple things when I'm sure no one is looking. I grab a dress of plaid with a belt and a pair of gardening clogs that are tucked neatly by the back door of the same home. It's not my overalls and Budweiser cap, but they'll have to do, and anything is better than the filth I am wearing now.

Moving quickly before my thievery is discovered, I double back the way I came. I had seen a church earlier, and once I reach it again, I duck inside and make my way over to the holy water. Murmuring a quick request for forgiveness from any supernatural eyes that might be watching, I wash my hands and face as best as I am able, and then duck into their toilet to change into my new dress. I feel like a new woman once I am moderately clean and shoed, but my contentment is short lived when I come face to face with a man of the cloth before I can make a hasty retreat.

"Hello, Father," I stammer. I tuck a wet strand of hair behind my ear and hope he hasn't noticed how muddy (and how pink) the holy water has become.

"Bless you, child." His eyes seem to be peering into my soul, or perhaps it is my guilty conscience that makes me think so, but in any case, I drop my gaze. They aren't angry eyes, but they are searching, which makes me nervous.

"Thank you?" I don't mean for it to be posed as a question, but that is how it comes out. Inwardly, I sigh at my own great awkwardness.

"Are you here for confession, my child?"

"I'm not Catholic, sir. I mean, Father." I am dreadfully embarrassed, whether at my lack of denominational practice or my thieving ways I am unclear.

"Confession is good for the soul in any religion, my dear." The tone in his voice suggests a wink in his eyes, but there is none.

"In all cases?" I wonder. I'm thinking of Rose, but it's clear he thinks I speak of myself.

"Of course. Forgiveness is a salve to heal all wounds."

"Some wounds will not be healed, I think." I falter. "Aren't there unpardonable sins, Father, sins that cannot be undone?"

"Those are two different questions." The man smiles. "There are no sins our Lord cannot forgive."

"But I am not Him."

"No." He cocks his head, curiously. "Are there sins you cannot forgive, or sins you've committed that cannot be forgiven?"

"I'm... I'm not exactly sure." I stumble on my words.

"Well, that is a quandary that requires thought and prayer, isn't it? Go in peace, child." He nods at me and walks away silently. I remember my silent monk, the one who taught me to read and write, and suddenly I miss him terribly. I could use a wise old sage in my life, and I nearly run after this man, but I don't. Instead, I exit the church and make my way back to Israel. I hope he will share his hospital meal, because I suddenly don't have the heart or the aspiration for stealing my supper tonight.

*   *   *

"That was an incredibly stupid thing to do, Sonnet!" I know Israel is mad, because he is using my full name. The tale of the Mickey Finn gone awry is not amusing him. Doctors have no sense of humor, it seems, when it comes to drugs and prescribing them to oneself. I probably should have left out that part of my sordid tale. It's been a day and a half, and I'm just now letting him in on the story of my trip to France.

"I know!" I say crossly between bites of a terribly bad pot roast. "I didn't claim it was my most genius idea. I simply said I was desperate to try to change what had happened. I couldn't just curl up for a little nap when I was scared to death you were dying on me. Don't pretend you would have done any differently. "

He just glares at me. "When I told you to run, I didn't mean a century and a country away, for goodness sake. I meant...well, I don't know what I meant. I was bleeding at the time. I was probably lightheaded and delusional. I don't know why you chose to listen to me then of all times when you never have before."

"I know, I know." I lean over and kiss his stubbly cheek tenderly. "Now if you're all done yelling at me, I'm going to eat your parsnips."

"Is that what they are? They look like sawed off cadaver's fingers. I thought my tray must have stopped by the morgue on the way up."

"Thank you so much for that lovely imagery. I'm eating them anyway, cad. How is that shoulder?"

Israel moves it experimentally. "Fine, really. Sore, but that's to be expected. I haven't been taking the medicine."

"What? You numbskull!" I frown at him and stop munching on the truly awful parsnip. Prue would have fried them. Everything tastes better fried in bacon grease.

"For one thing, smarty pants, I don't want to run the risk of you traveling without me, and I think drugs might interfere with the Lost, although..." Iz frowns right back. "You seem to have shot a hole in that theory since you traveled just fine with half a bottle of chloral hydrate in your system."

"More like two thirds of a bottle," I say sheepishly.

He closes his eyes for a moment, as if I am physically paining him. "Right. Okay. Now that I've had a small heart attack, the other thing I was going to say is, it's 1931, which means the pain killers of choice are opium and cocaine."

"Oh," my sheepish voice continues. "Yes, well, glad you passed on them then."

"Oh, I didn't pass on them last night! I was happy to let them shoot me up with something, anything, but now that I'm better and you're back, I thought I'd clean up."

"Fastest addiction kicking ever, I'd say." I grin. "You're wonderful."

"Glad you noticed. Anyway, I'm tired of being babied. What do you say to this?" He leans over, winces a moment at the pain, then rights himself again this time with a newspaper in his hand.

"What?" I take it and look. It's funny, because it's today's paper, of course it is, and yet I still handle it like it's an antique, like it will crumble in my fingertips. "This part?" Iz nods. "Hmm. 'Noted scientist Bartoli Giuliani takes Einstein's theories further.' That part?" Iz nods again. "What about it? I don't understand."

"Just read it!"

"Fine, fine! Don't get your knickers in a twist," I huff. "I'm reading already. 'Bartoli Giuliani of the University of Florence is making waves in the scientific world concerning the paradoxes of time and space. Considered a quack by some and an expert by others, Giuliani is fast becoming the world authority on the possibility, some say certainty, of time travel.'" I raise my eyebrows. "I already know it's a certainty, and I still say he's a quack."

Israel flicks the paper in response. "Be serious."

"What? I am."

"I think we should go to Newcastle Upon Tyne."

"Whatever for?" He's taken me by surprise, and I nearly choke on my last bite of parsnip.

"Because Florence is a thousand miles away."

"You're not making a single bit of sense."

"He was in Florence, but now he's in Newcastle Upon Tyne, which is much closer."

"I don't know why we'd want to see this fellow at all."

"Look at the photo."

"This tiny, black and white, blurry thing at the bottom? Yes, it's him, the ol' noted scientist himself. What of it?"

"Doesn't he look familiar?" Iz presses.

I squint and peer harder. "It looks like every other photo from this time period, grainy and in need of better lighting, and of course he's frowning.

Why can't anyone smile in old photography?" A thought, unbidden, comes into my mind, a memory of Luke passing me a photo of Rose. I had recognized her then with a burning in my chest and a gasp in my breath. When I recognize this fellow, it's not so dramatic, but I do cover my mouth with my hand in surprise. "Why, it's Bar!"

When you run into an acquaintance, but in a place where you don't expect to see him, it always takes a moment for your brain to adjust. I had said goodbye to Bar decades and decades in the future, and I never expected to see him again, hence the lack of recognition with his picture. Now, it seems obvious that it's my friend. That sad, young man straight from a Nazi camp, that I had befriended in a soup kitchen in modern America, had somehow turned up in Newcastle Upon Tyne in 1931. Well, it wasn't completely shocking since Bar is Lost too, but still running into one another is a strange and happy coincidence that makes me grin.

"How fun! I never knew he was a scientist!"

"Yes, well, so am I," Israel counters.

I cock my eyebrow at him as he lies in his hospital bed. "You are not. You're barely a doctor."

"That's what you think. If we are going to get access to Bar, a celebrated and somewhat infamous quack, we need titles. I'll be a scientist myself, and you can be my secretary."

"Why can't I be the scientist, and you be my secretary?"

"Can you discuss and dissect the paradoxes and intricacies involved in time travel?"

"No, but I can control it, which is more than you can do." I sniff.

"Don't remind me. Besides, we only need to bluff our way into Bar's presence, and then he'll recognize us, and we can drop the façade." He smiles smugly.

"Besides to have tea, and to view a town with such a fabulously strange name for itself, why do we want to see Bar?" Israel's train of thought has always been a track different than my own, barreling ahead in the same direction maybe, but on a different track.

"For one thing, he'll be delighted with your newfound abilities, and I'd like to pick his massive brain a bit. He may have some answers to your sister's condition and if controlling the journeys is dangerous." Israel shrugs, casually, as if to say, *not that it's important, just something do to, just an idea,* but I know he has hidden depth and reasons for his desire to speak with Bar.

I haven't even mentioned the nose bleeds and the screaming voices in my head during my hallucinations, and Iz already is suspicious about the aftereffects of what I can do. I stay silent a moment. It isn't as if I want to keep it from him, but I also don't want him to forbid me from trying again before I've reunited with Dad, at the very least.

Chapter 20

The doctor gives us his blessing and permission to leave the Royal Free Hospital, though he cautions us to keep Israel's dressing dry and fresh at all times. I reassure the doctor that I've had nurse's training, and he seems content. Israel doesn't like to lie unless he has to which is why this plan of posing as a scientist is somewhat surprising to me. He reminds us, as we exit the room, that morphine is easily accessible in any local pharmacy. I don't mention to either him or Iz that I know of an excellent pharmacy with a currently broken window.

Guilt surrounds me like a shroud when I wonder how the poor pharmacist is faring. Sometimes I dislike the lengths I go to and wish I could be a normal, boring twenty-year-old, on my way to college maybe or moving out for the first time. I sigh, feeling sorry for myself a bit, before shaking the whiney feeling off like a wet jacket.

Like I had before, my eyes scan the surrounding areas for the Rolls-Royce when we come out into the sunshine of London, but I don't see it. It's a rare sunny, bright day, the kind that begs for a picnic or a bit of sightseeing, unfortunately, we have no such pleasantries in mind. Instead, we have to think of a way to get to Newcastle Upon Tyne. We're both hoping to come up with a plan that doesn't involve thievery, he because his arm and shoulder would make a sudden getaway impossible, and I because having a run-in with a priest has me concerned somewhat for my soul.

I had considered letting the doctor continue in his mistaken belief that Israel had been robbed and then applying to his sense of decency and hinting for a loan, but I hadn't gone through with the idea. Hence, we've been dismissed from the hospital like a couple of kittens turned out from a yard or like Peter Rabbit chased from Mr. Macgregor's lettuce patch. I don't have the foggiest notion how to get to Newcastle Upon Tyne, besides walk, and then suddenly, it comes to me when my mind turns once again to the priest in the church down the way.

"Come on!" I grab Israel's hand and begin to pull him along. "I think I have an idea."

One thing I love about Israel is how he doesn't really question me or demand things of me I'm not willing to give up just yet. Most people, myself included, would refuse to budge until they knew what was going on, but Iz just walks along with me, a comfortable silence between us. Oh, he gets angry enough at my plans, that's nearly a guarantee, but he's willing to let me play them out first before the yelling and blustering about how I drive him completely crazy begins. Strolling along London does get us funny looks at times, even more than I got with a bloodied blouse. I ignore them for the most part until a snobby looking woman intentionally crosses the street after staring at our entwined hands with a look of distaste.

"It really is everywhere, isn't it? And every time," I wonder aloud. I hold Iz's hand tighter and debate the qualities of sticking my tongue out at the woman, who is still staring, this time in her perceived safe zone of several yards away.

"What is?"

"Her." I scowl and drawl out the word like it has a capital letter and a reputation. "Different face, same attitude. What's so impossible to believe about us?"

Israel shrugs but then winces, as it obviously pains him. "It's not always intended to be malicious, Sonny. I think sometimes people feel sorry for us."

"What?" I feel instantly offended. "What's to be sorry for? We're perfectly happy! We're meant for one another!" I feel like I'm speaking like Joe now, in overly dramatic and emotional exclamation points.

He smiles, like he thinks I'm sweet. Sweet and naïve. "Maybe they're worried for us. Maybe they know how hard a road a relationship between us will be, like Asha."

"What about Asha?" Once again, his train has gone off on a track, destination unknown. He's left me at the station this time, in fact, my skirt blowing in the breeze and a baffled expression on my face.

"The reason for her frustration with us."

"You mean with me?" I stop walking and wrinkle my nose. "She likes you fine."

"No, not really!" Israel seems surprised at my point of view. "She's actually pretty angry with both of us."

"But why? I never understood." We continue walking. I see the yard I pinched my dress from and hastily guide Israel across the street.

"She just knew what we were in for, knew we were setting ourselves up for hurt. 'Making life harder than it needed to be,' I think was what she said."

"I never knew that," I muse. "Not that it makes me like her any better."

"Well, she knows firsthand. Her dead husband was white."

"No way!" I stop in my tracks. "That does explain some things, I guess." I'm floored.

"He was killed by her brothers, who hardly approved."

"Oh." My voice has gotten very small. I can barely hear myself. "That explains the rest. I wish you would have told me."

"I thought you knew. I'm sorry. She must have mentioned it when you weren't there. In her own irritated way, she is only trying to protect you, I think. She thinks we're being foolish."

"Who would have thought?" I am genuinely taken aback. "I'll have to have a heart to heart with her when we get back to Africa."

"Not sure I'd go that far," Iz chuckles. "She also doesn't like you because you can't cook, and she doesn't understand your sense of humor. Better not push it."

We begin to climb the steps to the church. Iz still hasn't asked me why we're here. I pull open the heavy door and hold it open for him.

"Father?" I call shyly. "Are you here?"

The priest materializes out of the gloom of the church. It probably isn't gloomy, not really, but my eyes haven't adjusted yet from the sunshine of the outside world. I always get tripped up by solemn people in positions of authority, and I almost curtsy to him as I stammer a greeting.

"How can I help?" the priest asks calmly. He seems to see right into Israel's wound. I would think it was supernatural, except for the fact that there is an awful lot of dried blood on his shirt. I should have pilfered Iz something new as well when I got my plaid dress.

"We're in a bit of bind, Father." I choose my words carefully. I don't plan on mentioning Bedlam, though it wouldn't be the first time I've considered the need for an exorcism on my sister. "We know very few in London, but we would like to find an acquaintance. Would you happen to have a phone we could use?"

Immediately, I know my mistake. *Good heavens, Sonnet,* I mutter inside my own misfiring brain. *It's 1931!* But the priest only smiles and pats my hand.

"I'm sorry, child, but we aren't quite so modern here. I can, however, find a change of clothes for your companion here and take you somewhere where there is a telephone."

I grin at him. I can't help it. Now that I'm not so insecure at my lack of confession or my thievery of holy water, I am more comfortable and get a better look at him. He's a young man, most likely not a day over 30, but with the appearance of a more middle-aged one. His ginger-colored hair is thinning and probably always has been, and he's a bit heavy around the middle. I imagine he was a thin haired, chubby baby, and then a thin-haired, chubby teenager.

There's a scratch on his neck, and nearby a small square of cotton sticks, as though he has cut himself with a razor recently and needed something with which to stop the blood. He's probably forgotten that it is still there. He has a plain and homely look about him, and I am sure somehow that he was teased as a child, for ugliness or gentleness or both.

Behind his spectacles, he has merry gray eyes. He seems entirely trustworthy, but then again, I've been known to befriend murderers, so I'm the first to own up that I don't have wonderful instincts. I tend to believe the best in everyone until they prove me otherwise, by breaking my heart or the law, occasionally both at once. My smile fades.

"That would be absolutely perfect. Thank you so much. I'm Sonnet, by the way, and this is Israel." Since I don't know the social proprieties when introducing yourself to a man of the cloth exactly, I settle for presenting my hand. The priest's hand is warm and small, but it has a strong grip.

"What a fine name, an excellent name." The priest takes Iz's hand solemnly. "I am pleased to meet a friend of my young friend here."

Israel looks surprised but shakes the priest's hand firmly. "Thank you, sir, er, Father."

"You can call me Linus." He seems to know the word Father doesn't fall automatically from our lips. "I am new to the priesthood anyway, and I always get a start when someone calls me Father. I think I'll always be just Linus. In fact, I used to answer to that. Just Linus. My mother would proudly say my full name, Linus Arrealius Corcoran, and then she would follow that mouthful up with, we call him Just Linus." His eyes crinkle up at the corners when he smiles wider. "First, let me dig around for a fresh shirt. Are you in need of refreshments and tea?"

Israel declines politely at the exact same time I pounce on the offer like a vulture on a buffet. Anything to get the taste of parsnip out of my mouth is my excuse, but really I'm just always hungry. I should be done growing by now, but I've grown at least another inch taller this year. Iz rolls his eyes at my insatiable stomach and accepts the offer after all. We follow Linus to his kitchen, where he leaves us with the kettle on. I sit down gratefully and rub my ankle, which is only slightly swollen but still sore to the touch.

"Give it here," Israel orders, and I plop my foot on his lap obediently. He rolls it back and forth while I yelp in protest. "Well, if you would stop gallivanting off to distant countries in the dark ..." he trails off, making his point. "Um, did you know you have a toenail hanging on for dear life?" He stares at it like it's a scorpion.

"Excuse me for trying to save your life!" I grumble. "How is your shoulder, anyway? You look tired."

"I am, a bit. What are we going to do with a telephone, by the way?" He stops moving my foot and just lets it rest.

"I thought we'd call that girl from Bedlam, Mina Dobson. She seems involved in Rose's life. Maybe she'll be willing to finance our trip to Newcastle Upon Tyne. It's a shot."

"A long shot, but a shot," Iz agrees. "Although I'm not sure I want to run the risk of her reporting back to Rose and Luke."

"If they want to find us, they'll find us," I sigh. "I'm not going to run all my life. Grab the kettle, will you?" I hear it whistling, and it makes my head hurt a bit. Now that I'm sitting down and relaxed, I feel the aftershocks of what I've been through. It's a bit like recovering from the flu, or the bubonic plague. Everything is achy, and I feel as ancient as Old Babba. Remembering her gives me the willies, and I shudder. I bring my fingers up to my mouth to chew on my pinky nail, but stop abruptly when I realize what I'm doing.

"You're tired, too." Israel leans down and gives my awful toe a kiss. He really must love me.

Linus enters the little kitchen and presents a button down shirt to Israel with a happy look on his face. "Had to rummage a bit, but I found something! Will this do?" He looks anxious to please, and we both rush to exclaim our approval of his choice. It's actually a perfect shirt for a Lost man, nondescript, white, and able to blend in with any century. Not that we plan on leaving this one immediately, but still. Israel will be comfortable, and we just have to hope his wound doesn't seep. It'd be a shame to ruin such a nice shirt.

Once Israel has thrown away his old one and donned the new one and I've finished my last drop of tea (wishing it was a double mocha with whip) Linus takes us through the back door and presents to us his mode of transportation. I couldn't be more surprised. It's a motorcycle with a side car. Of all things!

Linus waits for our reaction like a small child who has presented an adult with a homemade gift like a handwritten card with backwards lettering or a macaroni necklace. He practically bounces from foot to foot, and his eyes are as wide as saucers. I hardly know what to say.

"I hardly know what to say!" I exclaim, finally. "I guess I was expecting something more..."

"Priestly?" Linus looks anxious, like he's displeased us. "I know, I know. I've been putting off getting rid of the old thing, but I just can't seem to find it a good home. I can't let it go to just anyone, you know."

"It's wonderful!" I impulsively hug the man, hoping that isn't some sort of religious no-no. He hugs me back with a grin, so it doesn't seem to be. "Just perfect, but I have to ask, you *do* know how to drive it, yes?"

"Backwards, forwards, sideways! Upstairs, downstairs, and in my nightgown!" Israel is still staring at the side car in fascination. Linus hands him a pair of goggles. "After you, my good man, and you, dear one." He passes me another.

"What about you?" I ask fitting mine on. I feel as though I'm peering through a pair of binoculars. Everything is a bit shadowy and tinted with amber. There's a scratch on the left side that makes my eyes want to cross. I tighten the straps. "There are only two pairs."

"Oh, I'll be fine!" Linus brushes away my concern. "I'll squint through my lashes. My mother always said I had abnormally long lashes. They should strain out the bugs quite admirably."

Israel is already folding his long legs into the side car. He would look a bit comical, especially with the goggles, except that I'm so head over heels for him that he always looks handsome to me. Still, I stifle a laugh as I try to fit myself behind Linus, the motorcycle fiend of the parish. I nearly kick him in the kidneys as I settle myself down, and though I should feel awkward hugging a man of the cloth, he's so kind and likable and dear that I wrap my arms around him without a qualm. He's another person I'll never see again; another person I'll miss. We could have been excellent lifelong friends, Just Linus and me.

"Ready then?" Linus shouts, as the motorcycle roars to life.

"Ready!" I shout back, delighted.

Israel shouts something as well, but I can't be quite sure what it is. It sounds something like, "Geronimo!"

Chapter 21

We race through London, as Iz would put it, like bats out of hell. It's the most freeing feeling I've had in a long time, and I already dread it coming to an end. I wish we could take this wonderful contraption all the way to Newcastle Upon Tyne instead of relying on Mina's goodwill, but I know Linus must have more pressing things to do than chauffeur two Lost strangers around Europe. He has souls to save, or confessions to listen to, or holy water to replace, I suppose. Where does one find holy water? I wonder. Do they dig for it beneath a holy stream, or do they turn ordinary water holy by mystical powers?

I content myself with the cheerful waves we get from people as we sail down the streets and the feeling of the wind combing through my hair, which is the nearest thing to a good brushing it has had in more days than I care to admit. I turn to the left and blow a kiss at Israel, who grins back.

"This is the best date!" I shout, but I can tell by his baffled expression that he can't make out the words. I imagine telling this part of our adventure to Joe. He'll be enthralled. It may even redeem my cooking and my lack of ninja skills. My heart skips a beat wondering if I'll ever see Joe again. I imagine myself telling this story, only it's me doing the driving.

Our ride is over far too soon. Before I know it, and really before my hands and arms can even relax around Linus' frame, he has parked us in front of a red telephone box. I climb stiffly off the motorcycle and pat it affectionately.

"What a marvelous contraption!" I say fondly.

Linus beams as if I've just complimented his first born babe. "Isn't she?" He agrees, running his hand through his windblown hair, which sticks straight up in meager little chunks. "You can see why I haven't been able to say farewell to it."

"I can, indeed. I hope you keep it forever; priestly duties be hanged."

He laughs heartily. "Well, what now my friends? Do I leave you in this telephone box, never to be seen again, or will I find you in my flock someday soon?"

"Stranger things have happened." I smile. "Thank you so much for your help. You've been wonderful."

"I certainly am not." He puts on the goggles I have just removed. "But thank you for thinking so. Israel." Linus takes his hand affectionately. "Take care of this young lady."

"I will, though she's rather difficult," Iz whispers loudly for my benefit. I sniff righteously and duck into the telephone box. I don't like drawn out goodbyes anyway, so I busy myself with the old fashioned telephone. In America, over a year ago for me, but of course eighty odd years in Linus' future, there were cell phones everywhere. I never had my own, but I played around a bit with my co-worker, Penny's once. My boss at the coffee shop, Micki, always griped about me not having a phone, but other than him, there was no one for me to call or text anyway. Penny's phone was pink and encrusted with fake and gaudy gemstones, but this phone is heavy and has the numbers in a circular wheel. I hear the clink before I see Linus' hand deposit money into it. I smile my gratitude. What would we have done without him?

Now to hope Mina Dobson proves to be just as accommodating and kind. I pick up the receiver.

A stiff, formal man named James answers my call, and I am in luck when he informs me that Miss Dobson is home. My stomach does odd flip flops and somersaults like it's full of moths, as I wait for her to come to the phone. I'm not exactly sure what I'm going to say, but I know it needs to be sincere and convincing, so that just adds to the pressure I feel about the whole conversation.

"Hello? This is Miss Dobson." Her voice is practical and crisp and businesslike, most likely because she expects me to be someone at the asylum. Dear old Agatha Helmes, perhaps, calling to ask if she would swing by to assist with a tangled strait jacket, or if she'd coax the woman in the hallway to come out for supper.

"Hello, this is Sonnet." I pause. Too long. I can practically hear Mina debate her options, hang up now or let curiosity win and hang up after I've explained? "Are you there?"

"Yes. What can I help you with, Miss Gray?"

"It's just Sonnet. I was hoping to appeal to you for help actually." Israel is mouthing something at me, and I shrug at him. *What?* I mouth back.

"You're sounding Scottish again," he whispers and smiles.

I roll my eyes and smooth out my speech. I don't know exactly what I sound like normally. Dad would probably be pegged as French, Prue was a crazy mixture and never settled on much of anything as far as accents go, Iz sounds mostly African with a British edge, and Luke has a bit of an Australian quip to his speech. Emme was always purely British, but she loved England so and most of her vocalizations were deliberate. She put on an English accent the same way she put on heels and lipstick.

"Yes? What is it?" Mina doesn't sound dismissing exactly, more like confused.

"Well, that is..." I stumble over my words and trail off. "I think it might be better if we could meet. Would that be permissible? It's just too much to tell over the telephone, I think. Could we come to you?"

"I could meet you at the hospital," she suggests.

At first I think she means the Royal Free Hospital which we have only just left, and I get a chill thinking she has known our whereabouts. A friend of Rose...but no. Quickly I realize she means Bedlam.

"Um, perhaps not there." Ever.

"My house then?"

"Yes, that would be fine. It's just—"

"Yes?" Now she does sound dismissive and a bit annoyed.

"Well, that is, I am without transportation at the moment." *And forever,* I add silently.

Mina Dobson is too well bred to sigh or gripe at me, but I can tell she probably wants to. "All right. I'll send a man for you. Address, please?"

I oblige, and we both hang up. I wipe my hands on my dress. They feel clammy from nerves and dirty from the public phone. "Well, that's that," I say with a forced cheerfulness. "She's sending someone to pick us up right now. How's your shoulder?"

Israel brushes away my question with one of his own. "Why didn't we bring along more currency? I don't like being so indebted to so many. It's irritating to not be able to provide for you, Sonny."

I make a silly face. "Are you going to beat on your chest next?"

"Very funny."

"Drag me by my hair to your cave?"

"Believe me. I've considered it on more than one occasion."

"Don't worry." I stand on my tiptoes and plant a chaste kiss on his cheek. "There will plenty of time for you to support me in the fashion I wish to become accustomed to. Until then, we're at the mercy of whomever, and whomever is dear Mina right now."

"How much are you going to tell her?" Israel kisses me back, but his is far less chaste, and I get that familiar tingle of happy anticipation in my stomach. The butterflies come back in a swarm.

"What?"

Iz repeats his question, looking indeed like a smug caveman at the stupor his lips have put me in.

"Not a thing," I reply airily, "until I figure out how much she knows already. Oh, fabulous!" I scowl in disbelief at the Rolls-Royce that has pulled up next to us. Then the window rolls down, and Luke grins at us.

"You rang?" he asks innocently.

"I was expecting the butler, not the lackey." I glare harder and refuse to budge, though the butter seats sound like they're calling me.

"Ouch! I am not Mina's lackey. I'm her friend. Now hop in. It's about to rain. Don't want Rhode's shoulder getting all goopy and weepy, do we?" Luke reaches across the seats and opens the door.

I turn and look to Israel. He looks flushed and aggravated, but not particularly surprised. Luke has become our own personal cat we can't get rid of. Fed him once, and now he won't leave. I petulantly kick the car door closed again. "Well?" I ask Iz. "What do you think?"

He uses his good side to reach up with his hand and wipe his face from the eyes down to the chin. His eyes stay closed for a moment as he thinks. He always does that smoothing out, wiping motion when he's thinking, usually right before he starts a surgery, especially if it's life threatening.

Which this decision just might be.

"What the hell," he mutters. "Might as well keep our friends close and our enemies closer." He opens the door once again.

"We have friends?" I mutter back, and we both get in the car.

The butter seats welcome me back with a gentle embrace. I am completely and utterly swayed by leather and can be bought with butter, it seems.

Chapter 22

It is at least two hours later, and we are still in the very precarious act of convincing Mina that time traveling is possible. Though she knows of Rose (not to mention Lizzie) and the oddness within her, she is skeptical of the rest. It's been a few minutes since I've tried explaining it the last time, and she continues to stare at me as though she'd like to bundle me up and take me to work with her as their newest inmate. Do they still use a cart to transport the lunatics?

"I know, it sounds crazy." I rub my tired eyes. "Maybe someday it will be commonplace and well known."

"Someday? Haven't you been to…" she struggles to get out the words, "to the future?"

"Well, um, yes."

"And is it commonplace and well known?"

"No, no… it isn't."

Mina sips on her beverage slowly. She had offered us something called a Gibson when we arrived, and Israel and I had declined, while Luke helped himself. Now I'm regretting my lack of imbibing. I'd even drink a bit of scotch if it were offered, I think, minus the chloral hydrate drops, of course.

"Someday they'll figure out it's only a matter of physics and science," Israel interjects. "Maybe it won't even be such a mysterious thing. People will look back and marvel that it took so long to discover and harness."

Mina responds with silence. She is definitely not coming around to our way of thinking. In fact, she looks as though she is going to summon James to turn us out on our ears as soon as she finishes her second Gibson. She swirls the contents of her glass and watches me.

"Luke, please tell her." I turn to my former friend. He pops a pearl onion in his mouth from the depths of his glass and regards me soberly.

"He may have a concussion from when he fell to the ground the other night." Luke addresses Mina. "Though that doesn't explain her." He moves his eyes in my direction. I want to stab him with his tiny onion pick.

"Luke." I speak as though I am talking to Joe, and he has just been caught doing something ridiculously naughty. "I swear by all that is holy, I am going to–"

"Just messing with you, Gray." He laughs. "I can't resist listening to you explain the particulars of time and space, is all. I especially liked the part about wormholes and folding space. It was H.G. Wells worthy."

"Oh, shut up."

Israel groans and rolls his sore shoulder, wincing. "We need to change this dressing, Sonny." I note, with alarm, a bright dot of red on his formally spotless white shirt. I move closer. "Can we have some privacy, Miss Dobson?"

She nods curtly and motions to Luke to follow her. She probably wants a word with him as much as we want to be left alone. They exit the luxurious sitting room that James, the butler, had shown us into hours before. I take out the roll of gauze that I had tucked into my pocket from the hospital and shake it out. "Off you go with that shirt," I say lightly. I'm worried about him. I hadn't expected the wound to start acting up so quickly, and I hadn't thought I'd need to change the dressing so soon. Israel unbuttons it, and I help him pull it off his shoulder. It sticks a tiny bit, and I remember my grandmother. Another twist of hatred in my gut for Luke Dawes appears like a cancer. I work quickly, un-bandaging the jagged scars.

"You'll need to clean it," Iz instructs. "The last thing we need is infection. The doc stitched me up alright, but still. Things aren't completely closed up yet."

"You think?" I mutter wiping away fresh blood. I am gentle, more gentle than my mood wants me to be, around the black threads of his stitches. "Stitches look nicer on you than they would on me." I smile, admiring the way the threads nearly disappear into his dark skin. "I would look like Frankenstein."

He laughs. "I'll remember to use the palest pink thread possible if you ever need stitches," he promises.

"What should I use to clean it?" I look around.

"That gin will do."

"Ick. Really?"

"Yes, it will work fine, though it will sting a bit, and I might cry like a little girl, so please avert your eyes."

"Okay. Here goes." I hover the shiny, silver cocktail shaker over his wound and bite my lip. That gives me an idea. "Do you want something to bite on?"

"I'm not in labor, Sonny."

"Just a thought." I hover the shaker and then right it again. "With or without onions?" I giggle a little wildly.

"Oh, for crying out loud, just pour!"

"Shaken or stirred?"

"Sonny!" he bellows.

Pour I do, or dribble really. The potent liquor runs merrily along his skin. It's probably my imagination, but it sounds like it sizzles, like his skin is slurping it up, but it's fighting back and scorching him. Israel gasps, but swallows any other sounds back. "Very manly," I whisper, and kiss his scar softly. I lick my lips. "Ugh. I don't think I like gin. I've had more alcohol in the past two days than I have my whole life."

"Party girl," he wheezes.

"I know." I dab his shoulder lightly with a napkin. When that's done, I use the gauze and wrap his shoulder back up like a Christmas gift, then help him back on with his shirt. "Think Luke has convinced Mina yet?"

"Let's ask, shall we?" Iz stands and offers me his hand. I take it like he's a prince asking me to dance.

Luke has convinced Mina, and I don't know why I'm surprised. He's always been a con artist, and with his handsome face and winsome ways, he could sell anyone anything. Mina looks a bit ashen around the edges, a tad pale, but otherwise normal. She's a pretty girl, with more bravado than most, if her relationship with my sister is any indication. Just when my thoughts shift to Rose, as they inevitably do, Luke begins to worry about her whereabouts.

"I'd love to stay and chat longer," he says shrugging himself into his suit coat, "but I really need to figure out where my wife is."

I still stay mum on the subject of having seen her last. Luke doesn't seem overly anxious, and I know he lets her go where she pleases for the most part. I assume he'll check Bedlam first anyway. We haven't even spoken of Israel's stabbing, but I don't much see the point of confronting Luke about it, so I continue with my silence. I certainly don't need to delay him. In fact, I'd love for him to leave.

Leave he does, kissing Mina affectionately on the cheek before doing so. When he's gone, there is awkward quiet, and the three of us don't quite know what to do with ourselves. At last Mina speaks.

"So, Newcastle Upon Tyne," she says flatly. "What good will this scientist do us?"

"I'm not entirely sure it will do any good at all," Iz replies. He is sitting in a way that looks uncomfortable and precarious in a fancy, delicate chair. "But I don't have any other ideas, I'm afraid. I'd really like to give the information we have to Bartoli and then hear what he has to say about the whole thing."

"And this Bartoli gentleman? He's one of your… kind? A Lost person, I mean?" Mina's upper crust British accent is sounding a little frayed around the edges, like she's a sweater we've been slowly unraveling.

"Yes. We met him in 2012," I interject. I am met with an unblinking gaze. She's still having trouble believing the story, it seems. I wish people were more apt to believe in things like fairy tales, unicorns, evil spirits, and time traveling… Why must everyone be so darn practical? It would save so much time and so much breath.

Then again, I have a hard time believing it myself, and I know one of those marvels exists. "He's older now," I continue to explain. "His life hasn't paralleled with ours exactly, if that makes any sense." I can see by her face that it does not. "Well, anyway, that isn't important. What is important is hearing what he has to say about it all. The science behind our journeys and what he thinks about the effects of our abilities most of all."

"You think controlling it is part of why Rose is insane?" Mina asks bluntly.

I'm surprised by the question. I would have thought Rose's only friend would be more defensive of her mental health. "I don't know," I say, honestly. "Our father says she was always this way, even as a little girl, before she ever traveled at all, much less controlled it. But having experienced it a little," I glance sideways at Iz, "I think I can safely say it doesn't help her sanity, and yes, it most likely makes it worse."

Mina fingers her empty glass carefully. She runs her pinky around the rim, and it's so quiet in the room that I can hear the soft humming of music it makes. She looks at me finally. "So, you're doing this for her?" It's a challenge, a gauntlet thrown. She is daring me to disagree.

I frown. Lies come easily to me, yet not this one. "Not precisely. That is, if the information can help her, I certainly won't keep it from her or you. Frankly, I need to know for myself, too. I think–" I pause, delicately, not sure how to proceed. "I think Rose is too far gone to help honestly."

"I disagree." Mina tosses her head defiantly. "You didn't know Lizzie."

"No. I suppose I didn't. What was she like?" Does she want to talk about her, reminisce? Wax sentimental over someone who didn't properly exist in the first place? It seems odd, bizarre even, but I can grant her that if she needs it, if it means she'll help us get to Newcastle Upon Tyne.

"She was funny, spunky, witty, pretty, strong... a lot like you seem to be actually." Mina's words seem to surprise her, but not half as much as they surprise me. "I'm not insulting you." She must read the look on my face accurately, and she sighs impatiently, as if it's irritating that I don't understand. "It's a compliment."

"Oh," I respond weakly. It hadn't felt like a compliment, though it would be hard to articulate why not. I'd rather be compared to someone else, anyone else. "Did you know her before she became Lizzie?" What a crazy thing to say. It sticks in my craw a bit.

"Yes, but we weren't really friends. More patient and nurse. She was there one day when I came to work..." Mina trails off for a moment, thinking. "I suppose she must have woken there after a time traveling spell? I didn't realize that at the time, of course. Luke must have paved the way with some sort of story.

Anyway, she was pitching a god-awful fit. None of the other nurses would go near her, except Miss Helmes, and even she was nervous. Rose would be meek and mild one minute and then fly off the handle the next. Luke would come close to taking her out, say he could handle her on his own, but then she'd act up again, and even he couldn't be around her."

"What did you see in her that made you think there was something worth befriending?" I am curious now, I have to admit. I almost wish I had been a fly on the wall during that time – almost.

Mina thinks for a moment. "She just seemed so sad and so lost, especially when she thought no one was looking. I knew she had a sweet tooth, so I would bring her bits of cakes and biscuits, talk to her like she was human, you know? She didn't like me, but she didn't hate me as much as she did the others. One girl she pinned to the wall with scissors."

I shudder. "Lovely."

Mina looks at me as though my answer has disappointed her. "You don't understand. She'll be washing that wall until the day she dies. Even when she doesn't remember why, she still feels a compulsion to wash it. That's why I think there's something deep inside worth saving. I know it!" She is vehement. The green and gold in her eyes seem to flash with righteous anger.

Israel, as usual, has been silent during this time. He has moved from the uncomfortable, feminine chair, to the floor, and his long legs are folded up like the legs of the chair he broke over Luke's nose. "She might have a better chance in a better time," he says, cautiously. "If we could move her…"

The look on my face must be audible because he trails off, and they both glance at me expectantly. I can hardly believe he's suggesting such a thing. The doctor in him must be overriding the man in him. "I think not!" I squeak. I clear my throat. "I'd rather not take her anywhere. Iz, just what are you suggesting exactly?"

Iz appears embarrassed. "Nothing. I just meant there are better medicines, better care, more understanding of mental health in more modern times, for the most part. I didn't mean we should personally escort her there. That is, I don't know what I mean," he finishes, lamely. If I didn't know better, I'd think he was blushing. Yes, there is definitely a pink to his dark cheeks.

"Aren't you the man who didn't want me messing with traveling not five minutes ago, much less take Rose Gray, of all people, with me? Have you suffered a concussion after all?" I stare at my not-husband and seem to have lost the ability to blink.

Iz swallows and has the decency to look embarrassed. "No, no, you're right. You're right, Sonny. I was only thinking out loud."

"Well, don't." I frown.

"I'm not allowed to have ideas?"

"Not stupid ones."

Mina breaks our little argument with a giggle. "Sorry." She covers her mouth with her hand. "It's just a funny thing to be having a row about, isn't it?"

Iz smiles and chuckles. I continue to glare. Evidently, everyone in creation has lost their ever loving mind, and I am the only sane person in this awful city.

I hate London.

Chapter 23

Mina excuses herself then to go smuggle a midnight snack up to her little sister, a girl she calls Amy. I think she's mostly giving Israel and me a chance to talk, since it almost looked as though we were about to have a heated discussion right there in her study. Rich, polite society probably wouldn't approve or engage in such nonsense.

"If my mother comes through, pretend you are from the Orphan's Aid Society and try to look businesslike, would you?" With those odd words, she disappears.

Iz sits up straighter, and I tuck my wayward hair behind my ears. It's as businesslike as the two of us can look, a pretty sad attempt, but it's all we've got. I'm suddenly completely exhausted. I hadn't slept very well at the hospital, curled up in a chair next to Iz, and I imagine the beds and pillows in Mina's small mansion must be awfully nice. My bones give a complaining sort of creak as I roll my shoulders and stifle a yawn.

"I only meant..." Iz begins to explain, but I wave it away.

"Forget it. I know you're a doctor and that pesky creed of yours gets in the way of common sense sometimes."

"Which creed is that?" He looks amused.

"You know the first do unto others what you'd have them do to you, all while not doing any harm to the birds and the bees and the flowers and the trees, or something noble like that. I should have thought about that before I brought you. Here I thought you'd be telling me, 'Sonny, stay away from her!' and instead you're encouraging sister bonding time. Just when I thought I knew you." I scowl, but it's a playful one, for the most part.

Israel shakes his head. "I just don't like seeing anyone suffer, even Rose. While nothing can fix her or cure her, I'd hate to see her go back in time to a really bad era for mental health – manacles on the floor and lobotomies and the like."

"And you were thinking to… what? Anchor her somewhere, sans manacles of course? Or maybe head over to the future and get her a lifetime supply of mind altering prescriptions?" I'm curious, I'll give him that.

He sighs. "I don't know. You're right. Let's drop it. We're both beat, and we'll have the whole drive to Newcastle Upon Tyne to talk it over."

"Mina still hasn't promised to help us," I remind him.

"I'll help," Mina enters the study again. Her arms are full of what look like clothes. "But you have to promise me something in return."

"You'll have to tell me what it is first," I reply. I know that prerequisite from Joe. Never agree to anything without knowing what it is first.

Mina hands me the pile. A pretty bottle green silk shirt slinks to the ground and puddles endearingly at my feet. "If you find out something that could help Rose, come back and tell us, and if you want to, you could read this."

I stare at the small journals, that are atop the stack of clothes. Red leather, they look antique, and I know in their own way, they are. As old as my sister anyway, and like any Lost person, she has lived several lives. Rose's name is printed on the first page when I flip it open. My heart does a little flip as well, and I frown. "Whatever for?"

"There might be something helpful inside somewhere. At least you can get to know your sister better, understand her a bit more. Don't you think? If not, I understand." Her voice clearly states otherwise and I know she is only being polite. She doesn't understand why I don't want to be privy to Rose's strange thoughts and writings and innermost desires, but I nod curtly.

"I'll try," I promise.

"And the other thing?"

I pause a moment. What choice do I have really? I can't hitchhike to Italy or ride the rails like the heroine in a child's novel, and I certainly can't steal Rolls-Royces the way Luke can. "All right. I promise."

"Good! Then I'll arrange a car for you."

"Without your last driver?" I respond drily. Luke is the last person I want to road trip to Italy with.

"Yes. Sorry about that. He insisted. I'll let you do your own driving."

I turn to Iz and widen my eyes in delight. He narrows his suspiciously at me. "She means me," he corrects.

"That's not what I heard," I say airily. "Besides, we don't want that shoulder moving around too much, do we? Don't want to pull your stitches out with all that steering. It's best that you stay in the passenger seat and look pretty."

"You're incorrigible," he growls. Growling again. I feel like a zoo keeper, not a girlfriend.

"Come along." Mina motions towards the hallway. "I'll show you to your rooms. James made them up for you, and you should be comfortable."

It's with a grateful sigh that I tumble into a wonderful bed in a room across from Israel. Evidently, we weren't fooling her with our pseudo marriage, or perhaps Luke had clued her in. Feeling more confident than I have in weeks, I still lock both the door and the window before falling asleep. Being a friend of Rose and Luke's, I trust Mina about as far as I can throw her.

*   *   *

I sleep in later than normal and would have slept longer, but Israel knocks loudly on my door. When I open it, he gives me a sheepish smile and says he is wide awake and can't possibly fall back asleep. Another irritating issue of being Lost. I mumble an incomprehensible reply and shut the door again. I hope James serves hot coffee. That's what butlers do, isn't it?

Yawning mightily, I sit back down on the comfortable bed and reach for the pile of clothes that Mina had provided last night. I pull out the bottle green blouse and pair it with a striped skirt. Since the stripes are the same color, it seems obvious, but I still feel a bit of anxiety thinking of Mina's reaction. I never put together outfits the right way, it seems. Still, everything fits well enough, and I have to admit to myself that the fabric and cut seems to be a higher quality than the plaid dress I had stolen off the line; I smooth it all out, finger comb my dreadfully tangled hair, splash some cold water on my face from the pitcher on my nightstand, step back into my shoes, and go in search of coffee. My mind wanders to the lovely imaginings of a toffee crème breve and maybe a croissant. Do they make croissants in England, or should I be conjuring up a scone or something decidedly more British? I'm distracted and nearly run into Luke's broad chest as I round a corner.

"Whoa there! Good morning to you, too, darling. I wasn't expecting a hug first thing in the morning." He steadies me by the shoulders, and it's all I can do not to slap him silly.

"Let me go. I need coffee. Why are you here?" I sound about as welcoming as I feel that is to say, not at all.

"Yes, ma'am, and I'll get you some. I'm here because..." Luke trails off and appears to be thinking. "Well, I don't have many other places to go, do I? My life is a bit dull at the moment."

I yawn again and continue walking. "Out of murderous energy, are we? Poor thing. I'll get my own coffee, thanks. You'd probably put strychnine in it instead of sugar. Where's Rose?"

He doesn't answer, and though I don't particularly want to, I look back. Luke is still standing in the corridor, and he looks a little troubled. He also looks like he slept in his clothes last night, either that, or he hasn't been to bed yet at all. He rubs his scruffy chin thoughtfully. A piece of sandy-colored hair has escaped the tie at the nape of his neck, and I have to stifle the urge to tuck it back where it belongs. Something about Luke Dawes brings out the mother hen in me sometimes, and it's maddening.

"I'm not sure."

I frown. "You haven't seen her for, what, two days now? Is that odd? Odd for her, I mean? Well, she's always odd, but odd even by her standards?"

Luke narrows his eyes at me, disapprovingly. "No need to stoop to insults, Gray."

I leave it alone and continue to follow my nose to breakfast. I smell bacon. He hurries to catch up with me.

"Mina told me about your promise to keep us clued in with ol' Bar."

"So?"

"So, I'm just making conversation is all. I'm worried and talking helps me keep my mind off things."

I sigh. "You never did answer my question. Is it really this strange for her to disappear so long?"

"She comes and goes. Sometimes she takes me with her. Sometimes she wanders off and sleeps far enough from me that I can't go. I respect that she needs her space. That's normal in relationships, isn't it?"

I'd like to offer a sarcastic laugh or quip, but he sounds so forlorn I stop myself. "I suppose in a way, sure. You checked the hospital, naturally?"

"First thing. She isn't there."

I nibble on my bottom lip, contemplating. She should have been there. I was there, and we would have traveled together that night after leaving France. After all, I was too out of sorts to steer myself anywhere. The only reason I ended up at Bedlam was because that's the anchor that brings Rose back. Isn't it?

"Hey." Luke reaches out and grasps my elbow, making me stop walking right before we reach the dining room. "I know that look. What are you not telling me?"

"Nothing! Let me go." I shove him with a force that is half what I really feel and enter the room.

* * *

"We're totally going to be pulled over and arrested for stealing this, you know," I grumble, as we pull away from the Dobson's lovely mansion later. We are in Luke's stolen Rolls-Royce Phantom, and even the butter seats can't relax me. Plus, Israel has insisted on driving, even with his weepy wound, so I'm doubly in a bad mood.

"Most likely," Iz agrees, "but since Mrs. Dobson didn't buy the whole Orphan's Aid Society story, this will have to do. Just try to look...inconspicuous and innocent."

"Whatever." I glower and sink down into the seats. "Can I please drive at the halfway mark?"

Iz ignores my request and points at the two diaries on my lap. "Don't you have some homework to do?"

"No. Don't want to."

"That's mature."

"Yo mama is mature."

In spite of himself, Iz laughs. "Just try. You did promise, and moral integrity is what separates the Roses from the Sonnets."

"Ha ha. Fine." I open the little red journal. "*Death came to me in a cornflower blue dress*," I read. I shiver, and abruptly shut it once more. "No, thanks. Not happening."

"Alright then, grumpy. Reach behind you."

After a moment of suspicion, I do, and my fingers feel something wooden. I turn around and peer behind my butter seat. It's a guitar.

"Israel Rhode!" I squeal. I really do squeal. I clap my hands over my mouth, and then on second thought use them to carefully lift the instrument into the front seat. "It's beautiful!"

Iz shrugs, but I know my reaction has pleased him. "Well, cars these days don't come equipped with music, so I thought you could make us some."

I settle myself in, guitar across my lap, and begin to strum. It sounds beautiful to my music starved ears. The strings bite into my soft fingertips with a delicious sort of sting. "It isn't stolen, is it?" I ask, anxiously.

Iz chuckles. "No, it belongs to Mina. She has an entire conservatory. I wandered into it when I was looking for bacon and eggs, and when I mentioned borrowing it for our little road trip here, she said it would be fine."

"Requests?"

"Surprise me."

I start off slowly, my fingers unused to the feel of strings again, my voice low and hesitant. Eventually, I settle into a rhythm of all my old favorites. Back when I used to work at the coffee shop as a barista during the day, I would play songs on our talent shows at night. My feet propped up on the Rolls' dashboard, I play and sing and forget my troubles. I even miss the halfway to Newcastle Upon Tyne mark, and Israel stays behind the wheel after all.

"I wanted to get you one in Africa," he tells me when I take a break to rub my sore fingers, "but they were hard to come by, and I couldn't quite figure out how to make one."

"You mean you didn't whittle me a guitar from a bush willow tree? Here I thought you loved me." I pretend to scoff. He just smiles at me and rolls his shoulder as if he's uncomfortable.

"Are you all right?" I set the beloved guitar in the backseat once again and move closer to him. "Is it seeping?"

"No, no, it's fine. Don't fuss. We're nearly there. Let me see your efficient secretary impersonation, if you please."

"I do not please, not until I see your wack scientist impression."

Iz laughs again. "Wack?"

"I picked up some things in the future, too," I say proudly. "That, my dear ignoramus, is a popular slang term."

"What does it mean?"

"I'm not entirely sure. I think it's a derivative of 'whacky,' from the Latin 'whackadoo.'"

"Whackadoo?" He laughs harder. I'm just proud to know something modern that he doesn't, so I let him laugh.

"Yes, whackadoo, and you're just distracting me from your infected wound and the fact that you haven't let me drive yet," I point out.

"It isn't infected so stop overreacting, and you can drive a bit in a while, I promise. Right now I need you to navigate. I think I took a wrong turn at that last wooly sheep."

So I do, and before I know it, we've reached Bartoli's address in Newcastle Upon Tyne.

Chapter 24

Bar is old, that's the first thing I see, of course. I saw that in his photograph, but still it comes as a bit of a shock. Now we know for sure that the Lost's timelines don't coincide with one another's. My head is already swimming with unanswered questions and paradoxes, and we haven't even started our conversation yet.

It takes him time to remember us, and when I feel a bit hurt, I squelch the feeling, after all, to him it's been a half century since he's seen us last. For Israel and me, it's only been a year and a bit.

His place of residence is the back room of a gentle, sloping English cottage, and from what I can gather, the lady of the house is some sort of distant relative to him. A cousin or a granddaughter, I assumed at first, but the young woman is old Bar's great grandmother. She can't be a day over thirty though, with a boisterous voice, and an apron dusted with flour. Evidently, she has a busy schedule, since she disappeared out the back door a few moments after seeing us settled with Bar and a pot of tea.

"I'm sorry, whose grandmother is she?" I ask confused.

Bar and Iz just chuckle at me, and I realize I'm already dead in the water as far as understanding the Lost goes. I consider absconding with the whole plate of cookies and just settling in with one of the old books that are strewn about the place, but on second glance they all seem to be textbooks and scientific publications, so I just stick with the cookies and my thoughts. I munch thoughtfully and attempt to follow the conversation. At first, we have the inevitable pleasantries to get over with, but Bar, naturally, is more intrigued with the description of my sister and her capabilities than he is with niceties and how-do-you-dos. Before long we are down to the nitty-gritty of why we have sought him out.

"I have never met anyone with the skills to steer their course," he tells me thoughtfully. His crinkly eyes are lit up from within, and he rubs his hands together. "This is extraordinary, a monumental milestone, to be sure!" His English is much improved since the last time we were together, and I'm glad to not be speaking Italian, which is a bit rusty at the moment from disuse.

Israel looks proud of me, but I don't feel particularly cocky myself. What good is my power if I can't change anything? I ask as much.

Bar stirs his cold tea, thoughtfully. "My dear, there is more to your life than correcting others' mistakes."

I frown. "But it all seems so pointless!"

"I don't understand." Bar frowns right back, his white mustache pointing downwards. "You have been given a great gift from the universe. You are not pleased?"

I feel like shouting or having a temper tantrum, but I settle for a shrug and reach for another cookie. I crave sugar when I'm feeling stressed, a disposition I blame on Joe's influence. We used to suck on sugarcane instead of taking naps in Nairobi. "I just wonder why I can do it if I can't change anything. It's all a depressing pile of poo if you ask me."

The old man smiles. "You can't change history, dear, because you haven't already changed it."

"Excuse me?" I drop some crumbs down the front of my green silk blouse and hastily brush them off. I don't need Mina's condemnation on top of everything else.

Patiently, Bar continues. "You can't change your history with your family because going back and changing it successfully would remove your motivation for going back and changing it in the first place. Thus, you'd never go back."

I try to look polite and intelligent, but I ruin the image by taking the last cookie and stuffing the entire thing into my mouth. I attempt to talk around it, but Bar has already turned his attention back to Israel.

"You understand?" he asks, eagerly. "It's what I've been saying for years. It's all about the impetus to change history in the first place!"

"I get it," Iz answers thoughtfully, and I glare at him. "If you can be successful at altering things, then your incentive to alter them would be taken away, and then you would never go back to alter them to begin with. I see."

I don't completely, but in a way, it's beginning to make a sort of sense. Hallelujah, I can be taught. "Wait. I think I'm understanding it now. If I could, say, help get Rose to sleep that night we left her behind and was successful at it, then our whole history would be changed, and there would be no reason for me to go back to that night to begin with. Yes?"

"Yes, something like that." Iz agrees. "But sir, what about changing one path at a time?"

"A divergent timeline?" Bar asks.

"A what, now?" I pipe up. "I'm just now getting the hang of the first suggestion."

Bar waves his hand. "I don't subscribe to the theory of alternate universes. There are some at the university who support that thought, but they are considered crazier than me. Two or more paths for each Lost? A dozen, a hundred, perhaps thousands of Bartoli Guilani's running through time, each on their own path, each making their own futures? No."

I'm not so sure. I was there and saw two Roses with my own eyes. I nearly saw myself, truth be told, though I was just a small lump in the blanket next to the hearth. "What if you're wrong? What if there are other versions of us?"

Bar grimaces at his cold tea and sets his cup down on the floor. Without warning, out of nowhere and nearly instantly, a large mass of fur is upon it.

"You have a dog!" I exclaim, and lower myself to my knees to see the pile of fur better. "I thought he was a rug!"

Bar chuckles. "Yes, Einstein does a wonderful rug impression, doesn't he? But he will stir himself for a spot of sweet tea."

I reach out and pat Einstein affectionately. "I'm so jealous you've found a way to keep a dog." I try to keep the wistfulness out of my voice, but it creeps in anyway.

"Well, it's unkind in a way, but I always seem to adopt a canine companion wherever I go. The inevitable leaving behind is something I never get over, and Einstein here will be the cruelest sort of loss. I've already made sure my neighbors here love him, so I'm quite sure he won't mourn me long. Besides–" Bar reaches down and rubs the sheepdog's ears. "I'm getting quite old and decrepit. Perhaps I'm done with traveling and can live out my life here with Einstein." The dog wags his tail in reply. The tea slurped up, he moves back to his spot behind Bar's chair.

"Can't you give him something? You know, a potion or something that turns pets into Lost animals?"

Bar chuckles again. Evidently, I'm the funniest thing he's seen all day. "I haven't stumbled upon that recipe yet, no."

I sigh. I would so like a dog to accompany me through life, or a cat, hamster, or a frog. Or a guitar. Or an espresso machine. I stare into my tea, pensively.

"We thought you'd be much harder to get an audience with," Iz tells Bar. "We were concocting cover stories about our identities."

"Were you?" Bar smiles. "I'm not really a celebrity, children. I had some fame in my time, of course, and I've rubbed shoulders with some who are truly geniuses. Hence, Einstein's namesake, of course."

"Name dropping, I see." I laugh.

"Crass, I know. It was Albert's Theory of General Relativity published in 1915 that started me on my journey of time traveling. Naturally, I have a bit of an edge myself, knowing that it's possible to begin with, seeing as how I've been doing it all my life."

"Did he believe you?" I ask curiously.

"Albert? Oh, it's difficult to tell. He was intrigued, and we had many interesting discussions. He didn't disbelieve, that's certain."

"I'm sure you were inspiring to him, as well, sir. Was it him who convinced you of the theory of impetus we were talking of earlier?" Iz inquires.

"No, no." He seems surprised that we don't know this. Surprised and disappointed. "That is part of Novikov's Self-Consistency Principal. That one didn't come along until the 1980s, I believe."

"Ah, yes, of course there is that." I long for another cookie.

"Novikov's theory is, naturally, that it is impossible to create time paradoxes at all," Bar continues.

"How many theories are there? Plausible ones, I mean?" Iz asks.

Bar settles himself deeper into his chair as he thinks. "Too many. Let's concentrate on the effects it's having on your sister, though. That's an area I haven't studied much. After all, the rest of us seem to be shouldering the effects well enough."

"We believe Rose was insane before, and their grandmother before them was also..." Iz pauses, delicately looking at me. I smile, in a wobbly sort of fashion. "...committed for psychosis. It's possible that the power they hold only makes things worse, not causes it, or is simply a coincidence completely."

"Possibly." Bar rubs his bearded chin, deep in thought. "Or the madness *is* the power."

"But I can do it." I object. *I'm not mad! Am I?*

"Coincidence then." Bar smiles grimly. "I'm sure of it."

I'm not, and I nibble on my lower lip, peeling back the skin with my teeth until I taste blood. "I wasn't sick when I caused our journey here, only the one to France, and it was nearly unbearable." I tell as much as I can, hoping that Bar will save me should Iz decide to go berserk since it's the first he's heard the whole story.

"I would assume that would be because you were too close to yourself, to yourself as a child. Being in two places at once that can't be healthy for anyone." Bar assures me.

"Yes, I suppose that must be it." I'm relieved, because if it's only that, I can avoid it and still use my abilities to steer my course, namely back to Africa, and possibly back to Emme or my mother, though so far, my mind flips a switch inside my head when I think about those ideas. I don't think I can change anything, and I can't bear to lose them both over and over again. "Since Rose has gone back there so many times, it makes sense that she is getting worse with each one while simultaneously being able to withstand the ill feelings. There's one more thing we haven't told you though. Rose loses her ability when the madness gets to be too much."

"That's not shocking. We've known the sickly don't travel like the rest of us do," Bar reminds me.

"I suppose," I agree slowly, "but it keeps her husband up at night, figuratively speaking, of course."

"I don't wonder. Well, for better and for worse. Some marriages have more worse than others." Bar stares off into the distance, and I remember how he accidentally left behind his wife in a concentration camp. I know I should ask his story, the ending, the middle, and the fate of his wife, but I can't. I'm too cowardly. My eyes are already filling with salty tears, and he hasn't even mentioned her yet. Was she too...sickly to travel, too? Their children? Were there children? I don't want to know.

"I'm going to refill the pot," I say and stand. Grabbing the teapot and the empty plate where once had been cookies. I scramble for the kitchen, hating myself all the way. I linger in there, in Bar's great grandmother's kitchen, boiling water, opening and shutting cupboards, and hoping against hope that I will miss the conversation I don't want to have. They can talk of Nazis and death and loneliness and madness and whether or not I'm heading in the same direction as my sister and my grandmother while I hide like a baby. I can't help it.

Einstein wanders in after me, probably eager for more tea, and I plop down on the tiled floor and scratch behind his ears. "Oh, to be a dog," I tell him, staring into his soulful brown eyes. He blinks, as if he understands. As if he's saying, *Yes, being a dog is the thing to be, much better by far than a confused, lost girl.*

I am lost. Always and forever Lost and lost, in every sense of the word. I sit down, cross-legged on the cottage floor, scratch Einstein's belly and ears, and tell him all the things I couldn't say to everyone else. I tell him that my sister is mad, and I'm afraid I'm heading that way myself, and that this responsibility is making me sick. I say I'm scared to marry Israel and scared that I will never see my father again. The sheepdog seems to understand, and I know he'll keep my secrets, although in a way, I wish he wouldn't. I wish he could say the things I can't.

Depressed, with a stomachache brought on by too many sugar-filled treats, I eventually make my way back to Bar and Iz with fresh tea. My new, furry friend keeping pace with me until he leaves my side for his spot on the floor. I feel his abandonment of me, and I know it's silly because he was only my dog for a few stolen minutes in the kitchen. The cracks in my heart, like caverns inside me, widen just a little bit, and I worry sometimes that I will tumble through.

Chapter 25

We have been at Bar's several hours when it begins to dawn on me how valuable a commodity I am to the Lost, indeed, to all of mankind when you think of it. At first, our old friend speaks of finding answers, traveling to places and eras where he can be the most useful, and then gradually, slowly, he replaces these scenarios of himself with me. I break into his next sentence, boldly.

"I am not some sort of super hero," I object. "Even if I could get to these places, we've already established that I can't change anything." I rearrange myself on the floral couch and take my aggression out on a needlepoint pillow. I fluff it up with more passion than is strictly necessary.

"He's not talking about killing Stalin or stopping bombs or curing plagues, Sonny. He's talking about research. Genes, DNA, codes, things like that." Iz smiles at me.

I had momentary flashes of myself saving people in the nick of time, lifting cars off of innocent pedestrians, halting planes full of villains and the like, so I smile back. "Whew. I was beginning to think we were heading to the roof for flying lessons next, in my cape and tights. The fact remains that I'm not a spy or a scientist."

"I know." Bar looks genuinely remorseful at those facts. "You were right all along, my dear. You can't change history, but I can't help being intrigued by the idea of being able to go further along in the future then I have ever been. When we met in the twenty-first century, that was the furthest I had ever been, and I had not yet begun my quest for answers concerning time and space. I wasted my time." Bar appears irritated with his twenty-something self.

"You did have other things on your mind," I remind him gently.

"Of course."

"How long did you stay? And," my voice gets soft, asking the question I had been wanting to ask since I had arrived hours ago, "when you left, did Harry and Matthias travel with you?"

"Ah, Harry and Matthias!" Bar claps his hands like a little boy in delight, remembering. "I had nearly forgotten those two scamps! Yes, yes, we traveled together for at least another, oh, three journeys or so, I do believe. When I was about forty years of age, I had to take a train cross country for work falling trees, you see. This would have been, ah, in the 1930s, I think. Just like now!" Bar chuckles. "Time is such funny, funny stuff."

"Yes, it's absolutely hilarious." I punch the pillow again.

"Anyway, I was in New York, working at a bagel shop for a Jewish family, but I heard about the jobs in Oregon. I think we all knew it would be the last time we'd see one another. Matthias and Harry stayed behind in New York, they would have been in their eighties by then. After a month or so in Oregon or was it Washington? I don't recall, I woke a couple hundred years in the past. I have no idea if they ever traveled again or if they lived the rest of their lives there." Bar steeples his old fingers together and rests his whiskered chin on them, remembering.

I smile, thinking of the boys, as we always referred to them. They were funny, energetic old men, lovers of television, especially game shows, and always looking out for others, first me, then Bar.

"They should make rest homes for the elderly Lost," Iz says with humor, "someplace to live out the end in style. Reminiscing with everyone else. Can you imagine the stories?"

"And the one-upping?" I add. "The fish tales would be extreme."

"Are you saying old people tell tales?" Bar pretend to look ferocious but succeeds only in looking like a mildly upset Santa Claus.

"Only when their mouths are moving." I wink at him.

"Let's get back to Sonny wearing tights," Iz suggests.

I toss the pillow at his head. "Let's get back to being serious. What about DNA and genes and all that, Bar? Do you think our answers lie there?"

To my surprise, Bar shrugs. "Your guess is as good as mine, I'm afraid. I have yet to concoct a theory as to why the Lost are the way they are, a faulty gene, a quirky chromosome, or an act of God?"

"The work of aliens?" Iz interrupts.

"Believe me, I've thought of that and have yet to discount it." Bar's eyes twinkle. "Not of this world we could be…"

"I didn't mean *we* were the aliens." Iz hurries to clear this up. "I meant well, I don't know what I meant."

I roll my eyes. "While you guys are keeping your eyes on the skies, I'm going to take a bath. Is that okay, Bar? It's been well, entirely too long. You don't need the sordid details."

"Of course, my dear, take your time! Israel and I will save the planet while you are away and fill you in with the details later." Bar smiles fondly, and I kiss the top of Iz's head on my way out of the room. The thought of a bath has me nearly giddy with excitement, and I stay in the hot water until it is cold.

* * *

The next day, Israel agrees to let me do the driving back to London. Combining that with my freshly washed hair and body, I am in an exceedingly good mood. Even the thought of having to report back to Mina about our conversations with Bar can't get me down. We have nothing much to tell her anyway. Besides, I'll let the esteemed scientist do the talking since he's insisted on returning with us. Even better, so has Einstein, and I'm secretly thrilled to have a dog.

The Lost pick up other Lost occasionally whether by accident or by design, but Bar is the first we've acquired in a while, and it's just another reason to smile. Dad will be pleased, too, I think. With that thought, my spirits plummet just a bit. I have to get us back to Africa, and Iz and I aren't discussing that as of yet. I know he thinks it dangerous for me to control where and when we go, but I can't just leave what little family I have. That was never part of the plan. Me and my plans... Sometimes I think I must make God laugh.

Driving the Rolls-Royce is different than driving the Blue Beast. It takes me ages just to adjust the seat and the mirror the way I like. Not to mention that the Blue Beast was an automatic and this, naturally, is a stick shift, or sort of.

"Step one," Iz instructs, as Bar waits patiently in the back seat, like a small child. "Push the timing lever up. That's this one."

"Here?"

"That's it. Okay, now move the throttle lever slightly down, no, no, down. There you go. Now, push the clutch in."

"The what now?"

"Right here." Iz points to one of what seems like a dozen gadgets.

"This is complicated," I admit slowly.

"Want to quit?"

"No! Look, the clutch is in. Now what? We still aren't moving. Where's the gas?" I search frantically, my body itching for a little bit of speed, a little bit of freedom.

"Slow down, Danica Patrick."

"Huh?" I squint at him in confusion.

"Never mind. Okay, step on the starter button and pull the choke out."

"You're so cute when you're speaking other languages." I blow him a kiss, only to release all the knobs and buttons I had just activated. "Darn."

"Start over," Iz sighs, "from the beginning, and try to go a little faster."

"Yes," Bar agrees from behind me. "I'm an old man. I don't know how much time I have left." I think he's being serious, not necessarily humorous. One thing I've already learned about this older version of Bar is that he only loves to converse about time travel and science. Any other subject bores him, and he gets a little introverted and cranky.

"You boys are hilarious." I clench my teeth determined. "I can do this. What's step one again?"

"Push the timing lever. No, up. Throttle down. Clutch, starter button, choke. Good! Oops. Not sure what happened there. Try again." I can tell Israel is holding in his impatience because he's using his doctor voice with me, slow and overly polite. He's probably going to give himself an ulcer before we roll into London.

I whoop a holler of victory when the Rolls-Royce roars to life. Well, it doesn't exactly roar, but it comes alive with something more than a gasp of annoyance, which was all it had done for me previously. I'm fairly certain there are bite marks on Israel's tongue, and his right calf is probably cramping from stomping on imaginary brakes, which is a little silly since we haven't even moved yet.

"I'm driving!" I shout. "Take that, you cranky pile of metal!"

"You're not driving yet," Iz reminds me. "The car has to be in motion for that."

"Trifles," I sniff. "Now where is the gas pedal, for goodness sake? It's like I need four more pairs of hands. These things were designed for octopi." I peer down at my feet, confused. In doing so, the car stalls and dies again.

Iz smothers a curse with a loud growl. So much for his professional bedside manner.

I groan, too. "This is the most dramatic, cranky old thing! Okay, okay, sorry, car. You're lovely, just lovely, ever so. I shall call you Cassandra. Please start. Please, Cassandra?"

Iz chuckles. "Cassandra?"

"Yes. Cassandra LaRue. That's her name. Now be quiet. You're making her nervous." I do the whole dance again, feeling like a well choreographed artist at this point. I hear a faint snoring from the back seat. The car comes to life again, and this time I hastily push on the gas pedal, which is cleverly disguised as a decorative knob next to the starter button. "Success!"

"Good job, honey. Ready to ease out onto the street?" I glance at Israel's hand which is clutching the dashboard with white knuckles. A bit of a worry wart is my Iz.

"Ready!" The car lumbers forward at about the same speed as a toddler on chubby legs carrying a watermelon, and Iz relaxes his grip. "This is great!" I beam at him. In doing so, the car lurches to a stop and stalls again. "Oh, come on!"

"Want me to take over?" IIe looks hopeful. I glower at him.

"Not even a bit. I'm definitely getting the hang of it. We'll be feeling the thrill of the highway soon, I promise. Now, where's that throttle thingy again?"

Eventually, I do get the hang of driving the old fashioned thing and even speed up a bit, to the speed of an elderly woman carrying a watermelon. At the rate we're going we won't be back in London before tomorrow, but I am in no hurry.

I still love driving.

Chapter 26

Einstein, we learned the hard way gets carsick, and after stopping a few times whenever his furry face looked a little more anxious than usual, we eventually come to the outskirts of London. Open air driving is for me, not the congested, busy streets of a city, and I'm happy to give the wheel back to Israel, who is just as happy to receive it. I think he acquired a new wrinkle.

Bar has slept the entire time or he faked it so as to get out of pleasantries and small talk. I can't quite decide if he's coming with us because he enjoys our company, or if he merely wants to visit old cronies in London. Perhaps he wants to be there when I make us travel intentionally somewhere. I think it's the latter though. He believes us, I'm sure, but the child in him wants to experience it.

My knuckles feel tired from driving, and my sore ankle feels stiff, but I don't complain. I'm absolutely famished since it's long past the supper hour, and I'm daydreaming about the concoctions that James, the amazing butler, might serve up once we reach Mina's. Maybe cold chicken, bread and butter, fruit…I hope she doesn't withhold our dinner as punishment for lack of information. We really don't have much to tell her. It was most likely a wasted trip, but then again I got a dog. I scratch Einstein's ears affectionately, and I hear his stomach rumble. He licks my hand halfheartedly. I think he still doesn't feel up to par.

Pulling up smoothly, I wonder where Iz learn to drive like this, and why haven't I asked? I am so unsurprised to see Luke seated on the massive front steps that I don't even react. I would have been more shocked if he weren't there. In fact, I would have been nervous about his whereabouts. Maybe there is something to be said for keeping our friends close and our enemies closer, though I shudder at the thought. Maybe we'll all retire at the Home for Aged Lost People, Rose and Luke, me and Iz, all in matching rocking chairs.

We all unfold ourselves from the Rolls, stiff joints popping and cracking the way they do after being cramped for too long, and I keep a close eye on Einstein as he runs around sniffing everything from the flowers to the trees to the fence. In spite of myself, I sneak a quick peek at Luke. He looks upset. He's still wearing the clothes I left him in, and even from this distance, I can see the exhaustion his face. He must not have found Rose then. My heart pauses its beating for a split second. Starting to really dislike the compassionate part of my nature, I climb the steps.

"Well?" I loom over him, as he hasn't bothered to stand up. It feels a weird position for us to be in, him meek and surrendered, and me large and strong. I prefer it. "What's the matter with you?"

"I can't find her," Luke answers bluntly. His eyes are bloodshot.

I suspected as much. Nothing else would get him so upset. "Has she ever stayed away so long? How long has it been?"

"I haven't seen her since the night of the stabbing."

"So..." I do the math quickly. All my days are running together. "Almost four days? How long has it been since you've slept?"

He stares hard at me and doesn't reply.

"Okay, four days." I grudgingly admire his resolve. I think I only stayed awake for three in the abandoned house Rose locked me in, and I was ready to throw in the towel and sleep on the side of the road, family forgotten by that time. Luke Dawes has more loyalty and sacrifice in his character than I do, apparently. Well, wonderful. "What are you going to do?"

Bar and Israel pass by us on the steps, carrying Bar's luggage. He actually has luggage. I wonder what is in it that he wouldn't leave behind. I hope he knows it isn't going with us when we go back to Africa. Iz pauses just a moment and looks hard at me. "Coming?" His meaning is clear. He's ignoring Luke and is irritated that I've stopped to talk to him.

"I'll be right there," I assure him. I hope he understands. In answer, he shrugs his shoulder and then winces at the pain it causes. That speaks louder than words, and the guilt I feel for his injury threatens to drown me. He and Bar move into the house, James removing the luggage from their hands as they approach the doors. Though I don't want to, I sit down on the step with Luke. "Well?" I say again.

Luke rubs his hands over his tired face and groans. "I don't know."

"You've checked the hospital? Bedlam, I mean?" I keep my voice light. I have more reason to believe Rose is there than he does. Luke doesn't know she traveled with me to France that night.

"Of course, but there isn't any reason for her to be there unless she's been controlling her travels again, and I don't know why she would." He looks at me pointedly. "You're right here. Who is she going to chase?"

"Dad, maybe?" I get a little chill at the thought and abruptly stand. It was stupid of me to go to Newcastle Upon Tyne. There's safety in numbers, and I should have gone back to Africa so we could stay together. "Do you think?" I can't believe I'm asking advice from Luke of all people, but I feel frayed and upset and am not thinking clearly.

Luke frowns, and then shakes his head slowly. "She doesn't know where he is, and she hasn't seemed as overly...obsessed with Noah as she is with you and your mother."

Mother. She went back to France to right her wrong, or more specifically, my wrongs. Is it possible she would go back to the night Mother died? I grimace. A change of heart? I never would have thought it, and yet she did hold my hand and let me sleep and refrained from murdering me that night in France. The bugs harmed me more than my sister did. I sit back down on the steps, and scratch my 200-year-old bug bites. Luke is watching me carefully, looking for changes in my expression. His eyes narrow.

"What are you hiding from me?"

I try to look as casual and uninterested as possible. "What? Nothing. Pardon me for trying to help you."

"If you want to help me, you'll tell me what you know, Gray." Suddenly, his large hand is covering mine, and he's unbearably close. I can smell his scent, spicy and smoky, like always. I pull my hand away.

"You're asking me to help find the woman who stabbed Israel in the back."

"It was the shoulder."

I glare at him. "She could have killed him, probably tried to kill him!"

"Don't be daft. If she had wanted him dead, he'd be dead. It's just a flesh wound. Don't be such an overly dramatic girl."

I bite my tongue so hard I taste blood. The flavor is familiar and reminds me of my nose bleed. "Okay, fine. Full disclosure. I went back to the night we left Rose behind, to see if I could change the outcome."

Luke looks interested. "Really? Way to show some gumption, Gray. Brava! And?"

I watch him carefully. Shouldn't he, of all people, know the results? Hadn't Rose herself tried it a hundred times? "Um, it was unsuccessful." Still no change in his expression. "I don't think I or anyone can alter history."

"Really?" Luke reaches into his jacket pocket and pulls out his ever present vice. He lights his cigarette as he regards me circumspectly. "Just once, and you're going to give up? Just like that? I'd expect more, oh, I don't know, stubborn determination from you. Never pegged you for a quitter."

He really is the most maddening creature on earth. I'd like to go back to his own personal past and advise his mother not to procreate. "I'm not quitting! Not exactly. I mean, it's not like that. I got really sick, and oh, never mind. The point is, Rose followed me that night." I can tell by Luke's face that he's still baffled. Or bored. "To France?"

"I don't get it. Wasn't she already there?"

I wave the smoke from my face, irritated. "What? Oh you mean three-year-old Rose. Yes, of course, but I mean, *your* Rose followed me, and it's not the first time she's gone back to that night. She goes all the time and never has any success."

Luke looks as though I've just ran over his cat. "That's awful. I didn't know. She didn't tell me."

"Whatever." My tone is harsh, but it's all an act, and Luke sees through me.

"Have a heart, Gray." Hasn't he told me that before? "Don't pretend you don't feel sorry for her. You can't hide the tears in those eyes of yours. They look like flooded swimming pools."

I wipe my eyes furiously. "I'll admit it may be a sad and twisted situation, but to get back to the point, she could be *anywhere*. I woke up in Bedlam, so I assumed she pulled us both back there, but now you're saying she's not there."

"I said they informed me she wasn't there. There's a difference. There are a hundred and one places to hide. We should know. Rose and I played hide and seek there often enough as kids."

I make a face. Who plays hide and seek in a mental asylum? Just my family. "Why would she hide?"

Luke shrugs. "Who knows why Rose does the things she does? She gets confused. She might not know where she is or what time it is." He holds his head in his hands now and stomps out his cigarette savagely on the step.

"Do you think she's Lizzie again? But wouldn't she be trying to get her job as a nurse back then or going to your flat?"

Luke gnaws on his bottom lip. I suddenly get a mental picture of Rose kissing that lip and feel a little sick to my stomach. "Well, anyway, that's all I know," I continue in a sudden rush. "That she was with me that night in France, and she didn't kill me, which showed a lot of self-control on her part, I suppose. I bounced back to Bedlam, which is her anchor, not mine, thank goodness. Now I don't know where she is, and I'm starving. Let me know if you find her." *Well, that was a stupid thing to say, Sonnet.* "Or even better, don't."

Luke doesn't answer, doesn't even watch as I leave him. I know because I look back, in spite of my head telling me not to. He just sits, dejected on the step, as I push open the door to the Dobson's house and let it slam behind me with a thud.

*   *   *

"Here, let me." I cross the room to Israel and reach out to help him. He's trying to peek at the dressing on his shoulder, but the angle is awkward.

"I'm fine." His voice is short, and I know he's angry with me, par for the course with us these days. I'm always screwing up it seems. I hardly seem the girl destined for romance, but Emme would not be surprised and would force me to try harder to be considerate of his feelings. I mean to, I really do, but I can't help it if my life is ridiculously complicated.

"You're going to make it worse. Let me see." Instead of feeling sympathetic and contrite because I know I'm in the wrong, I mostly feel defensive and bossy. "Hold still."

"I said I'd do it!" he snaps.

"And I said hold still!" I snap right back. I stand on my tip-toes and plant a big kiss right square on his objecting mouth. "Now, was that so hard?"

He glares at me some more, but since he also moves his arms around me at the same time, I think it worked. "You and your feminine wiles," he mutters. I grin, and he kisses me thoroughly this time.

"Have I ever thanked you for being my Bedlam?" I ask fondly.

"That's the most romantic thing anyone has ever said to me."

Breathless and disheveled, I only pull away when there is a sharp knock on the door. We are in the parlor or at least I guess that's what it is. It is the same room we were put in the night we came to talk to Mina. I haven't seen her since I came into the house, and I'd bet dollars to donuts that the knocker is her coming to find out what we've discovered. Sure enough, her pretty head pokes in and smiles politely.

"I thought I'd bring in a plate for you both, while we talk." Mina enters with two plates balanced on her hands, brimming with food. My mouth waters. Bar tags along behind her, looking out of place and self-conscious, and carrying his own plate.

"Mm, thank you." I snatch one from her and tuck into it as everyone finds a seat. I'm so busy enjoying some sort of dip with toast points that I only barely notice Luke's presence in the room also. It's practically a party.

Mina seems to be noticing the same thing and frowns, her pretty mouth turning downwards, giving us a glimpse of exactly what she looked like as a five-year-old who wanted her way. "We'll have to make this somewhat brief, I'm afraid. Mother is becoming annoyed with my odd choice of guests coming in and out. I apologize."

"No offense taken." I wave the request for forgiveness away, cheerfully. "We're an odd lot alright, and I'm afraid we don't have much to tell you. I think we came back with fewer answers than we left with. I guess it's my turn to apologize."

Mina looks crestfallen. "Really? Nothing that can help Rose? And the rest of you too, of course." Now she's sheepish. She's been raised to be polite, after all.

"Well, Bar may have more theories if you want to pick his brain a bit," I offer, "but all we really seem to agree on is that we can't change history, but Rose keeps trying. Which probably isn't best for her mental health."

"Will she get better if she stops?"

I look at Bar, who shakes his head as if to say, *Who knows?* "Just another question we don't have an answer to, I'm afraid. Hey, where's Einstein?"

"Who? Oh, the dog? Mother won't allow pets indoors. I have him tied out back."

"He'll get cold," I fret and so will my feet. I was looking forward to keeping him near me, in case of loneliness, cold extremities, and things that go bump in the night. Then I remember we can't stay here another night anyway, so wherever I end up sleeping, he'll be with me, and I cheer up and finish what's on my plate.

The next hour is spent with Mina firing questions and theories at Bar, who eats up her attention and intelligence. He may even prefer Mina to me, which is a little bit annoying. Then before we know it, the three of us, plus one sheepdog and one brother-in-law, are back out on the streets.

Chapter 27

Israel takes Luke's presence in stride, but that may be because Luke is being as silent as the grave. He trails behind us like a puppy. Our real puppy scampers ahead, pulling my makeshift leash taunt when he finds an especially intriguing scent. No one seems to know where we're going, but it's a nice enough night for a walk, so we don't complain. We had pulled into the Dobson's lavish driveway on the last of the fumes in the Rolls, and now it stays parked there in a forlorn sort of way. It would have been nice to stay another night at Mina's, but it seemed out of the question this time. Evidently her mother is a bit of a hard nose.

The Lost take people in and adapt so quickly and so casually that sometimes I forget others aren't like that. What must it be like to live all your life in only one or two houses? The same city? The same era? I can't imagine. I wonder if they get bored, coming home to the same house, the same people, day after day after day. Bored sounds lovely. I wish I could try it.

And so, we end up deciding to see if Linus will take us in at the church for the night. It seems as good a plan as any once we get to talking, and the only other viable option is making our way to Luke and Rose's flat, where she had lived the last few months as Lizzie. That idea gives me the chills, and the last thing I want happening is Rose waltzing in like she owns the place as we sleep peacefully like a row of sitting ducks.

Despite myself, I do feel badly for Rose, and I can admit, at least in my own thoughts, that I am concerned. Where has she gone? I should feel worried for our safety when she's out of my line of sight, but I'm also worried for her. She hasn't much sanity left to cling to. When Einstein pauses at a rosebush for a particularly long bit, Luke catches up to me. Israel and Bar are deep in conversation, something about bending space and time or some such nonsense except, of course, that it isn't. They don't seem to notice that Luke and I are now talking as well.

"Gray," he starts slowly.

"What?" I mutter my less than encouraging response.

"Stay awake with me tonight?" He rubs his eyes like an overly tired child, one who has stayed up past his bedtime and been spoiled all day. Joe gets the exact same look on his face pretty often. "Help me figure out where she's gone."

I don't answer. It seems too much to ask. Though, stealing a look at his face, I know he's right. He's going to need me to chatter incessantly, distract him, and possibly even smack him over the head periodically. He can't go much longer without sleep. I'd be happy to hit him with things in the name of a favor, so I end up being noncommittal, not really agreeing or disagreeing, just murmuring something that I hope sounds promising enough to drop the subject.

*   *   *

Linus is delighted to see us and happy to let us stay the night. He's been such a good friend to us, and that hurts a little knowing that we'll never see him again. It'd be easier to leave forever if I didn't like him so much.

It's the second time we've slept in a church, on hard wooden pews, Israel, Luke, and I, the first being that night in Zanzibar. We've become regular churchgoing folk, Luke jokes. No one laughs. He's exhausted, more so than he realizes. I know once he lets his body relax he won't be able to stay awake. In fact, he drifts off faster than even I expected, followed quickly by Bar, and Iz and I talk in hushed tones.

"Maybe if he stays awake long enough, he'll disappear forever, on his own with no Gray women to bring him back." Iz yawns.

"We can only hope," I agree drily, "but I doubt fate will be so kind. He's like a burr, stuck to us."

"Very leech-like."

"Maybe Rose gets away because she feels smothered by him," I suggest. "I've heard married couples take separate vacations sometimes," I pause, "but I don't really think that's it." Worriedly, I tell him of my passing thought that my sister could have gone to Dad, or even back to Mother.

"You think she's sadistic enough to continually push her off that cliff? Over and over?" I can't really see him in the dark, but I know his eyebrows are raised in a skeptical fashion. "That seems extreme, even for her. Carolina can't get any... more dead."

"No, not like that," I muse ignoring the crudeness of the suggestion, "but maybe, in a change of heart, to right her wrong? Especially if she's confused again. Evidently, Lizzie was a nice enough gal."

"But Lizzie wasn't Lost. So, she wouldn't be traipsing through time doing anything."

"Hmm, good point. Well, how do we know she doesn't have other personalities in there somewhere?"

Israel groans. "That's just what we need."

"Well, it's just a theory." When we are silent for a moment, I can hear Bar snoring and Luke breathing heavily. I can imagine the relief his body and mind feel right now, numb to the world and all its pain and confusion. He's going to be so angry with me when he wakes up though. I hear something else, Linus is going into the kitchen for a drink of water it seems. We're silent for a bit, and when Iz speaks again, he sounds sleepy, like he's about to drift off himself.

"Sonny?"

"Hmm?"

"Try to go to sleep with your mind a blank slate, okay? I don't feel like waking up anywhere weird, like the edge of a cliff or a mental institution."

"Ha, ha. Believe me, I've thought of that. Do you know how hard it is for me to go to sleep these days, now that I know what I can do when I put my mind to it?"

"Well." He reaches out in the darkness and takes my hand. "I'll go wherever with you."

"Romantic fool."

"But I would like some warning if that's all right."

"Agreed." I smile, even though he can't see me. "Good night. I love you."

"Love you back."

* * *

I wake what feels like only moments later, and it might be, it's still dark. Luke is standing over me, nudging me in a not so gentle fashion with the toes of his shoes. I don't need the light to know he's glaring at me.

"What did I say?" he seethes. I feel his anger radiating off him like static electricity. "Come on, Gray. I wasn't asking that much of you."

"Oh, come off it," I grumble keeping my voice low. I shove his foot away. "You needed a little bit of sleep. No harm done. You're still here, aren't you? You didn't wake up in the depths of an Egyptian tomb or anything." That would be a new one for Best and Worst, I think.

I hear Israel mutter something under his breath and know he's awake now, too. Bar, however, still snores peacefully a couple of pews away. I had tried to convince Einstein to snuggle up with me, but as soon as I fell asleep, he apparently abandoned me and went back to his master. The church is dark and full of shadows, but somehow it's still a serene enough place, or at least it was before I was so rudely interrupted in my slumber.

I feel, rather than see, Luke settle down next to me. In spite of myself, I scoot closer to Israel and glare, even though the invader of my personal space can't see it. I feel Iz's arm move around my waist, like a vise.

"I was dreaming of her," Luke says flatly. I'm surprised he's polite enough to bother with whispering, but I assume it's for the sakes of Bar and Linus. He never tried very hard to win points with Israel, and I wouldn't expect him to start now.

"So?"

"It was like she was calling out to me, searching for me, begging me to find her."

"It was just a dream." I sound heartless, though I can relate a bit. I've had those kinds of dreams myself, and they are disconcerting in their realism.

"We need to find her. She can't be alone. You know... you know what could happen. She can't be left alone."

"She isn't any less dangerous with you around," I remind him. "You've been there nearly every time she's done something terrible. I hardly think you're qualified to be her keeper, marriage or no marriage."

"Well, what would you have me do? Lock her up?"

I don't reply. *Yes,* is what I'm thinking, but I've been locked up, or very nearly so in Bedlam, and I can't say I'd wish it on my worst enemy. Sadly, my little sister is my worst enemy. If you don't count the one sitting next to me at the moment, that is.

Why does the list keep growing? I'm fairly certain Mina isn't too fond of me either, and Agatha Helmes seemed to think less of me than she ought.

"Is she on any medication right now?" Israel speaks from the crook of my neck, and his voice tickles. I stifle the urge to laugh since it seems inappropriate somehow. "Anything that could cause withdrawal if she misses it?"

Luke is running his hands through his hair, I know it, even if I can't see it. He always does that when he's thinking or angry or tired. Right now, he's probably all three. I'm sure his hair must be sticking up in a disheveled heap of sandy-colored strands. "Um, let's see. How long does that stuff stay in your system anyway? I give her whatever I have, whatever I can find, depending on when we are in time."

I feel Iz stiffen, and I can hear his teeth grinding together in frustration. "You're a piece of work, Dawes! Don't you have any sense?"

"I do the best I can!" Luke shoots back. His voice is enunciated and crisp and defensive. "Don't judge something you don't know. I'd like to see you smuggle a lifetime supply of the best antipsychotic drugs in your pocket through hundreds of years. I make do. We've been fine until now."

I resist the urge to point out just how not fine they have been. It seems pointless. Luke thinks his and Rose's story is beautiful and flawless, murders and all. To him, Rose's mental health, or lack thereof, is merely part of her charm.

"So, she's had what exactly in the past few weeks?" Luke stays silent. Iz continues, "This is the 1930s, and she's been here a while, so I'm going to assume you've had nothing more modern to give her. Bromides? Barbiturates? Hyoscine?" Israel lets go of his vise-like grip on my waist and sits up. His doctor tone is creeping in again. I can't help but smile. He just can't help helping.

"Yeah, all of those. She's been on them pretty steadily since we first got here, after the girl." Luke pauses to look at me. His voice is somewhat apologetic sounding. "After Emme, I mean. When she was Lizzie, it was harder to get them to her. I would find ways to get into her flat, leave them stirred into her jam and stuff like that. Mina was putting them in her lipstick."

"What? You mean crushed?" I don't like the tone in Iz's voice. He sounds concerned. More than concerned… scared.

"There wasn't any other way to get them to her without her knowing. Why? It isn't dangerous to crush them, Mina assured me."

"Mina is a volunteer candy striper in 1931!" Iz bellows. "What does she know? Yes, it isn't dangerous in and of itself, but it's a damn foolhardy thing to do. It's hard to measure, hard to know how much she's swallowing, and most importantly, it can react badly with whatever you put it in! Who knows what the hell is even *in* lipstick anyway? There could be more contraindications going on here than we could ever count!" His doctor voice is definitely gone now, and so is the delightful tickling of my neck. Now he's muttering curses under his breath, and I can see enough of the outline of his shape to know he's lacing up his boots.

"What is all the fuss about?" Bar shuffles over in the dark. I reach down and pet his companion lovingly.

"Sorry, sir." Israel apologizes. "I didn't mean to wake you. I apologize, but something has come up. Would you like to come with us as we search for Sonny's sister?"

"In the middle of London in the middle of the night? No, thank you. My adventuring days were over when I crossed the half century mark. I would, however, appreciate it if you would come back for me. I really have no cause to be in London without you." Bar sighs. I think we're beginning to get on his old nerves, and I can't see as how I blame him. I get on my own nerves sometimes.

"I'm sorry about this." I aim to give him an affectionate peck on the cheek, but miss in the dark, and kiss his ear instead. "We aren't usually so unreliable. Well, we are, but we don't mean to be. Please stay with us."

"I will, but only because you're the girl that rescued me from that soup kitchen so many years ago." He pats my head fondly.

It wasn't so many years ago for me. It was only a handful of months, but for him, it was most of his life away. It's nearly surprising he remembers me at all. I remember him vividly though, as a young man: gaunt and pale, sad and hungry. We spoke a bit of Italian as I drove him home the day that I had pinched the Blue Beast from Israel. He had been so mad, Israel, I mean, not Bar. He had shouted and completely ignored how nice I looked all dressed up in Emme's hand-me-down dress. I smile, remembering.

I'm forever making him shout.

Chapter 28

Moving through the city streets of London in the depths of the night is eerily familiar, and I stubbornly refuse to dwell on the reason. The last time I had done this was the night Emme died. We had been too late to save her, and I don't know what I'm afraid of now. Perhaps it's too late to save Rose, or that I'll be the one who ends up dead? All in all, whatever the reason, I have a heavy feeling in the bottom of my stomach that tonight's activities will end in disaster.

"Where was she in your dream?" I ask Luke, though it seems an absurd question, as if dreams mean anything. How stupid of me.

"Bedlam. I think it's best we go back. It's the only thing that makes sense really."

"Could Miss Helmes be keeping her there against her will? I mean, I know you and she were in cahoots with the whole Lizzie thing, but what if she's decided enough is enough? I did sort of let it slip that Rose had stabbed someone."

Luke stops and stares at me. "Thanks a lot, Gray."

"What? I'm not going to go around pretending she's sane, the way you do. I'm not going to cover up her crimes either, or conveniently forget that she tried to kill Israel."

"Enough. Just walk," he snaps shortly. He moves ahead of us in the moonlight, whether to lead the way or just to get away from us, I'm not sure, nor do I care. I have a fleeting thought to turn down another street and let him go on without us. I finger comb my hair as we walk, pulling it over my shoulder and fastening a makeshift sort of braid. I never really learned how to braid properly, so it's probably more like a series of knots that will make me yelp later whenever I get access to a real brush, but at least it gets it out of my face. I'm still wearing the bottle green blouse and striped skirt of Mina's, and it's becoming the worse for wear. She had given me more than this, but I've gone and left them somewhere. Bar's house? The Rolls-Royce? I can't even remember. I sigh. I can't even be trusted with clothing, and here I am pining for a dog.

"Are we just going to barge in and demand to look around? Peek in all the closets? Under the beds?" I grumble. I'm saying it only to keep some sort of lightness in the dark, pretending like I'm not scared of whatever it is we're about to do. Grumbling seems petty, but somehow it helps me feel better because it makes it seem as though this is simply a minor inconvenience to my night, instead of something that could end in life changing disaster.

Israel nods, curtly. "I suppose we'll have to. I don't particularly want to break in some back window or anything. They seem to be under the impression that Dawes is a doctor, so they shouldn't have any problem believing I'm one, too."

"You are a doctor," I point out.

"No, as your sister so eloquently pointed out, I am not, not really."

"You are in every way that matters. Just because you don't have some silly piece of paper –"

"Pieces of paper can be important, Sonny. I'd like to get one for us as well. What do you think?"

I'm completely confused until it registers with my slow brain what he's referring to. "Are you proposing to me?" My voice is squeakier and higher than usual.

"In a way." He stops, and laughs. "In a very bad way! I'm sorry, Sonny. Forget that. You deserve better than a night like this for your first proposal."

I'm about to say I'll take it, poorly done or not, but Luke has waited for us to catch up and now that we have, he frowns daggers at us. "Can you do this later?" he snaps.

I resist the urge to slap him, and we walk the rest of the way in silence.

* * *

Agatha Helmes is not any more pleased to see me than I am her. She looks as though she hasn't slept a wink since I saw her last. Her skinny frame is positively skeletal, there are dark circles under her wicked sharp eyes. Her hands appear to tremble as they rest on the door frame to the hospital. Even a bit of wiry hair has come loose from her pins, something which I daresay never happens to her. I'd bet even her hair is scared of her.

"It's about time you show up." She directs this at Luke, and her voice is like lemons, under ripe lemons with battery acid mixed in.

"I was just here yester…" Luke begins, but she cuts him off and waves us all inside.

"Never mind. I didn't know yesterday what I know today, did I?"

"Rose is here then?" Luke can't keep the relief from his tone, but it's still mingled with doubt.

"Oh, she's here, all right, or she's been here, at least. Left a mess behind her, too, for us all to clean up. You'd think Scotland Yard would be of more help, but no, they do their little search and then leave us all here to fend for ourselves." She wrings her hands, and I stare in disbelief. Miss Helmes does not seem the sort of woman to wring hands.

"Start at the beginning. I don't have any idea what you're blathering about." Luke gestures to a chair, somewhat rudely and impatiently, but she complies.

Miss Helmes takes a deep breath and glares at me. This display of petty immaturity seems to give her strength, and her voice is steadier as she begins to speak. "I found Mr. Limpet this morning, and then Marie later this evening. I didn't really put two and two together and come up with four until Marie. I thought maybe Mr. Limpet had done himself in, though I suppose pushing himself down three flights of stairs would have been a feat. Naturally we had the police brought in right away, though there's no one to care about the old man anyway. They were about as much help as they ever are here. They don't like being called here."

I sneak a glance at Luke, and he is resting his face in his hands. I'm not sure if he cared for Mr. Limpet or if Miss Helmes' beating around the bush is giving him cause for depression. I doubt it's the death of the anyone since Luke only loves Rose and himself.

Miss Helmes continues. "But when I found Marie I knew it had to be Rose. No one handles a knife like that."

I get chills over my arms, and I rub them with my hands. "Who were Mr. Limpet and Marie?" I ask softly.

"Limpet was the old man in the wheelchair. Marie was the girl in the hallway." Luke speaks through his hands.

I bite my lower lip and stubbornly refuse to become emotional. I remember the old man who reminded me of alfalfa sprouts, and the girl, Marie, grasping at my dress and asking me for help. "I should have helped her," I whisper. "I should have helped. Mr. Limpet... seemed so harmless."

"Rose must have felt trapped, surrounded. She was coming off too many medicines. Ask him!" Luke abruptly gestures towards Israel. Iz appears only taken aback at the attention. "There are side effects; contraindications. We should have been more careful." Now he glares at Miss Helmes. "We have only ourselves to blame."

"That's very big of you to spread the responsibility." Miss Helmes' words are tart, clipped, and very sarcastic. "But if you're done making yourself feel better about your wife's behavior, you can go about finding her, and in a hurry."

"You mean the police didn't take her in?" Israel asks.

"No. She hasn't been seen or heard from. It's only my word that it's her who's roaming around these halls, bent on death. I knew no good would come of this plan of yours, Luke!" She glares at him, and I see her hands are still trembling. "Even when she was Lizzie, she scared me a bit, sipping on imaginary tea and constantly scrubbing that wall. I know if it's revenge or death she wants, I'll be next. She always hated me, whether she's Lizzie or Rose. That much never changed." Her premonition wanders into a rambling sort of rush at the end. She sounds like a nervous, chattering squirrel.

I can't say I blame my sister for her dislike of Miss Helmes, but still I hurry to reassure her. "We'll find her. That's what we're here for. I suppose the police are here, as well? Searching? Protecting the other inmates?"

Miss Helmes snorts in disgust. "Not bloody likely." I doubt she lets her British slang creep in very often. We all lose our manners in times of crisis though. "They did their little search and left. Said to ring them if anything else happens. They hate coming out here," she repeats.

I share her disgust suddenly. I'd prefer the hallways of Bedlam were stocked with well-armed help.

"Well?" I turn to Luke. "We can't just let her pick everyone off, one by one."

"Don't be crude. If she killed them, it's because she felt threatened," he replies shortly. "I'd like to split up, but it's probably best if you stick close to me. I'm the only one she won't try to harm."

"I can handle myself against one small girl," Iz objects rolling his shoulder, "now that I know how quick she can be, anyway. I won't underestimate her again, believe me."

"Suit yourselves," Luke answers. Before I can chime in with my opinion of the situation, he is gone.

What would I chime in with? I ask myself. I don't have a better plan. I don't have a plan at all. The thought of fleeing seems tempting. Just leave them all here, get out, go anywhere else but here, but I already feel the weight of the deaths of the old man and Marie. If Rose were to hurt anyone else...no, I'll have to swallow my cowardice and do my part to contain my sister somehow. Maybe she'll talk to me. That night in France wasn't so bad, not even with her by my side. There is some humanity left inside, I think. Isn't there?

Is that what Mr. Limpet and Marie thought, as well, before Rose ended their miserable lives? The chills are back, and I don't bother to rub them away this time. I open my mouth to speak, but before I can I sense a presence in the doorway behind me, and I nearly jump out of my skin with fright.

"I got here as soon as I could get away." It's only Mina, and my heart slows down to a more normal rhythm. She hangs her shawl on a coat rack and addresses Miss Helmes. "It was difficult. Mother had heard what happened, and she's been keeping a close eye on me ever since. I had to sneak out."

I want to tell her she should have listened to her mother. I suppose I should be grateful for more help, but I don't really want Mina's death on my conscience either, and I kind of wish she had stayed home. "We're about to start a search," I tell her. "Do you want to come with me and Israel?"

Mina shakes her head decisively. "Too many people at once will only make Rose feel even more cornered. Miss Helmes and I have had training in subduing the patients if need be, and she and I are friends. I think it might be best that we split up." She seems to be taking this well, I think. She's snapped into nurse mode carefully keeping her emotions in check, and also carefully not bringing up the fact that she had underestimated her friend, as well.

"Splitting up in the movies never ends well," I mutter, but no one is listening to me any longer. Mina has taken Miss Helmes' elbow, and they have already left the room, Luke is gone, and only Israel is left in this large waiting room, left to stare at me with a bemused and somewhat baffled expression.

"You're going to give yourself new wrinkles making that face," I sigh in a poor attempt at humor.

"I'm only wondering if everyone else goes through this in their relationships. Burning the dinners, forgetting the anniversaries, leaving the cap off the toothpaste, chasing murderers through insane asylums."

"You're not funny. I already feel bad enough that I've dragged you into this hell."

He leans forward and kisses me quickly. "Don't be. Come on. Maybe the sight of you will bring Rose out of hiding."

"Oh, that's very comforting. Thank you for that. Shouldn't we have some sort of weapon? I wish we had Asha's rifle."

"As long as Rose doesn't have a gun, we won't need one," Iz replies practically. "She weighs approximately eleven pounds. We just need to find her, and I'll be happy to carry her, even if she bites."

"So the trick is just to find her." We begin to walk, slowly. I suppose we should be moving faster, but really, does it matter? I'm hoping Luke finds her first. He's the only one I think Rose won't attempt to kill, although I can't really be sure he won't just spirit her out a window or something. "She may have left, you know. She could be anywhere by now." I think of France, a hundred years ago. "Literally anywhere."

"I agree, but do you have any other places to look first?" We turn a corner and begin to climb a flight of stairs.

"Looking for Lizzie, too, are you?" Suddenly, a young man appears out a door at the top of the stairs and leans over the railing, casually. He's young, but dressed as some sort of worker, maybe even a doctor. He looks familiar, maybe I've seen him here before.

"Yes, that is, we're looking for Rose," I answer.

"Name's Mack." He holds out his hand and waits for us to reach him to take it. "Rose, huh? I only know her as Lizzie. Can hardly believe she's capable of being anyone else, actually. Whole story is a bit fantastical if you ask me, but no one is asking me." He grins.

"I'll ask you," I counter. "What do you think happened, and where do you think my sister may have gone?"

"Sister, huh?" Mack looks closer at me. "Oh, yeah, I see it now. Same eyes." I flinch as though he has struck me. "Well, miss, I don't really have many theories. Lizzie seemed right as rain to me. Guess she flipped some sort of external switch. It happens, especially here. I just never expected it with her. She never really liked me much. I always felt like she didn't trust me, but now it sort of makes sense. Me, being an employee here and everything. I'm a doctor." He puffs out his chest impressively, or at least it's presumably meant to be impressive. He probably doesn't even have hair on it yet, but I refrain from the temptation to look condescending. "Lizzie or Rose, doesn't care for doctors."

"You don't know the half of it. Mind if we look around?" Iz asks.

"Not at all. Be careful, though, and yell if you find her. I can help restrain her if you like. Oh, and the patients are locked in tonight. We've already checked all their rooms."

We both nod and begin to move again.

"Oh, and," Mack calls after us, "whatever you hear, don't let them out."

"Who?" I ask confused.

"The patients. Keep them locked in. It's for their own good."

"Of course," I whisper, but I'm not sure I mean the words. A part of me wishes to let them all go free.

What kind of a world would that be? Madmen left to roam the streets? I think of Luke, and then of Jack.

Would it really be so different?

Chapter 29

Trying knobs and finding them locked is all we've done nearly an hour into our search for Rose. We passed Miss Helmes and Mina once and they were a way down the same hallway I remember seeing Marie in. We gave quiet, little, ludicrous waves at one another from the distance. What a strange thing to do, yet we all did it. Our hands of their own accord, acting natural, as though we are meeting in the park or across a theater. We've also met and been warned to proceed with caution by a Dr. Ford. He obviously disapproves of us being given permission to wander his halls, but on the other hand, I could tell he was nervous himself. Perhaps he thinks we will capture and tame what his hospital could not.

I'm quite sure he's mistaken.

The halls, nooks and crannies, rooms and stairs of Bedlam are a fearful place. They were fearful enough in the daylight, when I was only slightly fretful for my own safety and no recent murders had taken place. Now the walls flit with shadows, and every corner seems to be full of some dark entity or threat. I cannot imagine even working here, much less being held here 'for my own good.' For their own good just may get them killed in their own beds tonight if we are not successful in locating my sister. I don't have too much faith in every room having been searched. Where else could Rose be hiding if not in some room?

My theory shows itself flawed soon enough. There are dozens of places to hide, closets, exam rooms, filing rooms, family waiting rooms, kitchens, pantries, libraries, studies. The list goes on and on. As unbelievable as it seems, I begin to let my guard down, and with it, the cold, prickly sense of fear abates. I can't say I'm getting bored peering into every corner we find, but it begins to look less and less like Rose is still here, and my heart stops skipping a beat with every sound. I somehow feel in my bones that she isn't here. It's the same feeling, and lack of feeling, that I have had other times I've searched for her. I knew when she was in that house she locked me inside of, and I knew when she wasn't. Instinct, of some strange sort, I guess.

The sounds of Bedlam are plentiful. They mostly come from behind the patient's doors, shouting as if there are dozens of people locked inside, though I myself had been in these rooms and they are not even big enough for two. There are whisperings that make my skin crawl, laughing, crying, knocking, scratching, rustling, yelling. Not every door, of course. There are plenty that are silent, but those silent ones worry me more than the others. Who knows what is inside? A dead body? My sister standing over it, a blade in her hand?

What was it she told Israel that day, that she could hold a knife steady?

We should have listened. Once again, I feel remarkably stupid.

After what feels like hours, but in reality is probably not quite so long, Luke finds us. His dejected, upset countenance tells me what his mouth does not. He hasn't been successful at finding his wife either. He runs his hands through his hair. As handsome and debonair and expensive looking as he had appeared to be only days earlier, that's how emotionally crippled and desperate and hollow he appears now. Amazingly, I very nearly want to reach out and embrace him, or at least pat him on the back like I would Einstein. I settle for a wobbly sort of smile, which is probably the kindest thing I've offered him in eighty years.

He ignores the gesture. "Think, Gray." He rubs his forehead like it pains him. He probably has a wicked headache. I know I do. "Where could she have gone?"

"Sonny suggested back to the night Carolina died?" Israel poses the suggestion like a question.

Luke ponders a moment and then shakes his head.

"You didn't know about her going back to the night we left her, either," I point out. "There might be a lot of things you don't know about Rose."

"Yes, there might, but there are things you don't know about her either. For one, she's terrified of Carolina. There's no way she'd seek her out."

I frown. "Whatever do you mean?"

Luke sinks down on the floor, tired. "She sees her mother everywhere. She's haunted by her, I guess you could say."

The chills come back. "I didn't know that. I can't say she doesn't deserve it, but still..."

"She sees Carolina everywhere, at train stations, in the street, across rooms. It's the only thing that stops her from getting places, doing things. There's no reasoning with her when she's had a vision of her, of your, mother. She gets shaky, can't stand still, begins to feel sick...in other words, she comes totally undone."

"What about Dad, then? Could she have gone to Africa?"

"She doesn't know that's where he is. Well, Lizzie knows, so I presume it's possible..." Luke trails off, thinking. "No, she's never been all that interested in your dad. I'm not sure she convinced he's her father anyway. She mentioned that once, or was that you?"

I remember clearly talking about that very thing with Luke, but I don't admit to it.

"Rose doesn't look anything like Noah," Luke continues, "and it would explain partly why she was left behind that night, if she's only half Lost."

"She didn't travel because she wasn't asleep that night!" I snap. "I know. I was there. It doesn't have anything to do with being half Lost." I don't feel like dissecting my parent's marriage and fidelity right now.

"Did you say the hospital was moved?" Israel suddenly interrupts. We turn to look at him, confused at first, then as the realization and possibility dawns on our tired brains, with understanding.

"Of course!" Luke stood so quickly that I hadn't even seen his legs fold out from beneath him. "That must be it, the old Bedlam!"

I understand, but I am still doubtful. "Whatever would she be doing there?"

"Hiding, feeling safe and alone and at home," Israel puts his arm around me, "wanting a sense of normalcy, I'd guess."

"But we already know she's been here. Hence the dead bodies."

"Yes, but everyone is looking for her here, and there's the stain..." Luke trails off. I stare at him, impatiently.

"What stain? What are you going on about?" We are already walking towards what I assume is the exit out of this horrible place.

"Never mind. It isn't important. The main thing is, I think the good doctor here may be onto something." Luke is rapidly several yards ahead of us. He's moving quickly, excited.

I hang back, unsure. "We should tell someone where we are going."

"We don't have time!" Luke throws over his shoulder, right before he takes the stairs, three at a time, and heads for a familiar way out of the asylum.

"Make time," I mutter to Iz, who nods in agreement. He snatches a piece of paper from the desk that Miss Helmes had been at an hour or two before and begins to write. Rolling my eyes at his chicken scratching, I pull it away, flip it over, and write a brief explanation to whoever may read it, hopefully Scotland Yard.

Once out in the cold night air, I am momentarily at a loss. Luke is nowhere to be seen. Has he left us then to rescue or capture his wife alone? I don't mind the thought. Now might be our chance to leave this place, this year, forever. I look at Iz, by my side as ever, and am about to speak, when a vehicle pulls up and nearly runs me down. It looks to be a hospital issued type of automobile, not particularly fancy. Sure enough, I recognize the sandy haired driver behind the wheel. He toots the horn, impatiently, and leans over to open the passenger side door.

"Hurry up already!" Luke commands.

My brain tells me *No, don't do this astonishingly dimwitted thing. Don't go wandering around an abandoned insane asylum*, but my body betrays me. I am already half in the automobile. Even Luke seems slightly taken aback by me getting in the car, though he quickly schools his face into his typical impatient scowl. Israel climbs in after me, and I am reminded, not for the first time, how much he will do for me. It should be a more comforting, romantic thought, but instead I only feel guilty. How long will this go on, this madness with my family? How long will he put up with it?

"Can we please at least swing by Scotland Yard first? Tell them we know where she might be?" I ask hopelessly.

Luke snaps out a rebuttal. "They won't care, and they won't follow us on a hunch. Marie and Mr. Limpet are hardly worth their time. They were society's rejects. No one cares that they're dead. Rose could diminish half the asylum's population before they'd start to get involved. People die in strange ways in Bedlam, and no one cares. It just frees up another bed."

He should know, so I shut up.

"Does withdrawal from or side effects of psychotropic drugs cause hallucinations?" Luke asks Iz as he drives wildly through London. The sun is beginning to rise, finally. It's very early morning now. I'm extremely grateful, as it means we won't be searching Bedlam in complete darkness. Thank goodness for small favors.

"Withdrawal could, or stopping and starting suddenly, only taking them occasionally, etc."

Luke drums his fingers on the steering wheel as he drives.

"You probably shouldn't be operating heavy machinery with as little sleep as you've had," I point out, wishing for a seatbelt as he takes a corner far too quickly.

He just glares at me. "I'm not going to fall asleep at the wheel, Gray. I'm starting to think I'll never sleep again."

"That would make some of life easier," I can't help agreeing. I'm back to making small talk to keep my mind from dwelling on reality. "Staying in one place forever…"

No one else seems too interested in playing this game though, and I end up trailing off when Iz and Luke don't respond. Awkward silence descends on us like a shroud. Even so, I am wishing it would take longer to arrive at the old hospital than it does. When Luke pulls the car over, willy-nilly, in his usual haphazard parking job, I stay motionless inside. That strange instinct is coming over me again, only this time with a reversal of feelings. I do think we'll find Rose inside this place, and I'm not too eager to see if I'm correct. Steeling myself, as if for a physical blow which, come to think of it, is exactly what meeting my sister feels like, I finally get out of the car. Luke is already ahead of us, naturally, he hadn't stuck around, waiting for me to find my nerve. Israel takes my hand and shrugs.

"Well?" he says.

"Are we walking into a hornet's nest?" I ask. "What if this has been their twisted plan all along? What if Luke has known her whereabouts the whole time?"

"Nah." Israel shakes his head. "He isn't that good of an actor."

"He had us fooled before."

"He had you fooled before," Iz corrects me none too gently. "I never liked the creep."

I laugh. "All right, smarty. We've established that your intuition is better than mine. What is your gut telling you right now?"

Iz takes a deep breath. "That we are absolutely and without a doubt, completely and utterly, bonkers for doing this. Also, your dad is probably going to kill me when we get back, and Joe will never believe it."

We continue to stare up at the huge building in silence, hand in hand. The sun is fully up now, but it hasn't done much to beautify the place. Maybe it's just its history, its macabre stories and ghostly tales, but I don't think any amount of sunlight, sparkling dew, or songbirds singing overhead would make this place anything less than a house of horrors.

Bedlam looms in the still, quiet morning like a demented dollhouse, my sister the unhinged doll who plays inside.

Chapter 30

I've never been in this particular Bedlam. Of course, I haven't, but it's exactly what I imagined it to be. The sunlight is no help to us once inside, as the windows are barred in places, covered in heavy draperies in others, and the whole thing is bathed in gloom and depression. The gray shadows and the heavy feeling overwhelm my senses. They must have overcome Luke as well, because he is hanging back waiting for us to catch up.

I'm not sure I'm grateful for his company. Israel may be convinced Luke is as baffled about Rose as we are, I'm still skeptical. He has always had the upper hand with us, and I have no idea who pulls the marionette strings in his strange relationship, Luke or Rose. Neither alternative is better than the other, but they are equally chilling. Luke is not as weak as he sometimes appears, and Rose has madness driving her. Well, so does he, doesn't he? He was an inmate here once, too, and he very nearly murdered me a year ago, a fact I haven't forgotten.

"Keep close," Luke instructs in a low voice. I haven't seen him smoke, since we came back from Newcastle Upon Tyne, and his hands shake a bit. Of course, mine are shaking too and it has nothing to do with a nicotine addiction.

In answer, Iz pulls me closer to himself, and to my shock, I see him pull out a very small revolver from his jacket pocket. "What in the world?" I whisper. "You said there was no need for guns!"

"I reevaluated," he murmurs. "Mina actually gave it to me. No questions asked. She pressed it into my hand when she arrived at the asylum, though she wouldn't even meet my eyes."

I'm surprised. I thought she was convinced we could rescue Rose from her own head and all be home in time for tea.

"Besides," he continues, as we turn a dark corner, keeping Luke in our sights, "I got to thinking about when Rose stabbed me. I never even saw her."

"What do you mean?"

"I mean I never even saw her! The knife came out of nowhere, like it was thrown. Whoever was standing next to me at the time pulled it out, which of course was the wrong thing to do, but I wasn't going to preach at him since I was busy bleeding."

"That's because it did come out of nowhere." Luke has very good ears and responds, drily. "That's how she does it. It's probably how she got Marie. She never even would have seen her. Miss Helmes said they found her in her usual spot in the hallway, sitting up with her head bowed on her knees like usual. No one even realized she was dead until Mack realized there was blood pooling beneath her."

My arms break out in chills, and I wish this day was over. There's no rehabilitating my sister now, not with so much murder on her hands. What will we do with her once we find her? What will Luke have us do? Even he has to know she can't go on living like this. There are too many people she has a vendetta against. What did Marie ever do to her? Probably nothing and she still died for her supposed sins.

We round another corner, and Luke stops still, staring at something on the wall partway down.

"What is it?" I whisper. I seem incapable of doing anything less than whispering in this godforsaken place, although there is a part of me that would like to make a lot of noise to drown out the haunts that I feel. It's my imagination playing tricks on me, I know, but the silence here is thick and swarming around my head. If I listen hard enough, I'm scared I will hear something like the ghosts of the insane perhaps swirling around my body. Maybe I'll see a cold presence with bony fingers that will play with my hair and run down my spine or pull on my hem like Marie did before she died.

Luke reaches out and touches the wall. There appears to be a dark sort of stain that drips down, like red paint. I very much doubt it's red paint. "It's wet," he says rubbing his fingers on his trousers.

"Is it blood?" I whisper again.

"Well, it was, once upon a time. It's only wet now because she's been washing it again. She's been here, and recently." His eyes swing towards the stairs.

Why do they even put stairs in these places, I want to ask, thinking of poor Mr. Limpet. It doesn't seem a very responsible thing to do when you're surrounded by aggressive patients.

"Why would she be washing it?" I mutter, but then I remember Mina saying something about that very thing. She was pointing out that she knew the girl named Lizzie had been worth saving, that Lizzie or Rose felt badly for that stain. I'm not entirely sure I share her conviction, yet it does soften my heart just a little, until I think of Mr. Limpet and Marie again. The warm feeling disappears.

Luke hasn't seemed to notice Israel's revolver. Iz is keeping it pressed close to his side, and it blends in perfectly with his pants and his black hand curled over it. "We'll try the ballroom," he says shortly, and leads the way.

The ballroom is full of dust that makes me want to sneeze, though I stifle it just in time. Sneezing seems ridiculous at a time like this, like giggling at a funeral. It's the brightest room we've been in yet, and the dust seems to sparkle through the air. It sparkles on its slow flight down to the floor, like glitter or snow. There isn't any furniture. It's simply a big, old room with a cold wood floor and windows that flank one side. One is broken, and it's probably where all the dust is blowing in. A bird makes a ruckus in the rafters and makes a break for the busted window, and I nearly scream at the surprise of all the noise its small wings make in the quiet.

It's very clear that Rose isn't here, and there's nowhere where she could have hidden herself. There are no furniture draped in sheets, no closets or wardrobes, but still Luke lingers with a far off look on his face. He seems to be remembering things, maybe memories this room holds for him. I don't think I want to know. Unfortunately, he doesn't hold with my desire to remain ignorant.

"We used to hold balls here. The staff would let us dance, and they would play music. We even had our own band! Rose always looked forward to those balls, even when an audience came in to stare. She was so carefree and young, so pretty."

He seems lost in memories now. His eyes have lit up from within, making them sparkle mischievously. "She would tease me by dancing with other boys, but I knew I was the one she loved best. Such an interesting cast of characters we met here." He runs his fingers through his hair. It's looking a bit greasy and the worse for wear. Even his expensive suit and shiny shoes are wrinkled and dirty. It strikes me that he doesn't look out of place in this mad, dusty ballroom. He fits right in here in Bedlam. The thought makes me stone cold.

"She isn't here. Let's move on," Israel says in a deep voice, not his doctor voice, but his no-nonsense one. The one he uses when Joe refuses to stay in bed or when I've absolutely annoyed the life out of him and he's trying not to lose his temper. It's kind of like the words are coming strained right through his gritted teeth, like the hard pebbly seeds of a raspberry that are left behind when you crush them for jam. All the sugar niceties are gone, and all you have left are rattling bits of gravel.

Luke obeys, though I think it's because he's still too lost in daydreams to notice he's being bossed around by Israel. We come out the way we had come in, and I have a feeling I'm going to miss the sparkling sunlight we leave behind in the ballroom. Sure enough, the darkness seems heavier now than it had before.

A scuffling, rustling noise by our feet makes me jump, but it's only a rat. A rat may normally make me shout and run for cover, but not when the alternative is something supernatural, and my relief outweighs my slight fear of rodents. I do think of the old expression about rats deserting a sinking ship though. I'd like to scamper behind it, right out the door and down the stairs and leave this place forever.

"What's this way?" I ask Luke, still in a whisper. I'd like to know where I'm headed, though I doubt it will help matters.

"Exam rooms are over here. I don't see why she'd go there. That whole wing is rooms, and I suppose we'll have to check them all. Then there's the kitchen. She tends to forget to eat, but she's probably hungry enough to remember. I hope." Luke seems anxious that Rose might be famished.

My heart sinks. This building is massive, devastatingly so. The other Bedlam, the newer one, is gigantic too, but we hadn't had to search all the rooms. This could take hours upon hours, especially if Rose is hiding. She would know this asylum like the back of her hand, and she's had too much practice haunting places. I take another step, and something breaks beneath my feet. I lean down to pick up the broken shards of the shattered pocket watch. The chain snakes its way through my fingers, and shards of glass trickle to the floor like rain. I look up.

"What's that way?" I point towards the hallway closest to where the watch had lain. What makes me do so, I don't know, since it's even darker than where we are now and all my gut instincts and common sense are telling me to stay away. Israel seems to agree with my body and not my words and glares at me.

"Really?" he mouths.

"Sorry," I mutter. I drop the watch, and it finds its place on the floor with a clatter.

"It leads to the baths," Luke answers.

"They let their patients take baths?" I'm a little surprised.

Luke turns on me with impatience, and disgust. "Don't be stupid. Not bubble baths, Gray. Cold baths, meant to shock the system. They usually left them in there for hours at a time, sometimes 9 to 10. You could spend the whole day, freezing half to death, while they took notes and attempted to ice the crazy away."

"Oh."

"Yes, oh, but we may as well look. Rose experienced these baths once in a while, though since it was a pain for the staff to keep her in if she didn't want to, they didn't try it often. She still doesn't like washing though. Didn't you ever wonder why she doesn't wash her hair often? Come on."

I hadn't wondered, though I had noticed, but that's not the same thing, is it?

Israel moves up the revolver and trains it in front of us. If Luke were to turn around, there would be no hiding it now, but he doesn't. He moves swiftly and surely, as if he's walked this hall a hundred times, which I suppose he has. My instincts of getting close to my sister intensify. It's the strongest it's been since we entered Bedlam, and it makes me feel nauseous. It's probably my imagination and anticipation that's making my stomach hurt, not some psychic connection to Rose and her whereabouts.

Or maybe it is, because the closer we get, the more I can hear her singing.

Humming really. No words, just a rambling melody that no one will ever find in a songbook, like the singing of a small child who has no ear for music and no ability to make it either.

"Darling?" Luke calls. "I'm here! Where are you?"

The singing falters a minute, but then continues. This time though, it seems to be coming from someplace else entirely.

I don't want to be here anymore, and I say as much.

"Don't be stupid, Gray." Luke's voice is harsh. "You don't even know how to get out of here, not quickly enough anyway. You'll have to finish the game the way she wants you to."

I hear Israel take the safety off the revolver and feel very grateful for Mina at this moment. The singing has stopped again.

Luke is several feet ahead of us, impatient, not masking his movements. Iz and I are quieter, though I doubt it matters or will do us any good. Luke is right, Rose has the upper hand. Retracing our steps will take too long, and I'm all turned around. The humming starts again and Rose seems to be everywhere at once.

We follow the sound of her voice, Luke moving faster than Iz and I, and we let him. At least she's alive. We know that much, and there is no one here for her to kill. She can't be anything but alone, can she? Still, my heart is thumping and my breath comes in shallow bursts that make my chest and lungs hurt. I'm scared to round that last corner and see her.

See her we do, or at least the tip of her head, with her yellow hair dangling out of the tub. One arm, rests on the edge, her hand trailing down. My eyes flit to her fingertips as we get closer, the nails are bitten down, and the cuticles torn with bits of dried blood on them.

There is no water, it was probably shut off when they left this building empty. I'm not sure what's stranger, my sister lying fully clothed in a dry bathtub, or the fact that we've found her at all. She smiles brightly at us.

"I know what you're thinking, what a silly place to sit! But my feet were tired from climbing all those stairs, and there isn't any furniture. I couldn't find the front door." Her voice is apologetic. She sits up and gathers her legs beneath her. Her feet are bare. "It seems to have moved."

"I was worried sick about you!" Luke leans down and kisses the top of her head, then her forehead, then her nose.

"Oh, don't worry about me. I'm just fine." She doesn't return the kiss and actually looks embarrassed to receive it. She pushes him away, gently. "Who are you?" She regards me curiously.

I don't know why I'm surprised. Half the time I've spent time with Rose she can't quite place her relationship to me. At least she isn't passing me empty tea cups and then tossing them at my head.

"Oh, never mind!" Rose adds musing almost to herself. "Sonnet. I remember."

"Why don't we go outside? We remember where the door is." Luke offers her his hand. If he's disappointed at his wife's less than joyful reaction to seeing him, you can't tell by looking. Of course, he's used to her mood swings, and I can tell he's treading carefully. Rose takes his hand after hesitating just a moment, and she stands. She is small, so small. It always takes me aback how innocent and sweet she looks. One would never peg her for a killer.

"What happened to Mr. Limpet and Marie?" I ask her firmly. We begin to leave the bath area. Israel's gun is still very much in sight, but if Luke and Rose see it, they don't react. Rose turns to look at me as Luke leads her by the waist. I watch her warily as she gently disentangles herself from his grip.

"Who?" She frowns.

"Never mind." What does it matter anyway? They'll still be dead, and there will be no one to care."

"Oh, those two." She waves the question away, as if it isn't worth asking, or answering. "It was a kindness what I did."

I open my mouth to reply but shut it again. There's no hope for getting her to understand, and in a twisted sort of way, I very nearly see her point.

We follow our own footsteps in the dust, back the way we came. Rose lingers at the ballroom with a delighted expression on her face. "I remember this place!" She claps her hand. "What fun!"

"I was telling them that just a moment ago." Luke looks down at her fondly. "You were such a lovely dancer."

Rose frowns a bit. "You were here, too? When was that?"

Luke reacts as though he's been slapped. "Of course I was. Rose? Rose, don't you know me?" He reaches out to touch her face, but she moves away gracefully.

She ignores the question, and moves into the ballroom. Twirling and spinning slowly, her red calico dress billows out around her. Luke stands, watching, confusion in his handsome face.

I think I've come to grips with Rose long before he has. It isn't that unusual for her to forget me, evidently, he's not accustomed to the same treatment, unless she's slipped into being Lizzie again, a turn of events he hadn't thought of perhaps. He should have, we all should have, I realize now.

Rose had been traveling again, at least once, back to France with me. Traveling makes her worse, especially when she controls the destination and especially when she meets herself coming and going, but Lizzie wouldn't remember dances in this place. She would know Marie and Mr. Limpet, even if she didn't recall killing them. She seems to be stuck somewhere between Lizzie and Rose this time.

Still I test the theory. "Lizzie?" I ask. Rose doesn't stop twirling. She's going to make herself dizzy. "Rose?" I try again.

"What?" She sounds impatient and irritated. Finally, she stops spinning and nearly topples over. She would have had Luke not caught her.

"Nothing," I stammer. "It's nothing." She is Rose then, but not exactly, or not entirely. She seems to have forgotten Luke altogether. A spot of compassion keeps me from looking at him, to let him grieve without my gaze. I doubt he would want my pity.

"Well, you're a funny one! You were going to show me that door, remember?" Rose moves out of the ballroom, quickly.

We follow, just as quickly, not wanting to let her out of our sights, though probably for different reasons. She trips lightly down the stairs, humming again. I pull on Luke's shirt and force him to stop, though his feet were barely moving anyway. Iz is the closest to Rose, and I can see the revolver in his hand still. He is watching her, so it's up to me to watch Luke.

"What are you going to do?" I hiss.

He looks at me with wounded eyes. All the sparkle is gone. "She doesn't know me," he states flatly. He sounds completely baffled.

"I know, but what are you going to do? What are *we* going to do? With her?" I press. My conscience won't let me just leave her here to wreak havoc.

Luke looks at me, but I can tell he's staring right through me. I could be anyone right now. There's no one in his world but him and Rose, and Rose is half gone. "She's left me." He sounds like he can't believe it. "It's happening again. She's left me." The man with the plan is completely confused.

I want to take him by the shoulders and shake him, but my pity stops me. "But she isn't Lizzie, I don't think," I point out, trying to bring him out of his stupor. "Lizzie wouldn't have killed those two patients. Lizzie was kind, wasn't she? Is she someone new altogether?"

"No, she's Rose... just not my Rose. She's left me. I can't keep doing this."

I wait.

"It's over." Luke's voice is so soft I'm not sure I heard him correctly.

I'm also not entirely sure what he means, but I don't want to linger on these stairs anymore, so I begin to walk again. When I look back, Luke still stands where I left him. "Come on!" I say impatiently. My pity is dwindling. I want to shout and shake him.

For a moment, I think he won't budge, that his feet will grow into those stairs like tree roots, and he'll become part of the architecture of this mad place, but then he moves. He takes a step down, pauses, folds his legs under himself and lights a cigarette, lies his head down on the stairs above him and blows smoke at the ceiling.

"Are you giving up then?" I say edgily. Whatever compassion I had is deteriorating like this old, awful building around us, and I don't want to stay another minute here.

Luke regards me not at all, and after a moment, I leave him there.

I round a corner and nearly bump into Iz. Rose is humming again and biting her nails, but she keeps walking. I have no idea if it's the right direction though, and the realization makes me sick. She thought we had moved the front door, but I'm beginning to get just as turned round. It must show on my face because Iz smiles at me. "I think this is right." He gestures with the revolver.

"If you say so," I mutter.

Rose stops suddenly and looks behind me. "You probably shouldn't have lost him, you know. Turned your back on him like that. You let him get away." She looks disapproving.

"Who?" I ask carefully. "Luke?" Maybe we were wrong about her not knowing her own husband. Maybe she'll answer correctly, and he'll hear her and come running back. Then they can live out their own demented life together, locked in a room.

She laughs as though I'm simpleminded.

"Jack, of course," she says, and she begins to move again.

My mind is reeling, but I am not about to go backwards to find Luke. Why would I? I can hardly process what I'm learning, and I don't have time to do so anyway, even if he had lightly called me the sixth canonical victim. Rose is moving quickly now, much more quickly, and though Iz seems confident that it is in the right direction, I'm not so sure. Where is the stain? Shouldn't we have passed it again? Or the shattered pocket watch?

Rose trails her fingers along the wall and hums. Abruptly, she stops and whirls to me. "Have you seen her yet?" Her voice is a whisper, like we're sharing a secret.

"Who?" I rub my arms to keep the goose flesh from appearing. I can't help it and I look behind me. There's no one.

Rose frowns at my stupidity. "Mother, that's who! She's here, with us. I've seen her, oh, I don't know, hundreds of times."

"Carolina's dead." Iz uses his doctor's tone. It's meant to be soothing, but the time for that is long gone. Rose won't be soothed.

She stomps her foot. "I know that! Don't you think I know that? I'm not crazy! But she's here, and she wants something."

My mouth is dry. I move towards Rose on feet that seem to be betraying me. On one side of me, Jack the Ripper waits in the shadows and on the other is Rose. There isn't much of a choice. Iz reaches out to me, but he isn't as fast as my sister. She pulls me close, her hand on my wrist, the nails digging into my flesh. She begins to pull me somewhere, and though I could overpower her, I feel as paralyzed as I had in my nightmare of Bedlam. Iz shouts something, but I am in front of Rose, and he undoubtedly can't shoot. We begin to climb another flight of stairs. This certainly isn't the way out.

"I only want to show you!" Rose says. "Stop being so difficult. Mother is down there! I know she is, look!"

She opens a small door that would usually be padlocked, I imagine, but not now when the hospital is abandoned and empty. It's small enough that even her small body must duck. She's let go of me now, and there's nothing to stop me from running away, nothing but concern now, for Rose, and the fact that Jack is somewhere back the way we came. Frantic, I stare at Iz, wondering what to do. He moves ahead of me and unbelievably fits through the little door. I follow.

"Look!" Rose instructs me, as I come through. I feel the warm sun on my skin. We're outside somehow, on a little slip of a balcony. A bell tower or something? A place for the window washers to stand? A resting area for gargoyles? It's the rotunda, and beautiful from the outside, but shaky and surrounded by scaffolding once you get closer.

On the one hand, I'm glad to be out of the stale, heavy air of Bedlam which made me feel as though my lungs were suffocating. On the other, it seems a very unsafe place to be. There's barely room for the three of us, and our bodies hug the wall behind us, while the scaffolding is at our fronts. Iz especially looks bizarre, his tall body dwarfing Rose's. "Look down!"

Every muscle in my body is taut and ready to spring. I don't move my head to look down. Out is the best I can do. Somehow I can't. It's ridiculous, but I'm scared of what I might see. Unbelievably, it begins to rain.

"She always wears that dress." Rose frets. "Every time I see her. Just like the day on the cliffs. Cornflower blue. She's come for something, you know. She's all alone. She wants her daughter." She pushes her windblown, and now wet hair out of her face.

I pull back, but it's unnecessary because Iz is at my side and has pulled me close to him. Rose still has my wrist though, and for a terrifying moment I think she will have supernatural strength and I won't be able to withstand her. She'll push me down to be with the ghost of our mother. That must be her plan, isn't it? Rose sees my fear and smiles at me, gently. "She's haunting me, you see."

"Rose, there's no one there." I pull on her hand, but her grip on my wrist is strong. She lets go then, so quickly that I stumble. Iz catches me with his free hand, the one without the revolver that is keeping steady aim on Rose. All three of us are so close to one another we share our very breaths. I'm sure mine has the bitter scent of fear.

Rose reaches up and touches her face. She pulls her fingers away, red. She sniffs and frowns. Her nose is bleeding. I frown, too. I remember that night in France, the closer I got to myself, the sicker I became. Why would Rose be bleeding now? I don't understand. She wipes the blood on her wet dress, and it matches the stain on the wall inside.

"Mother is my angel of death, I think," she muses. "Don't you?" She turns now, and looks down again, down, down. She seems so harmless and small standing there that I have to risk it. I have to look. I peer down, and all my breath is stolen when I see the phantom of our mother.

I gasp. Only no, wait, it isn't our mother. Very like her, yes, with that yellow hair and lithe frame. She could easily be mistaken with that uncanny likeness. In a cornflower blue dress that blows lightly in the breeze, it's no ghost. It's Rose Gray.

Rebounding back to her anchor, back to Bedlam, I realize with a shock. After some travel, who knows even which one. I look at the Rose beside me, who gives a soft cry of alarm and pain and stumbles. I remember the dizziness and ill effects of being so close to myself, in essence creating a paradox around me in France. I reach out then, to steady her, but she pushes me away and with such force that I'm surprised. Too surprised to react fast enough, and the old railing cracks with a loud sound, right before my sister tumbles down, a falling shadow of red calico and yellow hair.

Iz pulls me to him, even closer, so I'm wrapped in his coat as I cry out. He shields my eyes, and I feel his big hand shake. "It's over," he murmurs repeatedly until finally, I believe him.

It's over.

The End.

Epilogue

Getting back to Africa was the easy part. After saying goodbye to Bar, who had no interest in coming with when it meant traveling to Africa. He decided instead to return to his cozy home with Einstein. Telling our tale to Dad, Bea, and Joe was the hard part. It was very hard for even Israel and I to understand, much less tell it so that it made any sense at all.

It was a lovely spot and time for a wedding, and though our party was small, our happiness was not. Dad had been sober now for a while, and he and Bea tied the knot themselves very soon after we arrived back to them all in one piece. Dad walked me down the aisle very proudly. I had wanted Linus to marry us, but I was not yet confident in my ability to steer our course, and I wasn't sure I ever would be, or would even want to. The dreams of going back to Emme or my mother still plague me, and someday maybe I will try, if not to save them, at least to say goodbye. In the meantime, life goes on for those of us lucky enough to keep on living.

I think of Rose sometimes, and of Luke, sometimes Jack, too. I don't know whatever became of him. I could find out, I suppose, now that we are somewhere modern enough for computers and genealogy records, but I haven't looked. I think he probably disappeared, in and out of eras. Maybe he lived a long life, maybe his life really was over the day he lost Rose. Had he really been Jack? Had he gone back and forth through that year of murder, never being caught because he had Rose as his guide? I don't know what to believe.

As for Rose, the knowledge that she caused her own death saddened me, and yet the alternative was living a long life of insanity and unhappiness. I remember what she said about Marie and Mr. Limpet, and now I understand. At least in death they're both free from the madness that plagued them. I wonder if Rose remembered watching herself tumble off the bell tower. It's all so confusing. The Rose on the ground, what had become of her? By the time we recovered from our shock, and found our way outside, she was gone. The other Rose sprawled on the grass, like a Sleeping Beauty, where later Miss Helmes and Mina and Mack found her and transported her to somewhere where she could rest in peace. There was no funeral. Her diaries are gone, lost in time somewhere by now.

As for the two of us, Israel and I, we enjoy every moment. Even the dull, quiet ones. After everything we've been through, those are my very favorite moments indeed.

It's 1967 now, and my days are spent in a coffee shop, driving, and helping Iz study for that other piece of paper he has always longed for. Plus, there is a baby to plan for now, my belly has swollen so much that my guitar has no room on my lap anymore. I tried to learn to knit baby booties and caps, but not surprisingly, I don't have much knack for it. Prue would sigh and do it for me, and I wish she were here still, but I have memories, and by the hundreds to keep me content. I don't think we'll ever run out of stories, Israel and I. We even know how we'll start them, those stories to our sons and daughters:

Once upon a time, hundreds and hundreds of years ago, you were born...

Acknowledgments

Special thanks and all my love to the following people: Mandy, Heather G, Christin, Genesis, the Reed Women, MaryJane Butters, the staff at Home Educating Family, Andrea Johnson Beck, Tawni, Tybekah, the Rutkowski Clan, Mom and Dad, Kathleen Warren, Aerie, my Sonnet girl for the cover, Anna Martin, Hailey, Laryssa and the Gang, Keith and Alice, Chris, Cody, Coralee, Sarah, Coriann, the Shafes, Brian and Rachelle, Gary, Lauren, Peter, EJ, Marie, Nate, Konah, Calvin, and each and every one of my support staff. Your gleeful reactions, sweet notes, and support – online and in person – are what made me think maybe I can do this after all.

Everything else goes to Mike, Cora, Annalise, and Gianni, for cranky mommy moments, the hashing out of plots, and for saving the computer when I wanted to throw it out the window. Sorry about the nightmare, Anna. The next book will be less creepy...

I think.

Author's Notes:

In the writing of novels, sometimes for the sake of the story, facts and figures are tweaked. The incubation and diagnosing period for malaria is longer than what it took here, but for the sake of the book, poor Nora succumbed at a quicker rate.

Al Capone was captured a bit later than what was depicted in the newspaper that Sonnet reads, but for a more gripping headline, I blurred the lines a bit.

The Canonical Five victims of Jack, plus several others who are sometimes attributed to him, happened during the Spring through the Fall of 1888. The legend of Fairy Fay began on Boxing Day, 1887. Whether or not you believe our own Luke Dawes was Jack or if Rose simply likes to tell tall tales, dear reader, is entirely up to you.

About the author

Melyssa Williams is a mom, sister, daughter, wife, friend, ballet teacher, ex-contemporary dancer, writer, and blogger. She resides in Southern Oregon. She was homeschooled back in the day when it was slightly odd and eccentric, which came in handy when she decided to be a writer. She drinks coffee too often and reads fiction at inopportune times. She has parented inner city teens and wants to sky dive, but that's the extent of her excitement. Other than that, she finds baking bread and sipping wine to be the most thrilling parts of life.

She can be reached at: http://melyssawilliams.com

www.ingramcontent.com/pod-product-compliance
Lightning Source LLC
Chambersburg PA
CBHW072159130726
47910CB00010B/1539